STARK'S WAR

STARK'S WAR

JACK CAMPBELL

WRITING AS JOHN G. HEMRY

TITAN BOOKS

STARK'S WAR
Print edition ISBN: 9780857688613
E-book edition ISBN: 9780857689566

Published by
Titan Books
A division of Titan Publishing Group Ltd
144 Southwark St
London
SE1 0UP

First edition: September 2011
10 9 8 7 6 5 4 3 2

Visit our website: **www.titanbooks.com**

What did you think of this book? We love to hear from our readers. Please email us at: readerfeedback@titanemail.com, or write to us at the above address.

To receive advance information, news, competitions, and exclusive offers online, please sign up for the Titan newsletter on our website: www.titanbooks.com

A CIP catalogue record for this title is available from the British Library.

Printed and bound in Great Britain by Clays Ltd, St Ives plc.

To my father, Lieutenant Commander Jack M. Hemry, United States Navy, who enlisted as a Seaman Recruit and worked his way up the hard way, and to my mother, Iris J. Hemry, who stood by him through wars, overseas deployments, frequent moves, military housing, and four children.

For S., as always.

PROLOGUE

Once before, Americans had come here, riding to another world on primitive reaction rockets and a burst of national determination to be first across the final frontier. They came, staying briefly, exploring tiny patches of territory, and seeking knowledge. Then national will faltered and sought frontiers closer to home, frontiers less expensive, less risky, and less demanding. The Americans left a last time and did not return, leaving behind few traces that humanity had ever broken the bonds of its home world.

As the great Cold War that had dominated the last half of the twentieth century ended with an unexpected whimper and as economies around the world imploded during the post-Millennium Crash, America found itself the last superpower, economically and militarily supreme. Its corporations, backed by the most technologically advanced military in the world, dominated the Earth as no empire ever had before.

The Earth's riches foreclosed, other nations looked elsewhere.

Many years after the Americans had left, others came, from other nations and alliances, seeking the material and scientific wealth offered by Earth's consort. They built research labs, mines, refineries, low-G manufacturing plants, and colonies for their workers that soon became small towns. After great investment, the wealth began coming home and enriching the colonizers.

America finally raised its gaze once more, staring up at the Heavens and realizing they were now owned by others. So America resolved to return, and claim what she felt was hers.

PART ONE

OPERATION TRANQUILITY

The assault boat shuddered and jumped, a random pattern designed to foil fire-control systems but also annoying as all hell to the soldiers seated in their Armored Personnel Carrier. Regular motion could be expected and countered, but the wild jogs of the boat's course were always unanticipated. Sergeant Ethan Stark swore as a particularly violent jerk slammed him against the restraining harness. You never knew what waited at the end of a drop, but the drop itself always guaranteed bruises.

"Stand by for drop." The Lieutenant's voice rang through the comm circuit, piercing an otherwise oppressive silence. The dimly lit boxlike interior of an Armored Personnel Carrier was never a cheerful place to begin with, but going in for the initial assault ratcheted the tension a little higher. Stark closed his eyes, focusing inward.

"Drop!" Lieutenant Porter sang out, followed almost immediately by the ascending whine of the APC's lift units. They'd run drop simulations in lunar gravity conditions, and it was immediately obvious the real thing wasn't going right. The driver gunned the lift as the drop extended for tens of seconds too long, both of which meant problems.

Stark's eyes shot open, locking onto the Lieutenant where he sat rigid and silent with uncertainty. "Brace for impact!" Stark ordered his squad, barely getting the words out before the APC grounded with a teeth-jarring slam that wrested a volley of curses out of the waiting soldiers. With a sideways lurch, the APC shuddered back up and into motion.

The average grunt didn't rate an outside view, but Stark wasn't average. As a squad leader, he rated his own view, which was less a compliment than a recognition that Lieutenants could die or be disabled very quickly in combat, after which Sergeants had to be available for the brass to pass orders through. *Not that I'm going to let them keep me in the dark until then.* Stark toggled a communications switch, bypassing security thresholds to access the officers-only command circuit. Between the official view and his strictly unofficial pirate back door into the command circuit, Stark now knew as much as the Lieutenant—which, as usual, granted him no peace of mind whatsoever.

"Where the hell are we?" the Lieutenant complained. "My Tac can't get a fix."

"We're off your Tactical map preload." The laconic voice of the APC driver seemed deliberately modulated to enrage hyped-up ground soldiers. "Here's a dump."

The Lieutenant's gear took a few seconds to download the extra maps, seconds slightly elongated by Stark covertly tapping into the download to copy the maps into his own Tac, then Porter erupted in anger. "Damn! They dropped us twenty klicks off target!"

"Yeah," the APC driver came back agreeably. "And they dropped us way too high. Didn't seem to do any damage, though. I'm making best speed toward your drop-off point."

"Twenty klicks off and too high. And God only knows where the rest of my platoon is. Would it do any good to file a complaint?"

"Does it ever? I'd tell my own commander, but it looks like they dropped her so hard her vehicle lost comms." With that minimal comfort from the APC driver, silence settled over the circuit. Stark relaxed against his harness, studying the new maps, gut tense with anticipation. Sometimes you just waited. Twenty klicks would take a few minutes, even at best speed.

"Lieutenant?" The APC driver called again, considerably earlier than he should have to announce their arrival.

"Here," Porter responded, voice surly. "What's up?"

"Going to have to ground it. The power cells are overheating. They need a rest or they'll blow."

"I thought you said the APC didn't take any damage when we grounded."

"It didn't." The driver sounded aggrieved. "It's a design flaw. The cells overheat sometimes, and the only fix is to power down and let them rest."

"How far are we from the drop-off point?" The Lieutenant seemed torn between resigning himself to a totally screwed-up day or flying off the handle.

"Four klicks. Grounding now," the driver announced anxiously, maybe worried about the Lieutenant's reaction, or maybe just about his power cells.

"That's too far. What happens if you push the cells?"

"They blow."

"Can we ride that out if it happens? We have to stick to the Tactical plan," Porter insisted, "and the plan says we ride this vehicle to our assault positions."

Stark tensed, searching for the words necessary to convince the Lieutenant to follow the APC driver's advice, but the driver did the job for him.

"I wouldn't advise it, Lieutenant. You're sitting on the power cells, and if they blow they'll vent the blast into the troop compartment before the side relief panels pop. It's not supposed to happen that way, but it does. I've seen it, and it ain't pretty."

Lieutenant Porter paused, then replied in barely controlled tones, "I suppose that's another design flaw?"

"Lieutenant, I just drive them, I don't design the damn things. Are you gonna walk, or wait an hour for the cells to cool?"

"I don't know! Why the hell don't I have comms with anyone else right now?"

"I don't know, Lieutenant," the APC driver noted desperately. "Look, you either wait here or you walk. It's up to you."

"I need orders!"

Time to get this show on the road. Stark loosened his harness slightly, leaning forward to tap the Lieutenant's armored knee while he tried to project innocent concern. "Lieutenant, we've stopped moving. Won't we get off time-line?"

"Off timeline?" Porter questioned, horrified. "Oh, God. Damn. We'll walk," he informed the APC driver brusquely.

Stark began preparing for action unobtrusively so the Lieutenant wouldn't notice he'd been listening in even as Porter shifted to command broadcast. "Okay, listen up, everybody. The APC's broke and we're still four klicks from our proper initial drop point. We'll have to leg it. Get them going, Sergeant."

"Yessir." Stark ignored the chorus of groans that rose over the squad circuit in the wake of the Lieutenant's announcement. "You heard the Lieutenant. Move it! By the numbers and looking good, or you'll drill 'til you drop next time we're in garrison."

The access gaped and the soldiers went through, failing with eerie slowness to hit the dust and scattered rocks below, diving into an unnecessary but instinctive roll, then rising to scatter into the widely dispersed formation veterans always adopted in hostile territory. Stark stood by the hatch, using one foot to add downward velocity to bodies who had jumped out assuming gravity would do all the work. The last soldier went through, flailing comically as if trying to pull himself down to the surface by grabbing nonexistent atmosphere; then Stark followed, feet first, pushing on the access rim to gain speed toward the surface.

Dust, puffing up in small clouds where armored military boots had landed, hanging in slow-falling fields of fine particles. Stark scanned the horizon, eyes switching restlessly between the enhanced visual of the rock-littered plain before him and the eerie glow of symbology on his Heads-Up-Display. Friendly troop positions, solid green markers against the map projected on the HUD, stood out alone, no threat markers visible near them—which didn't mean there weren't any threats hidden out there. "Chen! Billings! Get the hell away from each other. You're not on a damn date."

The symbols of those two individuals jerked obediently as the soldiers scrambled to put distance between them. "Squad deployed, Lieutenant."

"Good job," Porter replied absently. "I still can't raise anyone outside the Squad!" he added with rising worry apparent in his voice.

Stark switched his own display to remote, finding nothing there. Even on his authorized scan he should have been able to see the movements of the rest of their Platoon. His unofficial back door into the officer's command circuit should have allowed him to view any part of the battlefield. "I haven't got anyone else either, Lieutenant."

"We've got to abort. There's something wrong with our communications gear. There's got to be."

"Lieutenant, if the comm gear's screwed up, how come we've got full displays for the Squad?"

"I don't know! The enemy must be jamming the higher-level comm relays. How can we operate like this? There might be major attacks going down against the rest of the Brigade right now!"

Stark swiveled to view the horizon in all directions. "Wouldn't we pick up something like that on our own sensors, Lieutenant? There'd be stuff getting tossed high enough to see, ground tremors from explosions—"

"I know that!"

"And the Tactical timeline is still active." On Stark's HUD, the numbers counting down that timeline glowed yellow instead of the pleasant green that would have meant they were on the schedule laid out by the planners. Porter still hesitated. Stark used his back door to check the Lieutenant's actions, finding he was frantically scrolling through comm circuits in search of a link to his chain of command. "I think my timeline is shading orange, Lieutenant."

"Orange?" Porter took a deep breath, torn between the need to meet plan requirements and the need to be linked to higher authority.

"Yessir," Stark prompted. "I'm sure there's some red there. We're way behind timeline."

"Stop pushing me, Sergeant!"

"Yessir." *At least I'm not going to push hard enough for you to know I'm doing it.* Stark spoke with a carefully modulated mix of professional stiffness and apology. "I'm merely trying to keep the Lieutenant properly supported and informed."

"Sergeant, I. . ." Porter's voice trailed off, then sounded again with obvious concern. "The timeline *is* orange. What'll we do?"

"Operate independently, Lieutenant. We have the plan in our Tacs."

"Okay. Good idea, Sergeant. Follow the plan. Just let me input orders for the Squad. . .. Bloody hell," the Lieutenant cursed a moment later. "I can't update Tactical."

Stark called up his own planning sequence, frowning as it refused to accept ground plots for his unit. "Me neither, Lieutenant."

"Great. Wonderful," Porter added in a voice that suggested that neither word held sincerity. "There's an inhibit on our systems. They'll only take updates from Brigade level."

Stark checked for himself, stifling an angry comment. "They said they didn't want anyone screwing with the Tactical plan, remember, Lieutenant?"

"They should have told that to the idiots who dropped us twenty klicks off objective, the idiots who designed that APC, and the idiots who are probably going to start shooting at us before long, since our chance of surprise has gone totally to hell!" Porter subsided for a moment, his battle-armored figure facing toward lunar northwest. "Okay, Sergeant. Our original drop site is somewhere that way. Let's just hoof it until we get close enough for Tactical to give us guidance."

"Yessir."

"Fast, Sergeant! We're already way behind schedule."

"Yessir. Follow me," Stark ordered his Squad, taking the lead, his HUD projecting a slim arrow toward where his suit's gyrocompass thought lunar northwest lay. He briefly hoped it hadn't been scrambled by the impact when the APC grounded, then concentrated on trying to move fast and spot threats at the same time. Every push from his feet seemed to launch him in a small trajectory, dreamily floating over the surface, a perfect target sweating desperately for contact with the lunar dust and rock again. Slowly he picked up the rhythm, transferring the force of his steps into forward thrusts, fighting off the Earth-gravity-inbred tendency to put strong effort into upward motion. Experience from a thousand marches over a hundred types of terrain gradually came into play, turning forward motion into an automatic process, leaving his brain to concentrate on the higher issues of scanning for threats and keeping an eye on his twelve Squad members.

Something felt wrong. Stark scanned his HUD, looking for whatever had aroused his instincts. Everyone and everything looked fine, but something about his Corporal's movements bothered him. "Desoto, what's the problem?"

Desoto's voice responded, a little too strained with fatigue, for the distance they'd covered so far. "Nothing, Sarge. My suit's just got a minor problem. No big deal."

"Minor problem?" Stark didn't try to hide his skepticism, calling up the remote readout for Desoto's systems. "Dammit, Pablo, I read your environmental system degraded thirty percent and dropping."

"Yeah. Yeah. It's stabilizing. I can handle it."

"No, it ain't, and no, you can't."

"Sarge, I'm okay."

"You negotiating with me, Desoto? Get back to the APC, on the double. I don't need you dying of heat stroke."

"Sarge, I can handle it," Desoto repeated in a beseeching voice.

"The hell. I gave you an order. Get going." Stark reviewed his Squad, mentally running through the rest of his troops. Corporals maybe didn't carry huge responsibilities compared to some General calling the shots in the rear, but as long as a Corporal was helping watch Stark's back he wanted to make sure he could trust the guy. "Gomez."

"Yeah, Sarge."

"Take over for Corporal Desoto." Gomez could be better positioned within the Squad's current formation for the job, but she was sharp. Very sharp.

"Sarge? I'm not senior. Somebody else ought to take it."

Stark grunted in exasperation. "Is there something in the air up here that makes you apes want to discuss orders instead of carrying them out? Gomez, you're acting Corporal. Period. Do the job."

"Yes, Sergeant."

"One more thing, Gomez."

"Yes, Sergeant?"

"Don't screw up."

He had barely finished speaking when Lieutenant Porter called in. "Sergeant! Where's Corporal Desoto going?"

"Back to the APC, Lieutenant. Suit casualty. Private Gomez is acting Corporal." He said it cool and firm, reporting a decision rather than asking for approval.

"Why wasn't I told?"

"Squad-level decision, Lieutenant. My responsibility."

"I'm in charge, Sergeant! Make sure I'm informed of your planned actions in the future before I have to ask, and get my approval before acting."

Sure. Just because you don't know your own job is no reason you can't try to do mine as well. "Yes, Lieutenant." Keep it professional, keep it calm, and keep it ambiguous enough to ensure that he could still claim enough freedom of action the next time he had to act.

Stark covered more distance, only slowly realizing the Squad was traversing something that looked like the Mother of All Shell Craters. It reminded him of one of the holes he'd fought across in the Middle East years ago, holes gouged by substrategic nukes, but much bigger. These craters, though, had been blasted out not by puny human explosives but by Heaven's own artillery. The Moon would be full of them, Stark realized, mentally tallying the advantages of defending in such broken terrain, marked by countless natural fortifications. Unfortunately, at the moment his Squad wasn't defending, but attacking. The shadows, so dark as to seem solid, suddenly seemed perfect hiding places for dug-in troops. Stark felt a growing pressure between his shoulder blades as muscles tensed. He fingered his rifle. The charges had been adjusted to fire at lower velocities than back on Earth, but he'd still have to aim lower than instinct directed to avoid overshooting his target in a low-gravity/no atmosphere environment.

"Thank God." Lieutenant Porter's delighted exhalation broke through Stark's growing disquiet. "We've got comms again."

"Oh, goody," Stark muttered. He called up the Platoon picture, shaking his head as he saw Sergeant Reynolds' Squad scattered some distance away. They'd obviously been dropped off target as well. Nonetheless, Stark grinned in automatic relief. Sergeant Victoria Reynolds, an old friend and one of the best soldiers Stark had ever served with, had made it down safely. "Hey, Vic," he called on the circuit Sergeants had long ago secretly jumpwired-in to allow private conversations. "Nice to see you. I feel safer already."

"Hi, Ethan. Likewise."

"Looks like you got dropped in the wrong place, too."

"Yeah." Vic didn't try to hide her disgust. "Everybody's used to the automated location systems on Earth doing all the thinking for them. Heaven forbid they actually have to navigate manually."

"What happened to the comms? How come we couldn't see you earlier? The enemy screw with our systems somehow?"

"Don't know. All the officers were running around in a panic without somebody to tell them what to do."

"Sergeant Reynolds?" Porter cut in, oblivious to the conversation he'd interrupted. "How are you doing?"

"Fine, Lieutenant. We were out of position but we're making it up and should be on our Tactical timeline soon."

"Good. Good. What was the problem earlier? Why couldn't we talk or exchange Tactical feeds?"

Reynolds spoke soothingly, trying to calm Porter's agitation. "Something scrambled comms in this sector, Lieutenant. Some sort of software failure in the relays. They just got it straightened out."

"Comms were scrambled?" Porter sounded horrified. "How did you command your Squad?"

"Just like Julius Caesar, Lieutenant. I used hand signals."

"Oh. Um, good. Where's Sanchez?"

"I don't know. His Squad may not have made it down." Stark winced involuntarily. Sergeant Sanchez wore a poker face like other soldiers wore uniforms, giving few clues to his thoughts, likes, and dislikes, but he knew his job and he had twelve other soldiers with him.

Porter obviously reached the same conclusion Stark had. "Oh, Christ. His APC crashed?"

"I don't think so. We should have seen and felt that. I'd guess it never dropped. During the run-in, Sergeant Sanchez told me his driver was complaining about some system failures."

"Why did he tell you and not me?"

"Lieutenant, I'm sure Sergeant Sanchez had a good reason, but I can only speculate as to—"

"Never mind. Stark?"

"Yes, Lieutenant."

"Are your comms okay? Did you receive the update to Tactical from Brigade?"

"Yessir." Stark scanned the new plot. "No threats?"

"None encountered so far," Porter confirmed. "We've got a long way to the objective. Keep moving. I'm going to head toward First Squad to link up with Sergeant Reynolds."

"Yes, Lieutenant." Stark switched to the private circuit again. "Hey, Vic, you got company coming."

"So I heard. You acting insubordinate again?"

"Just doing my job and trying to keep my people alive."

"Like I said."

"Vic, it ain't my fault the junior officers can't think without senior officers putting every thought in their heads."

"It's not really their fault, either, Ethan. Junior officers aren't allowed to think. Every action they take is dictated by senior officers monitoring their every move."

"Maybe if they held an assignment for more than six months at a stretch they'd learn how to think despite that, just like we do," Stark suggested. "Of course, if they thought independently and really took time to learn their jobs they wouldn't get promoted to be senior officers who think micromanagement is the only way to operate. What kind of system is that?"

"A self-sustaining one. You could still be more diplomatic, Ethan."

"Vic, I'm a soldier. I don't talk nice to hostile people. I kill them."

She laughed, the sound over his comm circuit oddly out of place amid the bleak emptiness of Stark's surroundings. "Okay. I'll calm the Lieutenant down, Ethan."

"Thanks. That's why the Lieutenant likes you best."

"Knock it off."

No threats. The once-ominous shadows held no enemy troops, fingers poised over hidden weapons, but now gaped empty on every side. Monotony replaced tension. Combat assaults weren't supposed to be monotonous, but this one lacked an enemy, lacked major obstacles, and lacked scenery unless you counted endless kilometers of gray rocks and fine gray dust. The stars probably looked nice, but any attempt to look up at them virtually guaranteed hooking an armored foot over one of the omnipresent rocks and sprawling in that dust.

Too monotonous and too damn quiet. Stark activated his pirate tap on the command circuit to see what the Lieutenant and the rest of his superior officers were up to.

". . . dull! We're losing audience points by the second!" That sounded, Stark thought, like the Brigade's Commanding General. *What the hell is he talking about? Audience points?*

"There's nobody to fight, General," someone else complained.

"That's because you're moving too slow! Take that unit. Who is that? Who's the commander?"

"That's part of Lieutenant Porter's Platoon," another officer reported. Stark felt a chill run down his back at the words.

"Porter! You're way off your timeline!"

"Yes, General," Porter responded immediately. "We were dropped twenty kil—"

"Why isn't your unit moving faster?"

"Uh, General, doctrine—"

"To hell with doctrine! I need some action here. Get those troops moving!"

"Yes, General. Right away." Stark braced himself as Porter called him over the official command link. "Sergeant Stark, advance at double time."

"Lieutenant," Stark stated with careful precision, "at double time we'll be moving too fast to react so we can evade any incoming covering fire."

"There's nothing to evade, Sergeant! Get them going, now!"

It all runs downhill, and I'm pretty damn near the bottom of the hill. Stark checked his scan once more, biting his lower lip, finding nothing there but friendly symbology. *No threat visible, and if I can't spot enemy positions at this speed we might as well go faster just in case surprise hasn't gone to hell.* "Third Squad, advance at double time." Groans and curses rippled up the circuit. "Stop complaining and move! Gomez, keep your end of the Squad up with my end. Don't let anybody lag."

"Yes, Sergeant."

Disorientation threatened as the pace increased. Dust and rocks skimmed by below, their height and distance distorted by the lack of atmosphere. Something that clear should be close by, but up here you couldn't count on that. Look down and you got dizzy from the dead-black and dazzling-white contrasts zipping past. Look up and the trillion stars seemed to be sucking you into space, so legs and arms started flailing as the mind convinced itself you were falling up. Looming over everything hung a white-spangled blue marble where humans by all rights belonged and where anyone with common sense knew they were supposed to fight their wars.

"Son of a—" Acting Corporal Gomez started to yell, the curse broken by a heavy grunt.

"You okay, Gomez?" Stark demanded, checking her suit's status.

"Yeah, Sarge. I just tripped and did a nose dive."

"Your suit looks fine."

"It's fine. How come that damn horizon is so close but we don't get anywhere no matter how fast we go?" Gomez demanded sourly.

"That's easy, Anita," Chen chimed in cheerfully. "It's like a nightmare, because you actually bought it and went straight to hell when our APC crashed."

"Sure. I'm in hell. The fact that you're here with me supports that."

"Kill the chatter, you clowns," Stark ordered. There shouldn't be any problem with the troops working off a little tension by bantering, given that someone had decided the threat was so low they could just run toward their objective. But he'd long ago learned not to trust any assessments from higher than company level, most especially those emanating from any place behind the lines. "We're on a combat op, not a walk in the park. Maintain comm discipline."

"Yes, Sergeant." Gomez sounded uncharacteristically abashed. "Sorry."

"Sorry?" Stark questioned sharply.

"I'm acting corporal. You shouldn't have to tell me that stuff."

"Right." Sometimes a little extra responsibility brought out a little extra in a soldier. Sometimes not. Gomez obviously felt the burden. "But don't apologize. Just do the job."

Stark cut into the command circuit again, worried about threats that might be developing elsewhere and half hoping to hear Porter being chewed out by his own superiors again, but instead heard a clutter of commands as officers continually passed detailed orders to units and individuals without regard to intervening levels of command. *Business as usual. What did officers do before they could use command and control gear to sit on our shoulders every second?* He switched over again, calling Sergeant Reynolds. "Vic? You busy?"

"Nothing special for a combat assault," she noted dryly.

"What's up?"

"What's this talk about audience points?"

"What about it?"

"I don't know what it means, and I don't like something happening during a combat op that I don't understand."

Vic hesitated before replying. "This attack is being broadcast back home on vid with less than a half-hour delay."

"What?"

"The audio and video feed from our command and control gear is being relayed straight to the public affairs office," Vic elaborated patiently, "who're shunting it to the networks. Congratulations. You're a vid star."

"I don't want to be a vid star. Why the hell are they doing that?" Stark demanded, outraged. "I don't want the enemy seeing vid of what I'm doing on our civ networks."

"There's supposed to be a long enough lag time to keep us safe. As long as we're on timeline."

"Which we're not. The damn planners are always too optimistic when they lay out those timelines."

"I know, Ethan. It's not my idea." Vic's tone changed, growing crisp and clipped. "Gotta go. We're closing on our objective."

"Roger. We are, too." Stark stared ahead, looking for visual on the objective his Tactical claimed would be nearby now. *Concentrate on the job at hand.* Something suddenly came into view as he crested a small crater rim, a large object set into the lunar surface that glowed like a neon sign on Stark's infrared sight. *Waste heat. A lot of it. Looks like they didn't expect trouble enough to worry about camouflaging their site.* That was good.

"I've got target on visual," Murphy reported.

"Me, too," Stark advised. "That should be the main entry hatch for our objective. Mendoza, check the door for traps or alarms. Gomez, hold back with Billings and Carter to cover the rest of us until we get the hatch open. Everybody else converge on it."

Smooth and easy, going through the motions they'd executed a thousand times before in a hundred different places, though none so different as this. Stark approached the hatch cautiously, crouched, weapon at ready, then covered Mendoza as the Private unlimbered his gear and scanned the access for any defenses or warning devices.

"There is nothing there but a standard arrival enunciator," Mendoza reported. "No sign they are expecting problems, Sergeant."

"Good. Now—"

Another voice cut in on the circuit abruptly. "What is that? What are you looking at, Sergeant?"

Stark checked the ID on the transmission before replying. Brigade Staff had apparently decided to devote their attention to his small part of the operation, at least for the time being. "It's a door, Colonel."

"A door? On the Moon?"

"Hatch, sir. The main airlock into our objective."

"Which is a laboratory, right, Sergeant? A research laboratory investigating, uh, new synthetic material fabrication techniques in low G."

Whatever that means. "That's what my Tactical says, too, Colonel."

"Good. Good. Well, gather your troops and prepare for entry."

Stark spoke with exaggerated patience. "They're already gathered and prepared, sir."

"Then get in there, man!"

Stark gestured roughly toward the lab airlock. "All right, you apes—"

"Wait a minute!" another voice interrupted. "Has that hatch been checked for booby traps?"

Stark bit his lip before answering this time. "Yes, General."

"It's clear?"

"Yes, General."

"I don't want unnecessary damage to that installation, Sergeant! Tell that Private—no, wait, what's the Private's name?"

"Mendoza, General, he's—"

"Private Mendoza," the General ordered, "run another check on that hatch for booby traps."

"Y-yessir," Mendoza stuttered. Seconds dragged by while he ran another scan. "It looks clean, General."

"It *looks* clean, or it *is* clean?"

"It is clean, sir," Mendoza amended rapidly. "Then get going," the General ordered. "Thank. You. Sir," Stark stated carefully. "And make sure you look good! Remember, we're on top of this!"

I remember when there was a chain of command, Stark thought darkly. "Yessir."

The hatch cycled open without protest, innocent of defenses, just as Mendoza had predicted. The Squad crowded in, weapons ready, while atmosphere built up. Just before the inner hatch popped, a small vid screen inside the airlock came to life, displaying an owlish visage blinking in surprise. "Who's there?

We weren't expecting visitors today, or this early."

"That's the point, Civ," Gomez said with a grin as the inner hatch swung open. "It's called surprise."

"Surprise?" The foreign civilian scientist blinked some more. "I don't understand. Who's the surprise for? Should I come escort you in?"

"You just wait where you are," Stark advised. "We'll come and get you." He faced his Squad, swinging an arm toward the inner hatch. "Move it! Round the civs up before they figure out what's going on."

His soldiers scattered into fire teams, heading down individual routes through the roughly hewn rock corridors of the laboratory in accordance with the plans in their Tacticals. Stark took two privates with him down the longest hall until he reached a ninety-degree bend at the end. He paused, weapon at ready, preparing to leap and then fire immediately if needed.

"Sergeant!" Stark jumped nervously, cursing as another transmission broke his concentration. "Be careful going around that corner!"

"Yes, Colonel," Stark grated out between clenched teeth.

"There may be armed opposition around that corner," the Colonel continued. "Make sure your other soldiers are posted to cover you."

"They are, Colonel," Stark assured his distant commander. "Now just go the hell away and let me do my damn job," he added under his breath.

"What was that, Sergeant? I couldn't understand the last thing you said."

"I didn't say anything, Colonel," Stark hastily assured him.

"I heard something. Major, didn't you hear something?"

"Yes, Colonel," another voice chimed in. "There was something there."

"There may be something wrong with your suit's comm system," the Colonel decided. "Run a diagnostic, Sergeant."

"Colonel, I'm in the middle of an operation—"

"Never mind. I'll order the diagnostic from here. We can't risk you losing comms with headquarters."

Stark opened his mouth to issue another frantic protest, then stopped as a blinking red symbol on his HUD announced that his comm suite had dropped off line to run the diagnostic. He slammed one fist repeatedly into the nearest wall, glaring threateningly at the two Privates, both of whom pretended not to be aware of his situation. Unable to advance while he couldn't talk to anyone else in the Squad, Stark waited and fumed while precious moments crawled by as the suit checked the entire hardware and software of his built-in communications system. "Please, sweet Jesus," he prayed, "when my comms come back on let the worthless Brigade Staff have found another little part of this big battlefield to micromanage to death."

Green lights popped up to announce the completion of the diagnostic. Stark held his breath, waiting for further backseat driving from headquarters, but silence reigned. *Guess they got bored waiting for the diagnostic to run and went off to tell some other poor grunt how to tie his shoes.* Stark eased toward the corner, motioning his two Privates along, then paused. All the training simulators insisted at this point you should stick a finger around the corner to scope out the scenery with the fiber-optic sensors in the suit's fingertip. That helped ensure you wouldn't be surprised, but unfortunately worked both ways in that it also told any enemies lying in wait that there'd be a soldier following that finger around the corner in the immediate future.

"Let's go," Stark grunted, leaping across the gap to plant his back against the wall, rifle aimed down the new corridor. Two civs were walking slowly toward him, apparently deeply engrossed in conversation. First one, then another, became aware of the armored figure menacing them and came to a gap-jawed halt. Stark waved his Privates forward, triggering his external mike. "Attention. This installation has been occupied by armed forces of the United States," he recited. "All personnel will be taken into protective custody. Any resistance will be met with appropriate force."

The Privates reached the two civs, both apparently too stunned by events to resist, and prodded them against the nearest wall with their weapons. "Billings," Stark ordered, "bring them along. Murphy and I will head for the lab." On his Tactical, the laboratory loomed as the largest room in the complex and as his final objective.

Deciding that speed was necessary to exploit the surprise they'd apparently achieved, Stark sprinted forward, following the map on his Tactical display, down another corridor, through a right turn, and then tried to turn right again, only to face a solid wall of stone. "Oh, hell."

"Sarge?" Murphy asked anxiously. "Isn't there supposed to be another passageway here?"

"Yeah, but there ain't. Guess they never finished building according to the plans Intelligence got their hands on."

"What do we do, Sarge?"

Doctrine was explicit on that point. No deviation from actions ordered by Tactical were allowed, which meant Stark was now supposed to call up the chain of command until whichever Colonel was calling the shots for his sector could confirm that Stark indeed faced a wall of rock, then download a new set of actions for Stark to follow. *Can't have grunts thinking for themselves.* On a hunch, he checked his suit's comm system for update delay times, then grinned. As he hoped, the blizzard of communications during the assault had grown so heavy that the Brigade comm system couldn't keep up. Delay times had grown from seconds to minutes, giving him precious moments to do something before anybody in charge realized he had deviated from Tactical.

"Follow me," Stark barked at Murphy, heading at a run for the next closest entry to the lab shown on his map. Stark's HUD revealed that his other fire teams had already covered this ground, so he didn't bother with caution, simply trying to cover ground in the few minutes available before some officer noticed he was off the track dictated by his Tactical.

. Sometimes that was a good idea. This time it wasn't. They came around a corner to find a man in what seemed to be a law-enforcement uniform, complete with a holstered sidearm, staring at them. A moment of mutual surprise ended as the man grabbed for his pistol. Stark, off-balance in the middle of a long, low-gravity step, watched as Murphy lined his rifle up, then hesitated. "Shoot him, dammit!"

"But Sarge, that pistol can't—"

Stark, finally stable, brought his own rifle to bear on the foreigner and fired, the round catching him in the midsection with enough force to fling the man backward a meter. "Get his gun," Stark ordered Murphy. "Don't ever do that again."

"But Sarge——"

"But nothing!" Stark's weapon didn't waver from where it focused on the wounded man, but his fury was aimed squarely at Private Murphy. "I don't care if that thing probably can't penetrate our armor. You don't take chances. You don't think. If they have a gun, you shoot them. I don't care if it's a water pistol."

Murphy, scooping up the pistol, avoided looking at Stark. "I'm sorry, Sarge."

"You sure as hell are." Stark fought down his anger, lowering his weapon as the blood from the wounded man's abdomen spread higher in the low gravity than Earth combat experience said it should. "Look, Murph. Take a good look. I don't want that to be you. Now use your med kit on that guy and then bring him to the lab."

"Okay, Sarge. Don't worry, Sarge. I know how I screwed up."

"Good."

Stark headed for his objective once more, sliding into the main lab just as an angry query resounded. "Sergeant, why aren't you following Tactical?"

"I am, sir," Stark responded in tones of injured innocence. "Tactical shows this as my objective, and I'm in place."

"But——" the officer began to object before apparently being distracted by some other display of unauthorized initiative. "Ah, okay. Carry on."

"Yessir." Stark sized up the situation. A large gaggle of civs, most in variations on the universal white lab coat but a few in whatever they'd been sleeping in, stood staring at his Squad members with looks of varying degrees of incomprehension. Stark singled out his acting Corporal. "Any problems, Gomez?"

"No, Sargento," Gomez reported cheerily. "Oh, a few of the civs didn't want to come along at first, but they didn't need much convincing."

Stark took another look at the scientists, at least one of whom seemed to be developing a black eye. "Any of them get hurt?"

"No, Sarge. Well, maybe a little."

"Fine. We'll let central processing deal with them." Stark switched to his outside speaker, broadcasting his voice to both the civilians and his Squad. "This facility is now under U.S. military occupation. You will be held here under guard for your own safety until a vehicle arrives to transport you to a central point from which you will be repatriated to your own countries back on Earth. No one will be harmed as long as—"

A civ stepped forward, interrupting Stark's speech, her dark eyes flashing with anger as she raised two hands in emphasis. "Leave here! You are interrupting our work and trespassing on private property."

"Ma'am, as I just stated, this property now belongs to the U.S. government."

"Pirates! Mercenaries!" Stark sensed his Squad tense at the second term, their pride affronted.

"Ma'am, we're not mercenaries," he corrected harshly. "We don't fight for money."

"I don't care what distinctions you draw about yourselves!" The foreign civ glared at Stark. "This is illegal. You Americans own everything on Earth! Isn't that enough? Do you have to come here and take this, too?"

"Ma'am, my orders are—"

"This is piracy!" she repeated, glancing around at the other civs in the room for support. "You have no right to seize this installation."

"Ma'am," Stark answered slowly, emphasizing each word, "that's not my department. You got a complaint, you bring it up with my Lieutenant. I'm just following orders."

"Then tell your Lieutenant you must all leave at once."

Stark hefted his rifle, its dull metal glinting evilly under the laboratory lights. The simple gesture drew the civs' eyes, which widened in fear and apprehension. "My orders are to take possession of this facility and secure any personnel here."

"I don't care about your orders!"

"That's your right, ma'am. But any resistance will be met with appropriate force." Stark canted his weapon so the barrel leaned in the direction of the civ scientists. "Your choice."

Most of the civs hastily raised their hands toward the rough ceiling, suddenly sweating despite the cool of the room. As the others were trying to decide, Murphy arrived, carrying the wounded man, who was white with shock but still breathing. Every other hand shot up as the scientists absorbed the sight, leaving only the angry female civ still defiant. "You killed him," she half demanded, half questioned.

"He'll live," Stark advised coldly. "Anybody else who threatens my people will get the same treatment."

The civ clenched her fists. "I will not grant legitimacy to your actions by cooperating."

"Whatever." Stark looked toward Gomez and hooked a thumb in the direction of the female civ. "Take her down."

Even with her expression obscured by her faceplate, Stark knew Gomez was grinning as she stepped forward, swinging her rifle butt in a swift blow against the civ's left shin. As the civ collapsed with a gasp of pain, Gomez reversed the weapon's motion to catch her on the chin, then dropped to one knee beside the dazed woman, expertly locking a pair of Dally-Cuffs around her wrists. The Dallys tightened automatically, their composite fibers forming an unbreakable second skin just above the civ's hands. "You can try cutting these off, *Senora*" Gomez advised the civ in a pleasant conversational tone, "but if you do, you'll bleed to death. *Comprendo?*"

The civ nodded numbly, allowing herself to be shepherded with the other prisoners into a corner of the room. "Lieutenant?" Stark called over the command circuit. "We've taken possession of the objective."

"Roger. Any resistance?"

"One apparent law officer wounded. Noncritical."

"Too bad. Brigade Staff is already complaining the assault lacks enough combat action."

Stark took a deep breath, staring angrily toward nothing. "We didn't suffer any casualties, Lieutenant."

"That's fine, Sergeant. An APC should be by your position in about thirty minutes to pick up your prisoners. Don't let them build any nukes in the meantime."

"Yessir." Stark's angry stare shifted to the civ scientists, standing next to stacks of equipment he couldn't identify. "Gomez, make sure they don't touch nothing. And I mean nothing. If one of them reaches to scratch their butt I want their hand broken."

"*Si, Sargento.* You guys hear the Sergeant?" Gomez asked the civs, all now standing so rigidly still that few even risked nodding in reply to the question. "Good. No trouble, then. I don't like fighting people who can't fight back. But I will."

Stark didn't relax, restlessly patrolling the halls of the lab complex, scanning for threats, until the APC had come and gone, running thirty minutes later than the half hour promised. Desoto showed up on the same APC, disgruntled at missing the assault despite the lack of action. "I should've been with the Squad," he protested to Stark.

"Sure, then we could've spent the whole action trying to keep you from baking inside your suit. I've got enough things to worry about during an attack without adding that."

Desoto stared at the floor for a moment, then nodded. "You're right, Sergeant. I shouldn't have complained."

"Hell," Stark said with a grin, "you can always complain, Pablo. That's the one thing the mil can never take away from you." The smile faded into grim seriousness. "In a combat situation I can't spend time thinking about anything but the job. My feelings don't matter and neither do yours. Neither do the likes and dislikes of every ape in this Squad. You're a Corporal, Pablo. You gotta remember that. I'll bust you if you don't and promote someone who can."

Desoto hung his head again. "Truth. I won't forget, Sergeant." He peered around, taking in the portions of the lab complex he could see. "How much longer we going to be here?"

"If we're lucky, maybe quite a while. They had about twenty civs billeted here, with a full kitchen in the bargain. All the comforts of home, plus the power plant that supplies this place got taken over by some combat engineers from Second Battalion, so we've got no worries there."

"Wow." Desoto's elation quickly faded into gloom.

"Some officers from staff will take it over as soon as they hear about it."

"Nah. I hear there's a lot of places nicer than this." The ability to see basic accommodations as a luxury was one of the few benefits of the living arrangements soldiers usually had to accept.

"Sarge?" Murphy called from the room they'd designated their command post. "We got a call for you from Sergeant Reynolds."

Reynolds looked comfortable on the comm screen, lounging in a chair that would have been nicely upholstered on Earth but was ridiculously overstuffed for the fractional gravity on the Moon. "Everything secure, Ethan?"

"No problems," Stark reported. "What's the word?"

"Might as well settle in," Vic advised. "Orders are to occupy the installations we seized until further notice."

"That's it? Not that I'm complaining. They've got some good rooms here. But no digging in?"

"No digging in. The brass don't want anything damaged in case we have to trade back some of what we just grabbed."

"Fine. When the counterattack comes, we'll just surrender quietly."

Vic grinned. "There's no counterattack in the offing, Ethan. It appears we're the only mil on the Moon right now."

"You think it's going to stay that way?"

"I don't know. It takes a while to get here, though, so you can sleep easy tonight."

"Maybe," Stark half-agreed, visibly uncomfortable.

Vic shook her head. "What's eating you, Ethan? Lighten up. Combat's over."

"Combat hasn't happened yet," Stark disagreed. "I'll lighten up when we're back home in garrison."

"Suit yourself." Vic mustered another smile. "My Squad occupied the supervisors' housing for this area. Civ bosses live good, Ethan."

"Figures. So where's the Lieutenant going to stay?"

"Here." Vic somehow kept smiling.

Stark smiled back this time. "Ain't that nice? A few months, maybe, with the Lieutenant breathing down your neck twenty-four hours a day. Have fun, Sergeant Reynolds."

"I will. But don't worry. I don't relax too much when I'm on the line, Ethan."

"You're not a new recruit, Vic. Sorry if I sounded like I thought you were. Hell, you're better than me." Stark chewed his lower lip, eyes hooded in thought. "I don't like this idea of not digging in. Do the brass really think the guys we took this stuff from are just going to accept it?"

"Apparently. Or settle for us handing back a little."

"Vic, we've fought against some of the people whose property we just grabbed, and alongside some of the others."

"Technically, by act of Congress, Ethan, it's our property. We just took possession."

"Sure. The corporations back home who own our politicians don't like the idea of all these First, Second, and Third World types getting their hands on all the goodies up here."

"They're the only goodies left, Ethan. We've got all the goodies back on Earth sewed up. There's advantages to being the only superpower. If you play it smart, you can stay the only one."

Stark grimaced. "Sure. Like I said, Vic, we know these people. They're tired of being held down so we can stay on top, and they're not going to take this quiet and peaceful."

Vic shrugged in reply. "Not our call, Ethan. Careful, you sound like a Third World symp."

"I'm just tired of being ordered to fight and die just so some big shots can get a little richer. Pax America, hell. There's nothing pax about getting ordered into combat everywhere on Earth and now on this godforsaken hunk of rock."

"I thought you liked your accommodations," Vic teased.

"Nothing wrong with the rooms. I just don't like where they're located."

"Wrong sector?"

"Wrong planet. Or Moon, or whatever. Vic, this is one ugly place. There's nothing living out there. It's dead. Totally dead."

"You better hope so. Would you be happier if a hostile battalion of mechanized infantry was outside your front door?"

"Very funny." Stark shivered, cold despite the calm efficiency of his battle armor's thermostat. "Vic, there's no grass or anything. Just rocks."

"I thought you didn't like grass, though you've never said why."

"I don't. But I like dead less." Stark fought down another shudder. "It doesn't help that it's such a big change. You know, from Earth, especially our last operation. I didn't like it there, but I like it here less."

× × ×

Five months before, they'd been on a peace-enforcement op on an island where the indigs didn't appreciate the efforts of outsiders to keep them from killing each other. An island crawling with so much life you had to fight your way through the vegetation and hope the assorted poisonous creatures that lived in it wouldn't also get in the way. So much life that losing a few pieces of it here and there didn't seem to matter one way or the other.

"History can be a terrible burden," Mendoza had observed, and that particular island had enough history to bury any trace of common sense. The one thing the locals were able to agree on was that, if they were going to be restrained from internecine murder, then killing peace enforcers was the second-best option. Especially since the peace enforcers were actually only there to keep things quiet enough for oil corporations hired by a corrupt government-in-exile to search for and exploit the island oil reserves that had become increasingly rare and valuable as the twenty-first century wore on.

It had been an ugly op, running patrols through heavy vegetation, scanning constantly for booby traps, worrying about when the next bomb would go off in the latrines. It didn't help that the island, like every other hot spot, was overloaded with ancient but still deadly firearms left over from the last century's Cold War. Stark and the other soldiers were used to encountering that state of affairs, but that didn't make it any nicer to deal with. "I thought the old M-16 had all these problems with jamming and stuff," Stark grumbled to Vic.

"Yeah," she agreed. "So?"

"So how come so many M-16s are still working good enough to throw lead at us?"

"Simple, Ethan," Reynolds said with a laugh. "We sold all the good ones to other countries. Probably made a lot of money. By the way, how's your ammo quota holding up?"

"Lousy."

Technically, the country benefiting from the peace enforcement ops was supposed to be paying for the soldiers, but that assumed the country either had a functioning government or that most of the available money wasn't being dumped into untraceable bank accounts. Since there wasn't enough funding to support much ammunition expenditure, the requirement usually got wished away. "It's a peace operation, not a war," one of the American officers lectured sternly. "You don't need excess ammunition. It will only encourage unduly aggressive actions."

Stark glowered at the ground. Lectures seemed to be as inevitable a part of war as bullets and beans. This one, derisively labeled Peace 101, covered the very important Rules of Engagement. Stark liked knowing the circumstances under which he could legally shoot back at allegedly pacified natives armed with heavy weapons and hostile attitudes. "If you are fired upon," they were ordered, "it is probably an attempt to provoke some military action that would discredit our mission. Therefore, you are not— repeat, not—to return fire unless and until actual damage has been inflicted."

It took a moment to digest all that. Then Stark raised one hand, his face stubborn. "So you're telling us that if the indigs shoot at us and miss, we can't return fire. We gotta wait until they hit us."

"That is correct."

"So, what if we're dead at that point? Are we allowed to, you know, bleed on them? Or are we supposed to die in a way that doesn't bother anybody?"

"You are completely missing the point," the officer declared with every evidence of exasperation. "You will not die, Sergeant. This is a peace enforcement mission."

A soldier in First Squad had raised her hand at that point. "If it's so peaceful, why do they need us here at all?"

Captain Disrali, their Company Commander of the moment, stood long enough to face his company, his expression put-upon. "There will be no more questions. Or comments. From anyone. Just listen to the damn briefing." He sat down again, back to the troops.

Stark leaned toward Reynolds. "Guess he won't be leading any patrols in person," he whispered.

"He wouldn't know how," Reynolds sniffed. "He's only here for his war-hero tour so he can pin on a Bronze Star he didn't earn and get promoted to Major."

"Just so long as he stays out of our way. We got enough problems with this op without adding obstacles."

Vic nodded. "Speaking of obstacles, did you notice the inhibits they've placed on our weapons?"

"Yeah. They'll only fire one clip per week. Not a round of ammo more. As if."

"Bullets cost bucks, Ethan."

"So do bandages and body bags. Anyway, the corporations pulling oil out of this rotting heap of dung they call an island are making plenty enough to fork over a few more dollars for ammo. I already got the work-around so we can fire on auto all week long if we want. That Corporal in Sanchez's Squad hacked it up yesterday. You need a download?"

"Yeah," Vic chuckled. "Thanks. You ever follow the rules, Ethan?"

"Only when they make sense to me."

"That must not be too often."

The only thing worse than the lectures were the patrols, trying to pacify chunks of territory where villages now consisted of marks on their maps that simply memorialized burned-out foundations and lost lives. Oil pipelines were blown up with such regularity that headquarters produced a standardized form to report the damage, every incident increasing the oil company demands for soldiers to be placed on guard every two meters along the lines, demands that headquarters had so far resisted, not out of any pure motives but simply because there weren't enough soldiers available to implement the ridiculous scheme.

Stark found himself covering twice as much territory as the rest of his Squad, trying to keep them dispersed enough to avoid providing tempting targets but close enough together that stragglers couldn't be picked off unnoticed in the thick vegetation. "Murphy, you worthless excuse for a soldier, if you drop behind again I'll shoot you and save the in-digs the trouble."

"I think I got a blister, Sarge," Murphy complained.

"You want me to call your mother so she can carry you for the rest of the patrol? Keep up with the Squad!" Stark checked the other soldiers' positions on his HUD, slamming a fist against the side of his helmet in exasperation as the display froze momentarily. The rudimentary field maintenance apparently jarred the right components as the symbology flickered, then jumped into current data. "Billings! I told you to patrol on the right flank. That doesn't mean heading for the damn beach six klicks in that direction! Get back in with the rest of us."

"Sergeant?" Corporal Desoto called. "My readouts keep breaking up, and comms with the Squad are erratic. You read me?"

"Yeah. I got you that time, Pablo." Desoto, up on point ahead of the rest of the Squad, had good reason to worry. The heavy, wet vegetation seemed cleverly designed to block the web of communications circuits that knitted the Squad together. The problem made patrolling even more hazardous than usual, besides generating hysterics among the officers sitting in the rear who wanted to watch the war go down from first-person perspective by monitoring the vid from individual soldiers.

A dull thump echoed among the greenery. Stark dropped into the mat of rotting leaves and mud that made up the ground around here, scanning for any casualties. A small patch of rough-textured grass tufted in front of his faceplate, bringing dark memories to mind and a shine of sweat to Stark's face. He reached to flatten the grass with one armored palm, grinding it viciously into the muck even as he called out to his Squad. "What was that? Anybody hit?" Silence reigned while Stark's HUD sat in the state of frozen idiocy that meant he'd lost comms with the other soldiers. "Ah, hell." Standing despite the possible threat so he could reestablish comms, Stark called again, this time generating a response.

"Land mine." Gomez spat the words. "I tripped it."

"You hurt?"

"Only my pride. The jungle absorbed the blast. At least it's gooid for something besides smelling like hell."

"Sarge?" Carter called. "I got one here, too. Spotted the trip wire while I was down after Gomez's mine went off."

"Let me call in." Stark switched circuits. "This is Third Squad, Second Platoon, Bravo Company. We've encountered a minefield."

"Roger." Headquarters didn't sound excited, which was reasonable given the number of mines lying around the island. "Continue patrol."

"We'd like the path swept for mines first. Our own counter measure gear is on loan to First Battalion."

"We know," headquarters responded in that tone that meant they'd forgotten but didn't want to admit it. "The mine threat is assessed to be minimal in that sector. Continue your patrol."

Sometimes it was hard to tell who was trying harder to kill you, the enemy or your own chain of command. "Request this patrol be aborted until the patrol route can be swept for mines," Stark insisted.

"Negative. Successful patrol statistics are already too low. Complete your mission."

"Sergeant?" Desoto called. "What's the word?"

"The word is we keep going," Stark replied. *So the mouse-pushers at headquarters can keep their damn statistics up.* "Okay, everybody, nobody's opened fire yet so this isn't an ambush. Get in single file and move real careful." It took a long time to clear the mined area, trying to pick out thin wires buried among all the junk a jungle keeps at ankle level. By the time they reached the supposed midpoint of the patrol, a village that might have been pretty before most of it got pounded into splinters and rubble, the afternoon was so far along that slanting shadows obscured the sullen faces of the few remaining inhabitants.

Weary and footsore, the Squad limped back into camp well after dark, too tired to worry about the snipers who periodically harassed any moving object. "You're very late." An officer stood there, tapping his hip-mounted mem-pad. "Staying on timeline is critical, Sergeant. Being out past dark can be hazardous."

"So can walking through a minefield," Stark replied in a steady tone.

The officer shook his head. "There aren't any mines along your patrol route. I saw the intelligence estimate this morning."

Stark's troops snarled like a pack of angry dogs, making threatening motions. The officer retreated in a hasty enough fashion to prove he wasn't totally oblivious to real threats, while Stark restrained his Squad. "Gonna frag that guy if I see him in the field," Gomez muttered.

"I don't want to hear it," Stark ordered. "Get back to your quarters and see to your gear. We might have another op tomorrow and I don't want anyone having to drop out because their battle armor is busted." He ignored the ritual under-breath grumbles, then headed for his own quarters, only to find Vic Reynolds waiting for him. "Hi, Vic."

"Hi, Ethan. Long patrol."

"Yeah, they get that way," Stark agreed savagely, pulling loose the seals on his armor with precise care despite his anger. "Coulda gone faster if I didn't care how many people I lost on the way. What's the occasion for your visit?"

Vic raised one eyebrow. "Good news, bad news, Ethan."

"Gimme the good."

"We're leaving the island."

"Hallelujah. Where we going?"

"That's the bad news."

"How bad can it be? There's no place worse than this."

"Oh?" Stark watched as Vic leaned back to stare up through the slit window toward the night sky. "Officially, it's very, very secret."

"Fine. So tell me."

"Guess. We have orders to ensure every suit of battle armor not only holds against bugs, gas, and assorted electronic threats, but also functions properly in an airless environment with no leaks. The environmental systems will be upgraded to operate in a totally hostile environment for an entire patrol cycle. And all the training simulators are being set to reproduce ops in one-sixth normal gravity. Where could we possibly be going, Ethan?"

Stark just stared. "Someplace bad." Then his mind fixed on one of the details Vic had provided. "One-sixth normal gravity? What is that, some other planet?"

"Close," Vic approved. "But not quite. There's only one rock within reach that has one-sixth Earth gravity. It's called the Moon."

"The Moon!?" Stark exploded. "What the hell is on the Moon?"

"Soon enough, you and I'll be."

Preparations matched Vic's predictions. Normally these days the many units that made up the First Division were scattered hither and yon, some on "peace" ops, some openly fighting dirty little wars in obscure little countries, some rented out to nominally friendly countries to do someone else's dirty work and earn a few bucks for the always-too-small military budget in the bargain. But now they came together, working toward an objective that officially remained Top Secret even as its identity became more obvious by the day.

"Sergeant," Desoto asked after one vigorous training session, "the Moon really like that?"

"How would I know? Besides, you're not supposed to know it's the Moon."

Desoto grinned. "I got a cousin in the Intelligence section. They've been watching the civ newscasts. Everybody knows what we're doing. There wasn't any way to hide building the transports in orbit and all the stuff going on here. But everyone thinks it's some kind of bluff to get what we want. That and some scheme to award big contracts to the space construction corporations."

"That last is real believable. Mil construction contracts are always first about the contractors and second about us, if that."

"Yeah," Desoto agreed. "So none of the foreign governments really believe we're actually going to the Moon."

"I can't quite believe it myself. What's your cousin say the reason for all this is?"

"Lot of money on the Moon, he says."

"Do tell. Maybe I'll pick up a few bucks when I get there."

"Really," Desoto insisted. "You know, we go places all the time because there's some, uh, economic reason."

"You mean," Stark stated flatly, "that there's something there some business tycoons need us to protect so they can milk it instead of some foreigners."

"Right. So maybe they want the Moon now. Since the post-Millennium Crash, everything here is pretty much owned by us. Pax America, right? That's why the other guys went to the Moon, to get stuff we didn't own the rights to. That's what my cousin says."

"He could be right."

"So you think we're really going? To the Moon?"

"Pablo, a word of advice. You've been in the mil long enough to know that you never really know where you're going until you get there."

"Everybody's spending a whole lot of money if they're not serious. Wonder where the mil found enough bucks to afford all this?" Desoto asked.

"Pablo, another piece of advice. Never ask questions you don't really want to know the answer to."

Finally, there were lectures. A military wedded to hi-tech video conferencing, able to link every soldier on every battlefield into a seamless whole, sharing every bit of information, still insisted on gathering large numbers of warm bodies into large, warm rooms to sit while another warm body paced in front of them and delivered large chunks of information in an authoritative and singularly dull fashion. They sat and slept through the latest versions of Rules of Engagement, Laws of War, the Uniform Code of Military Justice, Treatment of Noncombatants, and Military Courtesy, as well as the always dreaded update on Sexually Transmitted Diseases. Now the Battalion Commander himself, Colonel Danzel, usually glimpsed so rarely by the soldiers under his command that sightings of him were tracked like rare celestial events, stood before them with a hearty smile fixed on his face.

"Good afternoon. You've been through a lot of heavy training recently. I just wanted to tell you how proud everyone is of your performance. Especially during the uniform inspections. Everyone looks very good in the parade uniforms. Very good. And the barracks look great, too. Someone's doing a nice job of keeping the wax shiny on those floors. So, um, good job." Danzel shifted his feet, rubbed his nose, then nodded as if acknowledging a comment. "Any questions?"

A hand shot up. Stark craned his neck in an unsuccessful attempt to see who had been foolish enough to take the Colonel's offer seriously. *Must be a new guy.*

The Colonel also looked bemused, but swung an arm out to indicate the questioner. "Yes?"

Sure enough, a Private stood, licking his lips nervously. "Sir, we have been training a lot, and the equipment seems to be breaking down a lot."

Danzel frowned at the questioner. "That didn't sound like a question to me."

The Private gulped and tried again. "I mean, sir, these suits we've got aren't always reliable. Are we going to get anything new before we go into battle? Are there any fixes coming down the line?"

Colonel Danzel's frown deepened and darkened. "I am aware that rumors have been generated about the reliability of the Mark IV Battle Armor. This is the finest equipment any soldiers have ever worn into battle. There are no—repeat, no—serious problems with the Mark IV There are occasional minor malfunctions of subsystems. That's all."

Yeah, Stark thought sardonically, *minor subsystems like the temperature control and the oxygen rebreather. Nothing to get too worried about.*

The Private sat with a speed that suggested he'd finally figured out his error. However, a Corporal stood next, face fixed in a defiant challenge. "Colonel, sir, we understand what the Mark IV can do, when it works, but with all due respect, we're heading for the Moon, and when you're operating in a place with no air there's no such thing as a minor malfunction."

The Colonel's frown took on aspects of a thunderstorm. "I *thought* it was understood that our destination remains classified and has yet to be promulgated. Uninformed speculation about future operations will *not* be commented on."

The Corporal hesitated, face flushed, then sat back down.

Colonel Danzel scowled at his audience. "Any more questions?"

As an awkward silence stretched, Major O'Kane, the Battalion Executive Officer, stood up. "C'mon, soldiers, this is your chance to get answers." She was clearly expecting the troops to continue tossing out problems for the higher-ups to ignore, and seemed surprised at the lack of further takers. "I guess that's it, Colonel."

"Good." Danzel had trouble hiding his relief. "All right, then. Keep up the good work." He scuttled off the stage as O'Kane shouted "Attention!" and the Battalion shot to its feet in an automatic display of military courtesy.

"What was that for?" Murphy complained amid the buzz of conversation after the other Battalion officers exited with all due haste.

"I think they're trying to build up our morale," Carter offered. "Feel better?"

"Hell, no. I've been busting my butt on that damned combat endurance course, and all the Colonel cares about is how good the barracks floors look? Sarge, why wouldn't he at least talk about our objective?"

Stark skewered Murphy with a flat stare. "What am I, the Colonel's mouthpiece now? Why didn't you ask him yourself?"

"Hell, Sarge, I'm not that dumb."

Anything else that might have been said was interrupted by the harsh voice of the general announcing system: "All squad leaders are to report to their Company Commanders' offices on the double."

Vic and Stark exchanged glances as Sanchez came to join them, then wordlessly headed for the office of Captain Ringon, the latest Company Commander. On the way, two other groups of three Sergeants converged on them: Halstead, Two Knives, and Podesta from First Platoon; Greeley, Singh, and Rosinski from Third.

Ringon glowered at the nine Sergeants as they came to attention before her desk, nine impassive faces staring straight ahead. "The Colonel is very displeased over the disrespect shown by the enlisted personnel during his speech." She paused, looking from Sergeant to Sergeant.

"Permission to ask a question, Captain?" Sergeant Podesta inquired tonelessly.

"Permission granted."

"What disrespect is the Colonel referring to, Captain?"

Ringon's glower flushed red. "You know very well what disrespect. The questioning from the audience!"

"Neither of those questioners was from our unit, Captain," Podesta protested.

"And the Colonel invited them to ask questions," Stark added, drawing the Captain's attention squarely on him.

"Neither of those points is in any way relevant! Middle management is not properly supporting the officers of this command, Sergeant Stark."

"I am not a manager, Captain," Stark stated crisply. "I'm a combat leader."

"You're whatever I tell you you are! I expect no repetition of the events of earlier today. Is that understood?" Ringon waited for only a second before continuing. "That is all. Except for you, Sergeant Stark. I want to see you alone."

The other Sergeants filed out, closing the office door behind them, as Stark remained standing at attention, face professionally blank. Ringon raised one angry finger, shaking it in Stark's direction. "I've heard about you, Stark. I've heard you're difficult. I've heard you don't like to take orders." Stark stood silent. "Well?"

Stark kept his voice emotionless. "I obey orders, Captain."

"You question every one of them!"

"I express my opinion in appropriate circumstances, Captain."

Ringon turned an even darker shade of red. "There are no appropriate circumstances, Stark! You're a Sergeant. You don't have an opinion." She paused for a reply.

"Yessir."

"You do exactly what you're told when you're told."

"Yessir."

"You keep your mouth shut."

"Yessir."

Ringon glared in frustration, then pointed toward the door. "That's all. I better not hear any complaints from your new Platoon Commander."

"Yessir."

Stark saluted smartly, holding the salute until Ringon was forced to flip a quick salute in return, then pivoted on one heel to exit the office. There he found himself facing the impassive presence of Vic Reynolds waiting just outside. "Mind if I walk with you?" she asked.

"No problem." They walked for a few moments, past rows of identical doors ranked like faceless soldiers. "You hear what went on in there?"

"Every word."

"So what do you think?"

"I think you are one lying son of a bitch. None of those 'yessirs' meant anything."

"They weren't supposed to mean anything. I was just acknowledging her statements, not agreeing with them."

"Ethan, you can't keep pushing the edge all by yourself. Sooner or later some officer will call you on it for real."

"Not these gutless wonders. Besides, I gotta protect my people."

"You've got to lead your people into combat, Ethan. That's why we're here, to fight wars, regardless of how worthwhile we think they are."

"I know that. I also know there's more than one way to fight a war, and I'm going to fight the smart way."

"You may be right. People still talk about that stunt you pulled in the Mideast."

"Stunt?" Stark questioned. "Look, some Major who didn't know his head from a hole in the ground ordered me to do a head-on assault against troops dug into a damn mountain."

"Which the Major was told to do by some Colonel who was told by some General."

"Which is beside the point! If I'd charged straight in I'd have lost half my Squad, at least, and not taken the objective."

"So instead you suffered a mysterious communications failure, assaulted the hill next to the mountain, took the hill, looped around behind the mountain, and started pounding on the enemy headquarters, which panicked and pulled its own troops off the mountain to try to stop you."

"Yeah," Stark agreed. "We blew them away, climbed up the back of the mountain, and planted the flag. Objective taken. What's the problem?"

"The problem is that immediately afterward that comm problem of yours disappeared. The techs never did find out why your Squad couldn't hear any incoming transmissions for more than an hour, did they, Ethan?"

Stark shrugged. "I guess it was one of those, um, intermittent things. You know."

"Uh-huh. How did you explain not following the last instructions in your Tactical?"

"I thought I'd heard new orders that superseded the old Tactical before we lost comms. You know how our Tacs can get slowed down because of enemy jamming and our own clogged comm circuits."

She nodded, as if accepting the explanation at face value. "And where was your Platoon Commander during all this?"

"Bleeding to death." Stark made an angry face. "He'd tried to lead First Squad up that damn mountain like Tac ordered. Too bad. He actually listened to us sometimes when we offered advice. Unfortunately, he also did everything his superiors ordered, to the letter. With everything they do recorded in the Tactical systems that's the only way for officers to get promoted, right? And he wanted to make Captain something awful."

"Bad enough to die for it, anyway. Since all this happened before

I transferred to this unit, maybe you can tell me why you weren't court-martialed?"

"Heck, Vic, we won. That meant some General was a flippin' genius, right? The senior officers were too busy taking credit for their brilliant plans to blame me for some comm problem. I mean, how could they give themselves medals for winning the damn battle if what I'd done hadn't been what they wanted?"

"I see. You're a lot more devious than I've given you credit for, Sergeant Stark."

"I am not devious." Stark glared at her. "I do what I have to do when I have to do it. I don't sneak around planning things behind people's backs."

Vic held up her hands in a calming gesture. "True. Sorry if I implied otherwise, Ethan. But you take some major risks doing things without orders, or different than orders. Why?"

"Let's just say I owe somebody." He nodded grimly, as if to himself or unseen comrades. "Yeah. I owe somebody."

Vic peered at Stark as if she'd never seen him before. "I sometimes wonder. It's like you're fighting some other war the rest of us aren't."

"Maybe I am."

"You want to talk about it?"

"No, I don't want to talk about it."

"Why don't you want to talk about it?"

Stark glared at her. "How the hell do I talk about why I don't want to talk about it without talking about it?"

"Now you're being unreasonable."

"And now you're being a woman."

Vic pretended to be aghast. "You know I'm a woman? And here I thought the uniform had hid it all these years."

"Ah, hell, Vic." Stark started laughing despite himself. "Why do you care what happens to me anyway?"

"I don't want to talk about it."

Stark laughed again. "How much trouble can I get into with you looking out for me?"

"I shudder to think." She grinned maliciously. "Speaking of trouble, Ethan, you ever hear what happens when you cross a Special Operations Sergeant with an ape?"

Stark rolled his eyes with exaggerated disinterest. "I guess you heard I went on a date with a Sergeant from Ranger Company. Okay, Vic, I give. What do you get?"

Vic smiled wider. "A dumb ape."

Stark ducked his head quickly to hide an involuntary smile, then looked back up, face impassive. "I hadn't heard that one for, oh, a coupla years now."

Vic nodded back innocently. "Just wondering if it tracked with your experience, Ethan."

"Nah. There aren't any apes dumb enough to mate with the Spec Ops Sergeants I know."

"Oh, come now, Ethan. She's such a sweet little thing. Nice body, too."

"How do you know? Anyway, she also knows about twelve ways to kill a man with her bare hands without breaking a sweat. Speaking of breaking, she can do that to bones pretty easy, too."

Vic smiled again, this time pityingly. "Didn't get lucky, huh?"

"I'm still in one piece. I call that lucky. Besides, turns out she's just looking for a friend."

"Ouch." Vic winced. "Don't worry, Ethan, I'll be your friend."

"Gee, thanks. Will you go to the Moon with me?"

"Let me think about it. Mother always told me to avoid men in uniform."

"Your mother wore a uniform," Stark pointed out. "You told me she was a Sergeant. And, if I remember right, you told me your father wore a uniform, too."

"So? That just means Mom spoke from experience." The levity vanished from Vic's face as she leaned close, scanning their surroundings to ensure that no one stood close enough to listen in. "It's going down. We onload tomorrow."

"Damn. Where do you find out all this stuff?"

"A girl's entitled to a few secrets, Ethan. But if you've got anybody you need to say good-bye to, you better do it tonight."

Stark thought for a moment, then shrugged. "Nah. Everybody I'd want to say good-bye to is coming along, right?"

"Ethan, you need a life."

"Vic, I'm a Sergeant, and I've got a Squad of people depending on me. That *is* my life."

Sometimes that life was better than others. Right now they sat within a laboratory complex they couldn't use, under strict orders not to touch any of the equipment, chafing at the weeks of unaccustomed living in underground quarters. Not that Stark let them spend all their time in comfort there. "Chen, I could've put six rounds through you while you hung above the surface that time."

"I thought I was pushing off from dust, but it was rock," Chen complained, huddled behind a jagged boulder that apparently had been blasted out of some distant area before slamming into place here unknown centuries ago.

"Don't think," Stark ordered harshly. "Don't guess. Know what you're doing every second." He shifted to view another member of the Squad trying to advance under cover, bobbing among the rocks that littered the open area not far from the entrance to the lab complex. On his HUD, targeting data painted the soldier with an array of kill points. "Hector, keep your head down."

"I gotta see where I'm going, Sarge!"

"No, you don't. You memorize the route you're going to cover before you rush forward." Stark shifted to the Squad-level broadcast. "Listen up, people. This is just like back home. You know how to move under combat conditions. Do it!"

"Sarge?" Gomez asked. "It's really hard moving here. You know, every time I push or shove I either do it too hard or too light. And everything looks wrong 'cause there ain't no air."

"No kidding, Gomez. Here's a question for you, and I want everybody to listen to the answer. How do you get better at something?"

"Uh, you practice, Sarge."

"Very good. So guess what we're going to do until we know how to do it cold?"

"Okay, Sarge," Gomez agreed without noticeable enthusiasm. A ragged series of reluctant assents came from the rest of the Squad.

"Good. Now, we're going to run through another advance and another fall-back drill. If you apes do a good enough job on those, we can take a break."

Two hours later, soldiers still sweating from the exertion of moving under conditions alien to their every experience had their battle armor laid out for maintenance. Desoto moved close to Stark, indicating the other soldiers with a tilt of his head. "They're trying hard, Sergeant."

"I know that. But they haven't learned it all yet. They gotta try harder."

"They're tired, Sergeant."

"Would they rather be dead?" Stark raised his voice, addressing the Squad as a whole. "Anybody got any comments or complaints?" Soldiers exchanged glances but remained silent. "Come on. Open up."

Murphy looked at Stark defiantly. "None of the other squads is doing this, Sarge. They drill a little bit, but nothing like this."

"None of the other squads?" Stark asked. "Which squads in particular?"

"I don't wanna get nobody in trouble, Sarge."

"You won't. This stays in this room. Which squads?"

"Well, Second Squad in First Platoon. That's one."

"Uh-huh." Stark swiveled his head to view every member of the Squad. "Last op. How many casualties did Second Squad, First Platoon take?"

"Three," Gomez offered. "One dead, two wounded, right?"

"It was four," Mendoza corrected softly. "The fourth had a light wound."

"If they didn't have to leave duty, it don't count," Gomez argued.

"Knock it off," Stark interrupted. "Now, how many casualties did this Squad suffer?"

"None, Sarge. We were lucky."

"Really?" Stark demanded. "You think luck is all that kept you alive and in one piece? You guys are alive because I won't settle for less than the best from you. You're all alive because I drill you when your buddies in other squads are lying in their bunks playing vid games. And you know what? I'm going to keep drilling you until you're all perfect."

"But there's no enemy here," Billings pointed out. •

"Not yet," Stark agreed. "You want to wait until they show up to learn how to move and fight up here, Billings? Any of you want that?"

"Wouldn't matter if we did, would it, *Sargento T* Gomez mocked.

Stark bared his teeth. "No, it wouldn't. I'll kill you all from drill before I let one of you get killed because I didn't push you hard enough."

"We got any say at all in that?" Carter half joked.

"No. Anybody want a transfer?"

A long silence stretched, then Billings pointed toward an outside display monitor. "Hell, Sarge, if we transferred we'd have to leave here, and I'm starting to like this place."

The joke brought a scattering of laughs from the rest of the Squad, before the soldiers turned back to conducting maintenance on their battle armor. True to form, the Mark IV's were displaying their malfunctions in manners ranging from uncomfortable to potentially lethal. However, in a highly unusual development, spare parts flowed in an abundant stream whenever requested. While unwilling to look a gift horse in the mouth, Stark had been on too many underfunded and undersupplied operations not to be suspicious of such apparent wealth.

Billings, still grinning at her own joke, gestured to indicate a vague direction. "Seriously, Sarge. Any chance of seeing that colony? The one they're building out on the plain?"

Stark shrugged. "They're building it. Or digging it. Probably both. I doubt they need any sightseers hanging around."

"Are there people there yet?"

"Yeah. I hear a bunch of civs have already come up to help build and run the thing."

"Families?" Gomez wondered.

"Probably. Already or soon."

"So they maybe going to build a fort up here, too? Maybe have mil families around?"

"Maybe." Stark kept his response cautiously positive. He wouldn't dismiss the question out of hand, because having those families within reach, having a mil community within reach, would be very important to a lot of soldiers. "Too early to tell. I guess they'll get the civs settled in before they think about bringing mil families up."

"Any bars yet?" Billings asked eagerly.

"None that I've heard of," Stark stated. "And any that do exist are probably unofficial and illegal right now." That wouldn't last, he knew, not if the mil stayed up here. Stark had long since stopped being amazed by the many means people could find to manufacture booze or drugs out of any available materials. Somehow, some way, those who preyed on the needs of soldiers would set up shop to happily assist those soldiers in spending every dollar they could shell out. It was always that way, probably always had been that way, and probably always would be that way. "If any of you happen to visit that colony, you stay away from the civs, just like usual. That keeps them happy and you out of trouble."

"Speaking of civs, you know what?" Chen stated, drawing attention. "I heard from my folks yesterday. Back home the civs watched our attack here on the vid. Almost real time."

Stark stood silent, not willing to compromise the information he'd received from Reynolds and the command circuit during the assault.

"You're kidding," Carter replied. "You don't mean the news programs, do you?"

"No," Chen denied, shaking his head for emphasis. "It was special programs. Just a little time delay, and they showed us going through objectives and everything. Except when commercials ran."

"They made our attack a program?" Gomez spat. "With commercials?"

"That's not the worst," Chen added, reveling in the attention. "You know the guys in Second Division? The ones who are still committed all over the place back home? They're showing them, too. In battles and stuff. Soldiers getting wounded, dying, the whole thing. My folks say everybody's watching the shows on the vid. Better than that new no-rules hockey, they said. I guess there's more blood on a mil vid."

"I'm gonna shoot the next public affairs officer I see," Gomez vowed.

"They gotta just be following orders," Billings objected. "But why would the brass make our operations into a vid show to entertain the civs? Sarge, why would they do that?"

"I don't know," Stark admitted. "There has to be some reason, but I don't know what it is."

Carter slammed one of her tools to the floor. "Great. Now I'm not only going to have a lot of officers staring over my shoulder while I fight, I'm also going to have about a hundred million civs waiting to see me get hurt."

"Don't mess up those tools or you'll get hurt right now," Stark snapped. "Look, you know what a battlefield is like. Every soldier's got their own vid feed going back to headquarters. So there's no way any civs can be vulturing every one of us on their vid at the same time. Most likely, you'll never personally make the vid. Happy?"

"Not me, Sergeant," Desoto cracked. "I want to be a vid star!" Everybody laughed this time.

"Good luck," Stark wished his Corporal. "The rest of you, get back to work troubleshooting your battle armor. There's no sense getting worked up right now over something we can't do anything about." Silence broken only by the clink and buzz of equipment reigned for a few minutes.

"Sarge?" Murphy looked up from his maintenance work, mouth set in the determined fashion that meant he'd been thinking.

"Yeah, Murph."

"I heard an ugly rumor, Sarge."

Gomez barked a short laugh. "I hope it ain't as ugly as you, Murph."

"No. I mean, yeah. Hey, just knock it off."

Stark sighed heavily. "Okay, Murphy, what's this rumor?"

"I heard," Murphy declared pretentiously, glancing around the room to see how his words were received, "that they've run out of spares for the suits."

"Really?" Chen teased, hoisting a replacement rebreather cartridge in one hand. The genetically tailored living cells inside were amazingly efficient at converting carbon dioxide back into oxygen as long as you fed them current, but those cells also had a nasty tendency to die if any other organic matter contaminated them. "Then where are we getting these parts from, Murph?"

"I heard they're cannibalizing suits from outfits that are off the line. That's what I heard."

Mendoza eyed Stark warily. "Is that true, Sergeant?"

Stark shrugged. "What if it is?"

"It means we don't have a reserve," Mendoza noted. "If we need reinforcements, there won't be any."

Everyone watched Stark, trying to gauge his reaction to Murphy's and Mendoza's statements. He took a deep breath, choosing the right words. "I heard the same thing. So what? If you apes get in a firefight, who's the only person you can absolutely count on to look out for you? Yourself. After that, you can count on the other guys in this Squad. Don't forget that, and don't go into battle depending on someone else to save your ass because you're *never* sure that someone else will be there when you need 'em."

About half the Squad nodded back, reassured by the words, but the others still looked doubtful. "Sarge," Murphy noted, "sometimes everything goes to hell and you need help. It's kinda scary to know help can't come."

Help can't come. Stark fought down a shiver at the words, savagely tamping down memories he didn't care to confront. A vision of grass flecked with red specks of blood momentarily came between his eyes and the soldiers watching him. "Sometimes

. . ." Stark began, then choked off the words while his Squad looked puzzled.

"Okay," Stark declared in a harsher tone than he'd intended, drawing some more puzzled looks. "I could minimize all this, and make you all feel good. Or I can lay it out as bad as it is and make sure you apes are ready for the worst. Guess what I'm going to do?" Stark strode over to the vid panel on one wall, triggering it and calling up a sector map with American unit positions overlaid. "The situation sucks. See this? It's everything we hold right now. Mendoza, you're so smart, what d'you see?"

Mendoza gulped, obviously uncomfortable at the attention, then studied the picture intently. "Our forces are highly dispersed, Sergeant."

"Very good. Now put that in terms Murphy can understand."

"Yes, Sergeant." Mendoza raised a finger, pointing around the display. "Our units are spread out, a squad here, a platoon there. We're occupying a very large area for the number of personnel we have."

"Uh-huh." Stark glared at his troops, stabbing his own index finger at them for emphasis. "You know what that means? If everything goes to hell, if those foreigners we tossed out of here come back to fight for it all, it's going to be everyone for themselves at first. No one's going to have any support, from the rear or from the right or the left or anywhere else." Faces eyed the map grimly, years of combat experience measuring the situation and not liking the result. "So reserves don't matter. What matters is the grunt beside you. We hold, or we fall back, or if those idiots at headquarters order it we advance, but we do it on our own."

"What if we can't?" Billings whispered. "What if the odds are too bad?"

Stark glowered, putting everything he had into his performance. He had to convince his troops, had to keep their confidence in themselves, or he'd be letting them down as surely as if he let their equipment rust into uselessness. He also had to convince himself. Winning might require a lot of different things, but losing could be as simple as going in believing you were going to lose. "Not an option. There're no odds too bad for you apes. Period. So if everything else falls apart, you guys hold together. Understand? I won't accept anything less from you."

"*Si, Sargento*" Gomez agreed in the silence following Stark's words, a fierce grin illuminating her face. "We'll kick butt."

Stark grinned back, feeling his Squad's morale shoot upward again. "Damn straight you will." He pointed at the suits laid out for maintenance. "Now get that battle armor up to one hundred percent across the board. I want us ready for anything."

Time passed and eventually their chronometers said night, even though the lifeless rocks and dust were painted with the same harsh light and black shadow. Stark brooded over the view, alone now in the darkened cafeteria, a feeling of oppressive threat hanging over him. *Hope it's just nerves from living in this hole. We haven't received any warning of attack so far, but then the civs we took this place from didn't get any warning either. Lord, I don't want to buy a grave up here. If it all ends for me I want one somewhere less ugly. But above all, Lord, keep these apes of mine as safe as you can.*

"Sergeant?" Desoto stood nearby. "You about to turn in?"

"Yeah."

"Something bothering you? If anybody in the Squad needs straightening out—"

Stark shook his head, forcing a smile. "No, Pablo. The Squad's fine."

"I know Murphy's been a little harder to herd than usual these days. I'm going to have a talk with him."

"That's fine. Never hurts to put the fear of God in Murphy."

Desoto visibly hesitated. "You're not thinking of transferring Murphy out, are you, Sergeant?"

Stark's head shook again, firmly this time. "No. Murphy may not be the brightest star in the heavens, and he'll screw off any time he gets the chance, but if he knows it's expected of him he'll always be there when he's needed and he'll do a good job."

"He's a lot of work, though."

"Sure he's a lot of work. But if I sent him to some other outfit he might get a Sergeant who'd let Murphy slack off until it killed him. Murphy's my responsibility."

"*Verdad.*" Desoto nodded in agreement. "You met his parents once, didn't you?"

"Yeah," Stark recalled. "Back in the States somewhere. Nice folks. But that's not the point. He's my responsibility because he's mine. He's in my Squad. I send him off somewhere else, he's still my responsibility, because I sent him there. That's just the way it is."

"A lot of people don't see things that way. Officers sure as hell don't."

"Well, they gotta live with themselves, and I gotta live with me." Stark exhaled, long and soft. "Right now, I'm just trying to relax.

Got a bad feeling about things right now."

"Something coming down?"

"Not that I know of. Just nerves, I guess."

Desoto grimaced. "I know. It gets old after a while, doesn't it, Sergeant? That stuff about cannibalizing battle armor is bad news. One more mission on a shoestring, one more try at surviving without enough ammo or spares. God bless our leaders," he added irreverently.

"Don't forget whichever corporations plan on taking over all this stuff we grabbed for them. Oughta make them a lot of money."

"Yeah. Seems like all we ever do is go places to help rich people get richer. Did the mil always do that, Sergeant?"

Stark shook his head. "I don't know. Doesn't seem to have a lot to do with upholding and defending the Constitution like the oath says, does it? Go ask Mendoza." He pondered for a moment, then nodded. "Wait a minute. Mendo did say something about that once. The outfit was headed for some objective in the Pacific, and Mendo talked about how Hawaii used to be its own country."

"Hawaii? A country?"

"Yeah, only these American business types wanted it, so we went in and took it over for them."

Desoto looked puzzled. "When did this happen, Sergeant? Hawaii's been a state, like, forever."

"I don't remember. Long time ago, I guess."

"So why didn't we grab more stuff back then?" Desoto wondered. "You know, Korea or something."

"Somebody asked Mendo about that, and he said there was these other powers who wouldn't let us. Countries just as strong as us."

"Man, that was a long time ago. Not like now. Only superpower for what, a century?"

"Something like that. Ask Mendo."

"And nobody else can stop us when we really want something," Desoto continued, "so we've got everything we really want on Earth, and now we're taking the Moon, too. Guess the rest of the countries just got to roll over for that."

"Maybe. Maybe they'll just roll. But I tell you, Pablo, you back somebody into a corner and they might give up, or they might fight back real hard."

"You think they're going to fight, Sergeant?"

"Yeah. I think they're going to fight. I would." Stark eyed the impossibly barren landscape on the vid monitor, a landscape that already seemed to have been fought over for eternity by armies bigger than any humanity had ever mustered. "I hate this damn place, but I would."

"Wish the big bosses had to be here when the shooting started."

Stark laughed, the sound short and bitter. "That would be nice, wouldn't it? Too bad we can't swap places with them all next time it gets really hot."

"Sergeant, how come officers rotate in and out of assignments every six months? They never have time to learn their jobs. It'd be a lot easier on us if they led us better, but even the ones who seem okay—some of the junior officers, that is—they don't ever learn enough to be much good."

Stark held up three fingers. "Three reasons. One, there're too many officers for the number of grunts in the mil. They gotta keep them moving so it looks like they need them all." One finger came down. "Two, to get promoted, officers need to check off a bunch of jobs somebody decided were really nice to have. Only problem is, there're too many jobs on the list. So to get all the good jobs on their records, the officers can only stay in one job for a little while." Another finger dropped. "Finally, because an officer usually gets a medal at the end of a tour. The more jobs they hold, the more medals they get." The last finger fell.

Desoto screwed up his mouth in distaste. "I guess I should have known I wouldn't like the answer to that question."

"Then why'd you ask it?"

"To find out. Isn't that how you found out?"

"Yeah. Sergeant Reynolds drilled it into my head one day."

Desoto smiled quickly, there and gone in an instant. "You worried, Sergeant? About a battle?"

"I'm always worried. It's one of the things that keeps me and my Squad members alive."

"But this battle, Sergeant," Desoto insisted. "The one that's gonna happen sooner or later, when they fight. You worried we might lose?"

"Between you and me? A little. But, hey, vid wouldn't be very exciting if we didn't lose every once in a while, eh?"

"We won't lose, Sergeant. No way."

"I hope to God you're right, Pablo. If you and I have anything to do with it, we won't. Thanks for the talk. You'll make a good Sergeant someday."

"Thank you, Sergeant. Good night."

"'Night, Pablo."

Despite his resolution, Stark couldn't sleep, prowling restlessly through the hallways of the lab complex, dim "night" illumination leaving the far ends of the halls barely visible. The ache between his shoulder blades grew again, telegraphing a vague premonition of danger. *How long does it take to get to the Moon from Earth? How long to train the troops before they leave? Were they already training before we got here? Did they have transports ready, or did they have to build some in orbit first? How mad or desperate are they that we grabbed their last chance to break out of their boxes and maybe challenge the U.S. of A. for Big Dog status again? If enough of them stop fighting among themselves and get together, can they take us?* A lot of questions, none of which he knew the answers to. The rock-hewn passages of the lab complex held no answers, either, but at least they offered an endless path for restless feet.

"Sarge?" Billings called, her voice over Stark's comm. unit shocking in the silence of the sleeping halls. "Sergeant Reynolds is on the comm for you. Says it's really urgent."

"On my way." Stark checked the time as he ran, rubbing his face to calm himself. Everything about this felt bad, bringing new life to his fears. He headed for the comm terminal where Billings stood watch at this hour, past cubicles where the rest of his Squad still slept in the unaccustomed luxury of semiprivacy.

Reynolds' image on the comm screen started speaking as soon as she saw Stark. "It's going down. They're attacking."

"Damn. Why hasn't there been an official alert?"

Vic made a face. "The brass are still trying to find their heads with both hands."

Stark grabbed a packet of instant coffee, shoveling the powdered caffeine into his mouth for a fast jolt even as he mentally ran through the actions he'd take next. "How bad is it? What's going on?"

"I don't know for sure, because nobody does." Vic looked upward suddenly. "The Navy's getting hit hard, but they're trying to hold on as long as possible to give us time to prepare. There're definitely troop transports among the attacking ships, though."

"Okay, thanks." As the screen blanked, Stark turned to where Billings had been listening to the conversation, her own body tense. "Hold here and be ready for an alert to be passed." Then he ran back to the living areas, slamming the lights on at full brightness. "Everybody up, now! Company's on the way! I want you in full battle gear and ready to roll in five minutes! Go! Go! Go!"

It took more like ten minutes before the last member of the Squad fell in, which was still very good time. "Mendoza, relieve Billings on the comm so she can suit up. Listen good, you apes. The Navy's getting hit right now and there're transports bringing in enemy troops. I don't know how many, and I don't know what our orders will be, but we will be ready and we will kick butt. Any questions?"

"Who is it, Sarge? Who's attacking?"

"I dunno. But it looks like we finally pushed the First, Second, and Third Worlds a little too hard and they're pushing back harder."

"We're at war with everybody else on Earth?" Chen exclaimed.

"I told you I don't know."

Before anyone could say anything more, the comm panel buzzed frantically, then began relaying data to Stark's own Tactical. He immediately started shunting it downstream to his Squad at the same time as he read it. Full alert. Major attacks imminent. Tactical scrolled orders even as it painted a sector map on Stark's HUD. "Okay, everybody getting this?" Stark demanded. "We're falling back to form a perimeter around that colony they've been building up."

"Sarge?" Murphy called. "We're way outside that perimeter."

"The Sergeant knows that, Murphy," Corporal Desoto snapped.

Stark nodded. "Right. So, ladies and gentlemen, we are leaving as soon as Billings gets back. Say good-bye to clean living."

"Hey, Sarge." Gomez waved her hand around to indicate the entire complex. "The orders say we're supposed to destroy this place when we evacuate, but we haven't got any demolitions. It'll take forever."

"Yeah," Stark agreed. "It would, so we aren't going to try. On our way out we'll drop some incendiary grenades into the main computer room and call that good. If headquarters doesn't like it they can come do a better job themselves." Billings ran in, panting with haste as she fastened the last seals on her battle armor. "All right. Let's go. We're at war again, people. No screwing around and no screwing up."

Stark looked back as he cleared the main entry, the large airlock hatch still glowing clearly on infrared, remembering when they'd assaulted the lab several weeks back. He wondered briefly if the angry female scientist would return, complaining about the mess Stark's Squad had made of the place, then put it out of his mind.

"Sergeant." Stark looked over to Desoto, who pointed up wordlessly. He stared upward in turn, seeing strange new stars blooming far away against the lunar night. The Navy, fighting a desperate rearguard action. Suddenly a larger star erupted, growing into a ragged blossom that gradually faded. "Was that one of our ships?" Desoto wondered out loud.

"No telling," Stark noted grimly. "Given the odds up there, it probably was. Okay, those sailors are dying to buy us time, people. Let's move it."

Stark tried not to think about the distance left to be covered, tried not to realize how long it would take his Squad to reach the limited safety of the hasty perimeter that headquarters was trying to establish, tried most of all not to think about what would happen if they got caught by the enemy alone out here. They covered ground fast, the too-near horizon mocking them as it receded, endless vistas of rock and dust painted in shades of gray and black. "Sarge!" Hector yelled.

"Keep it down," Stark barked, watching on his own HUD as distant tracks arched toward the lunar surface—landing craft, well behind them but telegraphing the arrival of ground forces in large enough number to panic headquarters.

An ugly object suddenly jumped over the ridge before them, massive black armor glinting dully. "Hold your fire!" Stark shouted, "Wait for IFF!" even as his suit Identification Friend or Foe cheerily declared "friendly!" The APC pirouetted with absurd grace for such a mammoth object, coming to rest just before them.

"Get aboard fast," the APC driver called, her voice crackling with tension. Stark hustled his troops, ignoring normal dispersal routines, body crowding body into the cramped cavern of the troop compartment. No sooner did Stark haul himself in last than the access hatch slammed closed and the APC jerked upward, pivoted, then shot forward. The soldiers were flung into a tangled mass, cursing as they sorted out harnesses and tried to strap in.

Stark settled himself, checking suit readouts for the Squad.

"Anybody hurt back when we took off?" A chorus of grumbles answered him, intermixed with disparaging comments about the APC driver's ancestry. "Knock it off. How many of you would rather be walking?" Stark jacked into the APC's systems, trying to get more information, but its Tactical displayed the same scattered picture as Stark's. "Driver?"

"Yeah." Her voice reflected the concentration of highspeed driving through lunar terrain and the stress of impending combat.

"How far you taking us?"

"Not far enough, Sergeant." She stopped talking for a moment as the APC swerved violently. "Damn rocks. Don't wanna hit one. You get dropped a couple of klicks farther on."

Stark checked his Tactical. "That's still outside the perimeter."

"Uh-huh. I got more troops to collect, pal. I can't chauffeur you in all the way. No time."

"Roger." Stark settled back, trying not to think too much about everything that could go wrong in the next few hours. It seemed only moments later that the APC braked hard enough to provoke another torrent of curses from the Squad, then slammed to the surface. "Everybody out," Stark ordered.

"But Sarge," Chen protested. "We're still short of—"

"I know!" Stark roared. "Move it!" They moved, tumbling out with all the haste Stark's command could generate. "Disperse!" Stark snapped. "Maintain combat formation." He consulted his HUD as the APC jumped aloft and shot away, back toward where the enemy landing craft had fallen a short time before. *Good luck, buddy.* "People, we haven't got a decent map download of this area, but we know where we're going. Let's go."

As the Squad began legging it again, Stark switched to platoon-level scan, feeling a rush of relief as he spotted the symbology for Second Squad nearby. "Sanchez? You on?"

"Roger, Stark." From the lack of excitement in Sanchez's voice he could have been on simulated maneuvers instead of facing actual battle.

Stark checked his HUD again. "Looks like we're converging toward the same area."

"Agreed. My left flank should make contact with your right flank in about ten minutes."

"Great." Stark knew his elation was irrational in the face of the threat, but making physical contact with another unit meant that at least they were no longer alone on the empty. awful face of the Moon. "What about First Squad? Whereas Reynolds?"

"I think there's an APC trying to do a pickup on them now."

Stark felt a chill. "Damn. They were a long ways out. farther than my Squad."

"Relax," Sanchez advised. "You or me, we might be in trouble. Vic Reynolds will get her Squad out, though."

"Yeah, you're right." Stark fell silent, ushering his Squad forward until his right flank met Second Squad, until they reached the upwelling of ancient stone that marked the ridge they'd aimed for, until both squads flopped down, panting from their rapid movement, staring back down the way they'd come with dread anticipation.

Rifles came up as their HUDs pulsed, pinpointing a fast-moving object. "Hold on," Stark ordered as the vehicle shot directly toward them.

"I have no IFF," Sanchez reported.

"Me, neither," Stark agreed, fingering his rifle even as an instinct nagged at the back of his mind. "But what enemy would be crazy enough to charge ahead like that?"

"You think it's friendly?"

"Yeah. Maybe something's wrong with its IFF."

"Then my Squad will hold fire until you say otherwise."

Rifles lined up, aiming toward where suit combat systems estimated the unknown vehicle would be when it came within range. They made an odd sight, almost thirty barrels individually moving in sync with each other as each soldier's combat system reached the same targeting conclusions. "Sarge?" Carter called. "How close does that thing have to get before our rifles can punch through its armor?"

"Depends on what it is," Stark stated. "But nobody fires until I say so. Remember, that vehicle might be ours, and it might have friends on it."

The vehicle finally came into sight, glimpses of a dark shape weaving through the rocks like a huge beetle in a gravel pit. Stark gradually realized the weaves were too erratic to all be deliberate attempts at evasion, staring as the armor grated against outcrops, then steadied to come on again with the determination of a badly wounded animal seeking shelter.

"Man, that is one beat-up piece of metal," Gomez whispered.

Stark nodded silently, wondering how many of the dents and holes he saw marked penetrations of the troop compartment. The APC reached the spot where terrain began climbing and tried to rise with it, but staggered, grinding against the foot of the ridge, then came to a shuddering halt as bodies began leaping free.

"Who's there?" Stark demanded.

"First Squad," Vic Reynolds answered crisply. "Lieutenant Porter's been hit."

"What happened?"

"Firefight. Some enemy troops dropped almost on top of us. The APC yanked us out just before we got overrun. Unfortunately, it got shot up in the process."

"Jesus. Get the driver and the gunner."

"We've got the driver. She's been nicked but is mad as hell and has a sidearm. The gunner's dead."

"Hell."

Reynolds paused, then spoke again. "We'll have to leave him."

"But . . ." Stark gritted his teeth. *Have to leave them.* The words echoed someplace where memories forever lay too close to the surface. *No, just him. One guy. One too many, but what else are you going to do? Hold back all your living soldiers to help one guy who can't be helped anymore ?* Too much mass to lug around even on the Moon, not when you had to worry about moving really fast. "At least nothing will happen to the body up here."

"Yeah," Vic agreed shortly. First Squad members were coming up the slope, two with damaged battle armor being helped by other soldiers. "Can we hold here, Ethan?"

"I doubt it. The position's not bad, but there's nobody here but us."

"Sanchez? Anybody on your flank?"

"Not in contact, no," Sanchez noted coolly. "There is a gap of perhaps half a kilometer between my left and the next unit."

Big enough to drive a brigade through, Stark thought, but at least Sanchez had somebody providing support on that side.

"This is Lieutenant Porter speaking." His voice wavered oddly, possibly from shock, certainly from weakness and the effects of the drugs his suit's medical kit would have been automatically pushing into him. "We will hold here in accordance with our orders."

They waited, for moments that seemed longer than they should, until threat symbols popped into life at the edges of their HUDs. The symbols came on, flowing forward and to the side, marking infantry and vehicles moving ahead with deadly determination. Stark noted the numbers of oncoming threats, matched it against his own Platoon's firepower, and breathed a silent prayer.

Textbooks laid it out clearly. To defend a position you needed to be able to prevent the enemy from attacking you from the side or the rear. It was as simple as the truth that a soldier could only aim and fire in one direction at once. If necessary, you could try forming a circular defensive line, much like the surviving companies of cavalry had at Custer's Last Stand. That could work if you were strong enough, if the terrain you occupied was strong enough, if the enemy didn't try hitting you harder than you could hold against. It helped to be a little crazy and keep fighting long after logic said to give it up. Mendoza had talked once about how the British had done that a long time ago at a place called Rorke's Drift, but then Stark had always thought most Brits were born a little crazy. But those were exceptions. The cavalry companies actually with Custer hadn't been able to form a strong enough circle and had died to a man. So had a lot of other people on a lot of other battlefields. Stark had known some of them.

Stark could feel it, feel something that wasn't there, the absence of any other units beyond his last Squad member. The void worked at him, mocked him, told him his Squad had been hung out without support. Finally he could take it no longer, trying to speak without letting his ragged nerves show. "Lieutenant, I got nobody on my right."

"I know that, Stark!" Porter obviously wasn't in a very good mood, doubtless nursing considerable pain from his wound, pain no doubt aggravated by the rough ride here on the crippled APC. "I've told headquarters! What do you want from me?"

Stark licked his lips, fighting off another wave of anxiety, choosing his words with care even as he triggered a channel to ensure Reynolds and Sanchez were also listening to the conversation. "Lieutenant, I've got threat readings popping up steadily on the right. They're already behind us on that side. If we don't fall back we'll be outflanked and surrounded."

Before Porter could answer, Reynolds called in, voice innocent as if she were unaware of Stark's last statement. "Lieutenant, recommend falling back to the next ridge. We need to buy time for reinforcements to cover our flank."

It hung in the balance for a moment, Porter's fear of not following orders to the letter warring with his fear of losing his unit. The fact that he'd narrowly escaped capture or death a short time before may have tipped the balance. "Yes. Fall back by fire teams to the next ridge. I'll inform the chain-of-command that we're, uh, shortening the line to ensure we can hold."

Thank God. Stark had barely formed the grateful thought when Vic called him. "Ethan, you okay?"

"Yeah. I'm okay."

"You sound really bad. What—?"

"I told you I'm okay!"

"Fine," she snapped, breaking off the conversation.

Stark ordered his Squad into motion. Soldiers scampered back in pairs, dropping to cover the next pair as it retreated through them. They hadn't reached the next ridge when Stark's Tactical flashed with an update. Caught in midstride, Stark went to one knee to study the map, an involuntary whistle escaping his lips. They were going to shorten the line, all right, and for the first time the planned perimeter looked small enough to hold with the forces available. "De-soto, you get the new Tactical plan?"

"Yes, Sergeant. The planned perimeter has shrunk quite a bit."

"You might say that. The brass is finally getting real about this situation. We got a lot of falling back to do. You stay on the left and keep that end of the Squad moving proper while I watch the right side." Stark paused, then called up his command circuit tap to see if he could receive the big picture again. It took a moment to make sense of the chaotic picture that sprang to life. Apparently they'd had it easy so far, while units on the other side of the perimeter had taken heavy blows, been driven back, but were now hanging on. A cluster of unmoving enemy symbology apparently marked an attempted raid into the heart of the U.S. position, a raid which had cost the attackers their entire force thanks to the warning time the ground forces had received. *Thank you, Navy. I'll never slug a sailor again.*

"Sarge?" Private Hector called.

"Yeah, Hector."

"What's up? I mean, we almost got trapped back there, and now we keep falling back. How far we gonna go? What's going to happen?"

Stark stared ahead, seeing on his map display a long array of interlocking crater rims and ridges leading back toward the colony core of the perimeter. "Who do I look like, Hector, God? Stop worrying about what happened or almost happened. It's gone. Stop worrying about anything in the future. All that counts is that next ridge. Once we get to it, all that counts is the ridge beyond it. Understand? All of you, I want you thinking about *now*, because now is all that matters."

"Yes, Sarge," Hector answered, audibly abashed.

Something fast sped by far to the right, perhaps an enemy APC trying a risky maneuver to outflank the retreating American infantry. Even as Stark tracked the symbol, his jaw tense, hidden U.S. guns spat out heavy shells, and moments later a distant flash announced the destruction of the vehicle. *Thank God. There's somebody to our right now. Hang on, guys, we're coming.*

They made the next ridge, a feeling of pressure growing behind them. Threat symbols flickered in and out, there and not there as enemy forces came on, closing the distance. On into the next shallow valley, the pressure real now as a few shots ripped overhead, enemy troops unfamiliar with lunar conditions firing too high. "Don't stop," Stark commanded. "Get to the ridge."

They moved to reach the high ground, diving over the crest to keep silhouettes to a minimum, rifle rounds kicking up spurts of dust or shards of rock as they spattered all around like a rainstorm growing in intensity by the minute. Stark checked his HUD. One more ridge back to meet the planned perimeter, but the enemy was pushing hard now. Static fuzzed around the edge of his display as jamming began interfering with signals. "Stark, Sanchez," Vic called. "I sent Porter on ahead with the APC driver. We'll do this last fall-back by squads."

"Vic, they're on us," Stark objected. "One squad won't hold."

"They don't need to hold. They just have to make the enemy pause a little." Vic's breath exhaled suddenly, the way Stark knew it always did just after she'd fired a shot. "Now, Third Squad goes first. Get halfway back, drop and cover us. Second Squad will follow, go all the way to the ridge and cover this ridgeline. Got that, Sanchez?"

"Roger." Laconic as always. Stark felt an absurd annoyance, a wish that something would break Sanchez's calm outer shell.

"Go." One word.

"Third Squad, fall back with me." Stark scrambled backward, coming to his feet as he got far enough beneath the ridgeline. Fast, through showers of gravel falling along with them in lethargic tandem, as if the Moon were insisting it would not be rushed regardless of human priorities. They reached the midpoint, breathing heavily now, turning and aiming to where Sanchez's Squad came down off the ridge in another series of small slow-motion avalanches.

It took a little something extra to hold in place while Sanchez's Squad stampeded through them, not running but feeling like it all the same. "Everybody hold still," Stark grated, hunching his own body a little higher to make himself a solid symbol of stability. It made him an obvious target, too, but that was part of the price you paid. His Squad held their position, waiting as HUDs began calling out new warnings, tracking heavy rounds coming in high over the ridge. Artillery, looping in deadly tracks to gouge new craters where millennia of meteors had once worked alone.

Mortars, arching high overhead to drop almost straight down. The Squad held again, trusting to their myriad of deceptive camouflage devices and active jammers in every suit to throw off or fool smart munitions, hoping no dumb round would blunder its way right on top of them.

The enemy barrage hesitated, as Stark knew it had to. The enemy had come up too fast for supplies to keep up, and now they'd have to pause until new ammunition arrived. First Squad came down, faster than Sanchez's had moved, leaping in long, flat arcs, three figures now being partially carried by their Squadmates.

"Hold on," Stark urged as First Squad passed through. Sergeant Reynolds waving a quick salute as she passed. Shots rippled across the now vacant ridge, questing for targets, then ceased. *Here they come.* Stark aimed toward the ridge, canting his rifle high momentarily as he did so and seeing the targeting symbol flash red. *Can't shoot if I aim too high. Must be an inhibit to keep us from throwing rounds into orbit.* "Stand by," Stark cautioned his Squad. "Make every round count."

Figures showed momentarily as enemy troops rolled over the ridgeline. Stark's and Sanchez's Squads opened fire in a prolonged volley. In Stark's rifle sight, magnification and enhancement revealed vague outlines, ghostly images of soldiers with their own camouflage and jammers. He centered on each outline, his rifle slamming against his shoulder as rounds went out. Small clouds of shrapnel spread their deadly rain as Desoto used his auto-launcher to drop grenades among the enemy with cool precision. The outlines fell or tried firing back, only to fall sooner as they attracted more fire. "We gave them a bloody nose," Vic called. "Get your Squad back here with us, Stark."

"On our way. Let's go, Third Squad. Desoto, you and I bring up the rear." Run, all out except to keep herding the slower Squad members before you. Run, as more figures boiled over the ridge line behind them, firing as they came despite a murderous barrage from First and Second Squads. Chen slipped and fell, his suit broadcasting damage to Stark's display. He slid sideways, grabbing Chen as the Private tried to rise, propelling him forward even as Chen grunted with pain that the motion intensified.

Then the artillery came again, chasing at Third Squad's heels as they gasped up and over to the relative safety of the final ridgeline. Stark lay, breathing heavily, checking his own stats as well as the rest of the Squad's. "Mother of mercy. Chen, looks like you're our only casualty."

"Lucky me." Chen's voice had a slightly delirious quality, wobbly from the drugs his suit med kit was busy shoving into his system. "It's not bad, is it?"

"Bad enough, but you'll live." Stark switched circuits, grateful for the welcoming presence of friendly unit symbols on either hand, trying not to dwell on the increasing amount of threat symbology crowding in front, trying not to feel the steadily increasing drumroll of artillery slamming onto the ridge where they lay. "Vic, we got any more orders?"

"See anything new on your Tactical?"

"No."

"That's what we've got. We hold this line, Ethan."

Stark looked back over his shoulder, noting for the first time that behind him lay only a long, gentle slope, leading for kilometer on unobstructed kilometer to the American rear areas, to the new colony city being dug and raised by civs adventurous or desperate enough to come to the Moon voluntarily, and to the only spaceport left in their possession. "Yeah. I guess we do hold here. Otherwise, it's all over for us, and for the civ colonists who're depending on us."

It had been somewhere between Earth and Moon, months ago during the too-long lull between loading into their assault ships and reaching the objective. Stark and Corporal Desoto were strapped in, staring somberly at the many-shaded grays of their lunar target, talking about the small things and the big things soldiers discuss in quiet moments.

"Never thought I'd leave Earth," Desoto offered at one point.

"Me, neither," Stark agreed. "They say we'll be able to see it again when the ships do a turn-around to brake for arrival at the Moon. Not that I expect it'll be all that much to look at by then."

"Long ways from home," Desoto observed, then, after a pause, "You ever go home, Sergeant?"

"What do you mean?"

"You know. Home. Parents. Brothers and sisters."

"Home." Stark repeated the word slowly, then shook his head. "Nah. Haven't been there since I joined. Civ neighborhood, you know."

Desoto's eyes widened in wonder. "Your parents were both civs? You weren't born on a fort?"

"That's right." Stark looked out the port, his eyes focused somewhere else. "I tried going back once, right after I made Corporal. Pretty proud, let me tell you. I made it in only three years."

"Three years?" Desoto demanded in amazement. "How'd you make Corporal in only three years?"

"Uh . . ." Stark hedged with obvious reluctance, then shrugged. "Just lucky."

"Sergeant, it takes more than luck to make Corporal that fast. You get a battlefield promotion or something?"

Stark stared back at the Moon, avoiding Desoto's gaze. "Or something. Look, that's not what this is about. I made it."

Something about Stark's attitude finally got through to Desoto, who nodded in silent assent to change the subject. "So, what happened when you tried to go home?"

"Well, I was passing through the old town and I thought, *Why not?* Hopped a ride to the old neighborhood."

"Bet it'd changed."

"Uh-uh." Stark grimaced at the memory. "Same as always. Me, I was different. Wearing a uniform. Civs stared at me, fish out of water." He'd been around uniforms so long he'd forgotten how rare they were in the civilian world, insulated from the small band of military that sufficed for America in the twenty-first century. "Like I was some kinda alien with two heads, you know?"

Desoto nodded. "Yeah. Been there. Like they expect you to start shooting them or raping their sons and daughters or something." He suddenly smiled sadly. "Or maybe they're afraid seeing us will make those sons and daughters want to join the mil, too."

Stark laughed sharply. "Could be. Look what happened to me. They don't know us, Pablo."

"Mendoza told me that once upon a time lots of people knew someone in the mil, or had even served themselves. That was before the long drawdown. Now that there're not too many mil, and we're all pretty much in for life, most civs never meet a uniform. What happened when you got home?"

"Never did." Stark remembered the cops, alert and wary, who had faced him at the bus station. You lost, soldier? The base is back that way. If you're looking for a drink, take the number twelve bus to the military bar district. No, he'd protested, I'm just passing through. Fine, keep going, but don't pass through here, soldier. It's a peaceful place. A civ neighborhood. "Some cops stopped me. Made it clear nobody wanted me there. I said, 'Hell, what do you think, I'm gonna kill someone?' And they said, 'That's what you do, isn't it? Kill people?'"

"*Bastidos.*"

"Damn straight."

"So you let them stop you?"

"Not like that." Stark smoldered, old slights rising to the surface. "But I turned around. Didn't go home."

Desoto tried to make a joke of it. "Never thought Sergeant Ethan Stark would be afraid of a couple of civ cops."

Stark stared at his hands, not rising to the levity. "I wasn't afraid of them, Pablo. I was afraid my parents would be the same way. That's what scared me away."

"Sorry. Why they got to be that way, Sergeant? We put our lives on the line all the time, but they treat us real bad when they see us. Why?"

"Because they don't know better, I guess. Civs like the mil to protect them, but they want it done from far away."

"I wonder why we do it, sometimes. Why not do something else?"

"Something else?" Stark laughed. "Like what? You gonna get a civ job? Wear some kind of suit to work?"

"No. I guess civs are as alien to us as we are to them, huh?"

"Yeah. I grew up civ, and sometimes I can't even remember what it was like anymore. Other times it's like some weird dream where everything is different from what you know."

"Different? Like, how?"

"You know." Stark fumbled for words. "Different."

"I grew up on a fort," Desoto stated. "I don't know different. Like in school, everybody's mother and father, or maybe both, were in the mil and maybe off fighting. And we all knew we'd grow up and join the mil like them. Is that what civ kids are like?"

"No." Stark lowered his head, staring at the metal flooring beneath his feet. "No. Civ kids . . . okay, their parents do a lot of stuff. All different jobs. But hardly any of them run around saying, 'I'm gonna do what my dad or my mom does.'"

"How come?"

"They just don't. I dunno. Everything's confusing. You got all these . . . options . . . but most of them ain't real and you don't have any way of really understanding what the others are like. I mean, the mil, it's your life. Everything you do is mil. But civ jobs are all different. Maybe you understand what your parents do for a living, maybe you don't. Maybe you want to do the same thing. Maybe not."

Desoto nodded, his face puzzled. "You didn't want to do what your father did?"

"No."

"It was a real bad job?"

Stark looked up finally, face set in an unreadable expression. "I used to think so. I used to know everything when I was a teenager."

"We all did, Sergeant." Desoto laughed.

"Yeah. Now, I dunno. Maybe Dad didn't have the most important job in the world, but I guess he did it as best he could."

"You got an important job."

"I like to think so, but I know civs don't understand it. I was there, Pablo. One of them. Didn't have a clue what the mil was like." He shrugged. "Doesn't matter now, I guess. My life as a civ ended a long time ago."

"But you still have a home there."

"I guess. Sorta. Like I said, that civ life doesn't seem real anymore." Stark slapped Desoto on the shoulder. "Why do I need to go to a civ neighborhood to get home? Hell, I'm home right now."

Sensory overload threatened, even through the filter of the battle armor's systems, as the final American defensive line on the ridge got pounded by everything the enemy could throw at it. The lunar soil shuddered repeatedly as enemy rounds and submunitions hit, dust thrown up to hang in slowly falling curtains that were quickly ripped by small-arms and heavy-weapons fire.

Stark's Tactical glowed serenely, displaying no changes and no updates. It looked like the brass had locked up again. No decisions, no brilliant stratagems. Just hold until there was no one left to hold. Not the first time a unit died in place because no one could figure out how to extract them. But now that kind of thing was being shunted to the civs to see on vid. Great drama. Blood and guts. Now the civs would get to see them buy it, not staring in sick fascination at a rain of death displayed on their HDDs but watching all nice and comfortable in their media rooms with pretzels and cold beer.

Can't run, not without screwing every other soldier on the line. Can't stay, unless dying in place counted, which sometimes it did but not now. Stark hugged the rocks and dust and felt death's impacts trembling through them. The ghosts of trampled grass blades seemed to wave in front of his face shield, vibrating in time to the explosions. How many of the soldiers on this ridge might already be down, how long was left until the enemy pushed again and cracked the line wide open?

A unit could take only so much punishment, throw out only so much destruction at the enemy before ammo started to run low and battle fatigue ate at their brains. Too much combat, sustained too long, and you reached a point where the incoming rounds started to overpower resistance, a point where your own stuff couldn't hit back hard enough. Then it was just a matter of waiting until the unit's line started crumbling like cardboard under rain, falling apart into individuals and breaking away.

Stark had been here before, in another place, where grass grew. Lots of grass, tall and wild on the open hilltop, grass that had been trampled by heavy boots and matted down with blood as a long afternoon turned into despairing sunset. A place where the indigs had outside backing, a place where his unit had found itself on the downside of the firepower game, the manpower game, and the tactical thinking game. He could see it still, the tree line on all sides flashing with gunfire, those deadly flashes only partly obscured by the haze of battle. The soldiers to either side dying in sudden silence or long agony, their final duty to have their bodies plundered by those still living for desperately needed ammunition and medical supplies.

Not this time, Stark thought with rising rage. *I'm not gonna sit here while everyone dies around me. I don't care what happens to me. But what can I do?*

Over the squad net Hector called, his voice distorted with strain. "Sarge, it's getting *mondo* bad over here."

Stark came back quickly, trying to sound as sharp and cool as if he were on inspection. *No panic. Keep their fear, your fear, under control.* "You need me to hold your hand? I've been through a lot worse than this."

There was a long pause, then Billings came back, unnaturally calm. "Hector's down, Sarge."

Startled, Stark checked his HUD. No unit casualty stats showed. *Sonofabitch. They're screening out casualties. Damn. Damn. Damn.* Brigade had started sanitizing the information available to lower-level systems. That meant the brass expected heavy losses and didn't want them to know they were being torn apart. Never mind that filtering out the information at squad level meant Stark couldn't keep track of his own capabilities.

Like hell, Stark thought with redoubled fury. *I'm not playing that damned game. Not here. Not now.* There was another way. No orders? Fine. He'd make up his own. Maybe for the last time. Save his Squad if he could. If they were going to buy body bags anyway there wasn't much sense in not trying.

Stark raised his head, fighting down fear that the movement would attract instant fire, and scanned the ground ahead slowly, concentrating to block out the panic that threatened to break free.

The intensity of the enemy barrage had grown so bad it actually provided some cover, the rocks, dust, and other junk tossed into slow-falling lunar trajectories that confused or blocked enemy targeting systems. Stark squinted, matching what he could see with the partial map on his HUD. If he could just cover that flat area between him and the next ridge, he'd be in among the enemy grunts and at least he wouldn't die cowering here. At least. Do the unexpected. The enemy had been pushing them hard, trying to make them break, and by now the enemy had to be tired, too.

Okay. Get to that ridge. Maybe one hundred meters. Piece of cake on an exercise track, but impossibly far here and now. He and the Squad would need cover, and they didn't have the bullets left to provide suppressive fire.

They did have the damned dust, though. There was plenty of that.

Stark called up a personal circuit, one jump-wired so the command channel and the vid monitors couldn't access it. "Pablo," he called his Corporal. "Need you. Get ready to put a string of delay-fuzzed eggs along this line." As he spoke, Stark used his helmet sight to draw a ragged series of impact points along the far ridge and through the low terrain before it.

"Okay, Sarge." Desoto wasn't happy, but he didn't question the order. "That's going to use up all the grenades left in the autolauncher."

"If this doesn't work, we won't need them." Stark switched back to the regular circuit, ready for the chain of command to track his actions again, now that it would be too late for them to veto anything. "Third Squad, stand by. Okay, Corporal Desoto. Fire."

Stark's HUD suddenly tracked a dozen grenades flying toward the points he'd designated. Every round on target despite the intense enemy fire. *Good shooting, Pablo.* The rounds hit, and, after a pause, detonated from below the surface, throwing up a dense cloud of dust along and before the ridge. 'Third Squad! Follow me!" Fighting down the voice screaming in the back of his brain to hide-hide-hide, Stark lunged forward, rolling headfirst down the slope before him, running, staggering back and forth to confuse aiming in case the enemy could somehow see him, trying to hold a course toward the next ridge. His HUD flickered, staggering under the load of enemy jamming, then blanked out, blinded by the dust, picking up incoming small-arms fire and energy pulses close by, here and gone in a blink through the obscuring cloud. He kept going, hoping his Squad had followed, trying not to think beyond the next step.

His feet hit an upslope and Stark surged forward, putting all he had into a final burst of speed. He cleared the cloud of dust and debris, sudden stars and black night seeming unnaturally bright, bursting out with the top of the ridge before him and in a single motion dove low down and across the rocks, turning to glide down into the dust of the reverse slope, head down on his back, bringing his rifle around and triggering its two grenades to either side, lining up the sight to aim-squeeze-fire, aim-squeeze-fire at the figures scattered here. Enemy soldiers fell, atmosphere venting from ruptured armor, firing across at him from each side, rounds passing above his prone body to inadvertently engage their own forces on either side.

Stark slid to a halt, aim suddenly jittery as he tried to keep shooting, feeling a long, slow moment of despair as enemy fire steadied, knowing he had only seconds left and panic frozen inside. *Didn't work. At least I tried. Sorry, you guys. I guess the civs will get to watch us buy it after all. Hope Mom and Dad see this, know I did 'em proud, if they can stand seeing me die out here.*

Another figure loomed, shockingly close from over the ridge, and Stark swung to fire, freezing his finger on the trigger as IFF shouted "friendly!" Then there were more friendlies coming over the ridge. His Squad, shouting and firing at enemy ranks already disrupted by Stark's charge. The enemy began falling back in confusion, ranks torn and broken.

"Jesus, Sarge," Murphy screamed as his armored body flopped down near Stark, his weapon jumping as rounds ripped out in an almost steady stream, "why the hell'd you do that? Next time give me a heads-up!"

"Sure," Stark shouted back, automatically rolling away from Murphy to avoid providing a clustered target. Stark's comm system was screaming now, too, commands from up the chain tangling with each other and enemy jamming. "Get the heavy weapons!" he ordered.

Murphy and the rest of the Squad turned, targeting the weapons pits that were finally reacting, shifting aim to target Stark's Squad now that their own troops weren't intermingled. Some of the Squad scrambled up, trying to get in among the enemy once again, but dropped rapidly as the heavies opened up, raking the area with firepower the Squad's own small-arms fire couldn't match. The charge's momentum faltered, events hanging in the balance as the enemy tried to figure out what had happened and how to crush the unexpected assault.

A huge object jumped the ridge to Stark's left, gouging out a swath of terrain as it shaved the top, then slid ponderously down in a slow avalanche of rocks and dust, turret swiveling and secondary rounds going out, enemy weapon pits erupting into clouds of debris as the tank took out local targets. Whoops of triumph filled the comm circuits. *Of course,* Stark realized. *We cleared the troops manning the ridge, so a tank could get across without being targeted.* He suddenly loved all tankers, especially the one who'd risked his or her machine and life in that mad leap to join them. The turret steadied a moment and the main gun jumped, followed seconds later by a massive detonation in the distance.

More infantry came over the ridge. Stark's overloaded HUD painted a flickering picture of tentative IDs that indicated the rest of his Platoon had followed his Squad. "Stark!" Lieutenant Porter's outraged voice rang out in a moment of comm clarity. "What the hell—?" Then it was overridden, Tactical clearing momentarily to shift in a wild update, ordering an advance all along the ridge. Someone up the chain had seen the opportunity offered by Stark's Squad's charge, had broken out of paralysis long enough to shove everything available after them.

The enemy line had fallen apart. Some of their infantry were still running, others stopping and dropping their weapons to await capture. The tank continued methodically chewing up every target in sight, shifting position as the second and third tanks in the squadron heaved up over the ridge to join it. On the HUD, Stark watched as more troops poured into their penetration, widening the hole and peeling away the edges like a river in flood tearing open a dam. Then the river faltered, slowing to a trickle as the stream of troops ran dry. *Nothing left to exploit the success,* Stark noted bleakly. *We used up everything we had stopping the enemy.*

Stark came up to one knee, trying to judge the status of his Squad from their position markers, knowing he couldn't yet trust their health or readiness readouts. Somewhere up ahead, a sudden flurry of fire marked the enemy rushing in reinforcements to stabilize their front and seal the penetration, the two armies clashing in drunken exhaustion like punch-drunk fighters still trying to land blows but too worn out to achieve much without rest. His HUD displayed tangles of estimates warped by jamming, comm delays, and enemy deception, but the lines seemed to be holding on both sides even as Stark's Tactical ordered another advance against the rapidly solidifying enemy resistance.

"Gimme a break." Stark checked his own ammunition, noting less than a half-dozen rounds remaining, and extrapolated that to the rest of the Squad. "Lieutenant Porter?"

"Stark!" The signal came through so clear that Porter must have somehow gotten himself onto this side of the ridge as well, maybe with the assistance of the dismounted APC driver who still had to be thirsting for revenge over her gunner's death. "If you ever take off without orders or Tactical again I'll, I'll—"

"Yessir. Lieutenant, I've got orders from Tactical to assault, but my Squad's out of ammo."

"So what? Follow orders for once! Just do what you're damn well told!"

"Lieutenant," Stark corrected, trying to project regretful innocence, "doctrine states exhaustion of ammunition requires holding in place until resupply."

"It does? Damn. Sergeant Reynolds?"

"Reynolds here," Vic's voice chimed back. Stark ducked his head in gratitude to hear she'd survived the assault as well.

"How's your ammunition?"

"One or two rounds left per weapon, Lieutenant."

"Sergeant Sanchez?" Porter called, sounding increasingly vexed.

"Yes, Lieutenant." Sanchez might have been reporting in a routine roll call. "I have no ammunition remaining."

"Whatever happened to fire discipline?" Porter demanded. "What about casualties?"

"Unknown," Stark declared coldly. "Casualties are being screened out at our level. We can't trust our Tactical picture."

"I—" Porter cut off his own reply, then spoke again as if with difficulty. "I'll report our status up the chain. Stand by for orders."

Stark, trying to fight off a giddiness born of unlooked-for survival, switched his own comms to talk to Reynolds directly. "Hey, Vic. What happened to all your ammo? You been in a battle or something?"

"Look who's talking. How many angels you got looking out for—? Oh, God."

"What?" Stark checked his HUD, spotting incoming through the mess of symbology. *Careless. It's not over. Too damn careless.* "Third Squad! Take cover!" Enemy heavy artillery had finally reacted. Massive rounds started dropping along the ridge, perhaps called in on their own position by the now-fleeing enemy infantry. Stark held on to the rocks beneath him as the lunar soil shuddered with impacts so heavy he seemed to be on the verge of launching into the empty atmosphere, wondering why the artillery had concentrated on this site, then cursing wildly as one of the reasons rumbled by.

"Third Squad, get out of here!" Stark bellowed. "Away from the armor, now!" Tanks were magnets for enemy fire, and there were three of the metal monsters scattered among Stark's own Squad's position. He rose and dashed to the right, downslope, taking only a dozen steps before his suit shrieked another warning. Stark dove for the ground again, forgetting where he was, forgetting to pull himself down instead of depending on gravity, falling with agonizing slowness until a column of fire blossomed close by and a great hand reached over and slapped him with shrapnel fingers.

Darkness without stars cleared abruptly, Stark's ears ringing with comms and suit alarms. Battered but somehow still intact, pitted with shrapnel scars, the armor had absorbed the impact without suffering a major rupture. "Third Squad. Follow me." He rose, limping as either his leg or the battle armor protested the movement, leading the way down off the ridge.

"Sarge?" someone called, voice distorted by screeches of static. "We gonna attack again, Sarge?"

Stark checked Tactical once more, glaring at the red digits demanding his Squad assail the enemy again immediately. "No."

"But our orders—"

"Screw our orders. We're digging in."

Stark stood awkwardly, helmet in hand in traditional deference to the dead as he stood in the field hospital. A medic who looked like he hadn't slept in a week stared bleary-eyed up at the Sergeant. Stark nodded to indicate the medical wards down the hall. "I'm here to see Gomez."

"Gomez?" The medic made an obvious effort to concentrate, typing with careful precision on the laptop before him. "Anita? Bay 25B."

"Thanks." Stark headed in the direction indicated, keeping his hands well clear of the unadorned white paint that sealed the rock walls here. Bay 25B held more of the same, a white curtain strung across the entrance, white ceiling, white sheets on a bed where Gomez lay with a white cast covering most of one leg. Even Gomez seemed whitened, drained of color by shock.

Stark sat and waited, patiently. Sleep was important, more important than his words, so he waited until Gomez finally stirred, blinking up at the whiteness all around with a dazed expression.

Gomez stared, unable to speak, until Stark finally quirked his lips in a small smile. "Guess I finally found out how to shut you up, eh, Anita?" He leaned forward to peer into her eyes. "You don't look too drugged up." Stark gestured toward her leg. "A heavy round went off right next to you, they tell me, close enough for the pressure wave to hit, but so close you were inside the shrapnel pattern. Concussion broke your leg and bruised the hell out you, but no suit penetration. Lucky."

Gomez drew in a breath, half sigh and half sob as the gesture apparently brought pain. She used one hand to raise the sheet covering her, wincing at the sight of one side of her body painted in patterns of purplish-black, which seemed doubly awful amid the whiteness all around. "Damn. Thought I was dead." Gomez winced, looking embarrassed at speaking so frankly to her Sergeant.

"We all ought to be," Stark agreed.

"You told us to follow you," Gomez pointed out.

"Yeah, I did. Damn fool stunt, but I didn't think we had any other choice."

"Yeah, well, you did good, Sarge," Gomez offered. "Saved our butts."

"For now, yeah, maybe I did."

"What's going on out there right now?"

"Digging in," Stark stated. "Everybody's going deep, laying minefields, building bunkers. There's talk of us trying to retake the areas we lost. Seems the civ politicians still want to claim the whole Moon. They got one helluva appetite for territory."

"Great. What about the other side? They willing to let us?"

"Nah. The enemy seems to still be interested in pushing us off the Moon completely. They're tired of getting kicked around. Fighting all-out back on Earth would be too dangerous, but up here they're willing to face off with us."

"Man," Gomez noted ruefully, "looks like everybody's drawn a line in the dirt."

"That's right, and we're sitting right on top of that line. Looks like it's going to be a long war."

"Lucky us." Gomez grinned. "Hey, I'm alive."

"Yeah, lucky." Stark took a deep breath, avoiding Gomez's eyes. "You've been doing good lately. Real good. Reliable. Sharp. Looking out for other grunts, not just yourself."

She blushed and looked away, unable to deal with the praise. "Just doing what I'm supposed to. You always said we need to look out for each other, Sarge."

Stark leaned back, now gazing at her steadily. "You've been field-promoted to Corporal. Congratulations."

Gomez stared back at him, alarmed. "Corporal? Sarge, I'm happy as a Private. I'm no Corporal. No, thanks."

"That wasn't an offer, so you don't get to refuse it. We need a new Corporal," Stark added bluntly, "and you'll be a good one."

It took a moment to sink in, then Gomez's face fell as the meaning came clear. "Pablo? He was hit, too?"

"Hit, yeah." Stark kept his face impassive, his words flat. "They were able to reconstruct what happened from the vid feed. One of the heavy rounds they were throwing at us, probably a two-hundred-millimeter, hit him dead on. You and I, we had good luck. He had bad. They found enough of him to do a DNA match, but not much more."

"Damn," Gomez whispered, blinking rapidly. "Pablo, he always said he was scared of the body bags, scared of being fastened in one while he was still alive. Funny, huh? All the things we got to worry about, and that's what scared him. Now he won't need one, not scattered in a million pieces across . . . where was it? That last fight?"

"The Sea of Tranquility," Stark replied. "Near it, anyway."

Gomez nodded. "The tanks that saved us, came over the ridge, they also attracted the fire that killed Pablo?"

"Probably. My fault. I should've realized quicker, gotten us moving faster."

"Nah, Sarge. We needed those tanks, but nothing ever comes free or easy, right?"

"Right."

"We lose anybody else?"

"Hector's gone, nailed during that barrage before we attacked, and Carter got her head blown off, maybe before the enemy weapon's pits got taken out. Chen's wounded, took a round in his left hip, but the docs have replaced the joint and he'll heal up fine." Funny thing, the battle armor protected pretty well, which meant that when something did get through, it was likely to be lethal. Fewer wounded. A higher percentage of dead. Sort of a good deal.

Gomez nodded, face stricken. "Could've been worse. A lot worse."

"Yeah, could've been." Stark stood, feeling heavily burdened despite the light pull of Luna. "I'll leave. You gotta rest. Just wanted to be here when you woke." He turned, then looked back before he left. "Real sorry about Juan Hector, and Susan Carter, and Pablo. I know you were friends. Pablo was my friend, too, and a damn fine Corporal. Would have made a good Sergeant someday." *I should've done better. Somehow.* He left the last unspoken, the thought lying across his shoulders like an invisible burden.

Gomez nodded, wordless once more, as Stark left. The white ceilings, walls, and curtains spoke of peace and healing in the hushed silence of the medical ward, yet as Stark walked down the hall, the chaos of bygone battles raged in his mind, and pain filled him.

PART TWO

WHERE NO LARKS FLY

The news swept through the front line, leaping from bunker to bunker like a swift, dark messenger heralding pain and loss. "Popularity ratings on the war are down, big time."

Stark cursed softly, his face lit in sharp patterns of light and shadow by the glow of the comm screen in the darkened bunker. Predawn calls were never pleasant, but some were worse than others. "Five points down is one hell of a big drop."

"Sorry to be the bearer of bad tidings." Vic Reynolds didn't look any happier than Stark felt.

Stark shook his head tiredly, shaking off the last traces of sleep. Each of the past few years had seemed to add a double ration of age, as if the gravity up here were twice that of Earth instead of a small fraction. Earth. A place so physically and psychologically distant they simply called it "The World" now. "Real bad, Vic.

Why hasn't word of this spread around official? Vid ratings aren't classified."

"Because official ratings aren't out, but the brass got advance intelligence."

"Good to know those apes in Intelligence do something with their time, even if it is just watching the vid." Stark closed his eyes briefly, thinking through the implications. "Thanks for spreading the word fast, Vic. There's only one way headquarters will think of for getting the ratings back up."

Vic nodded, her expression now matching that of someone who had bitten into a very foul-tasting object. "Something dramatic." Her image glanced to the side as someone passed her cube over in the command bunker, a momentary shadow tending an unknown midnight errand, then focused back on Stark. "Brass likes to plan things to death, usually."

"Uh-huh. And when the enemy sees the overnights they'll know we'll have to do something to try to boost the ratings, so they'll go to full alert." Stark shook his head again, this time wearily. After years of military and diplomatic stalemate in the lunar war, the patterns of action were so well set that they almost matched the predictability of Earthrise. "Yeah, Vic, headquarters will grind out a plan just after the enemy goes to full alert, so anything we try will be real dramatic and real dangerous. Appreciate the heads-up, though. Maybe for once headquarters will give us a pleasant surprise."

"Want to bet any money on that?"

"No. You tell the Lieutenant yet?" The way it was supposed to work was Lieutenants got the word from up their chain of command and passed it on down to their Sergeants. In practice, the Sergeants heard about anything important first through their own grapevine, given that they trusted neither their Lieutenants nor their chain of command.

Reynolds quirked a humorless smile. "No, nothing there. Kilroy's still too new to have a feel for things up the chain of command, or good contacts. She'll be fat, dumb, and happy until official orders come down." Their last Lieutenant had headed back to the World— Earth—only a couple of weeks before, after sliding through the usual six-month officer tour without committing any particularly horrible mistakes. Stark already had trouble remembering that last Lieutenant's name. The new Lieutenant's real name was Conroy, but the Sergeants only called her that to her face and before the troops. Kilroy had been an inevitable and irresistible nickname for an Earthworm new to the front. Maybe, if the Lieutenant did a good enough job, the Sergeants would call her Conroy in private before her six months were up. Maybe. Nothing came to you up here without earning it. "Sweet dreams, Ethan," Vic added.

"Thanks a lot. You, too." The screen blanked, leaving Stark with the darkness and a large stack of misgivings. There had been plenty of similar events during the past few years, but something about this one felt especially ominous. By no means a superstitious man, Stark still had come to trust his own premonitions for better or for worse.

The rest of the night passed slowly. Sleep wasn't possible anymore, not after Reynolds' warning. Stark thought, running through the sector of the front his Squad faced, visualizing enemy strongpoints that any attack might have to bypass or, Heaven forbid, assault.

Now, there's a way to boost ratings. Watch our brave soldiers prove once again that, even inside battle armor, flesh and blood lose big time against entrenched heavy weapons.

The stars moved and Stark waited, but no orders came. Eventually, humanity's time declared morning's arrival, in a place where the concept had no meaning otherwise. The event was trumpeted by a brief enemy artillery barrage, whose shells sailed overhead to die in sudden glory against the ebony lunar sky as American defenses sought them out, or fell to detonate in soundless fury, the tremors of their detonations coming as brief vibrations against the rock into which Stark's bunker had been dug.

Stark had dressed and shaved long before, moving quietly in the predawn silence of the darkened bunker. Now he sat, listening to his Squad stir. Soldiers moved, exchanged greetings, went for" breakfast, or checked the plan of the day for work and sentry duty assignments. He heard Corporal Gomez chewing out a Private for sloppy appearance. Gomez had an intensely precise way of spelling out the many personal and professional shortcomings of anyone who didn't meet the standards she thought Stark expected. It was unlikely that Private would risk her wrath again.

Finally, Stark rose and entered the corridor, actually a narrow shaft through the bunker granted dignity by the term. A quick breakfast first, he decided, despite his lack of appetite, then roll call. *Have to make sure I don't look nervous. That'd make everybody else nervous, too. So, do I tell the troops action might be around the corner?* It seemed absurd, after the night's quiet, that the silence from above had made that possibility more hazardous. *The brass never panics into action when inaction can cause us more trouble. Now we get to wonder a little longer just how bad it'll be and who'll get hammered. The Squad deserves to know about the ratings, though, even if the sentry hasn't already gotten a dump on them from another bunker and spread the word.*

Even after all this time, his first step was too strong, so Stark had to catch himself on his desk to keep from rising off the floor. The body never quite accepted it wasn't home, habitually acting as if it were the Earth beneath it. The first misstep was almost a daily routine here on the lunar perimeter, defending America on its current and only front lines.

0730, Lunar Adjusted Time. Morning roll call, like every morning on the line, his Squad falling in for work assignments, updates, and whatever else Stark felt like tossing in. Not like back on the World, the cloud-bannered Earth that floated overhead in distant reminder of home. There, roll call caught the occasional soldier off-base and Absent Without Official Leave with a new "friend" or maybe in a ditch with a major headache and empty pockets. That couldn't happen here, where the only things within walking distance were more bunkers and enemy defenses itching to conduct target practice on any American soldier who wandered close enough. But you called the roll here anyway, to keep things structured, to keep a routine.

Corporal Gomez snapped a salute as Stark approached. "All present, *Sargento.* Work and sentry details assigned."

"Fine." Gomez had developed into such a good Corporal it was tempting to let her run things on auto sometimes, except he'd seen that trap before. Good noncoms ran things well as long as you respected them and pulled your share. "Got some word."

A ripple of disquiet ran through the ranks. That meant something nonroutine, and nonroutine usually meant more work or more risk, if not both.

"I guess it's been quiet lately." Awkward beginning, but Stark had never claimed to be a great speaker. "Got word last night that mil vid ratings are down. Five points." A staggered reaction ran through the Squad as each soldier processed the information. "That big a drop is going to hurt revenue, and that means things are likely to get exciting soon. Maybe not for us, but maybe so." Worry, excitement, tension showed on individuals, sometimes chasing each other across a single face. "Whatever happens, we'll deal with it. Make sure your gear is at one hundred percent, because it might be real short notice. Questions?"

The veterans knew enough not to ask for details Stark didn't have, while the two newer soldiers hesitated to speak and show ignorance. Private Kidd, one of the recent replacements, finally half raised her hand. "Sergeant, when will we know if we're on tap for something?"

"When we know." The vets smiled derisively as Kidd looked abashed. Stark unbent enough to elaborate; he'd been a new recruit once and asked his own share of dumb questions. "I'll pass on any word I get, soon's I get it. If we're lucky, somebody else will get handed this one. Anything else?" he asked the room. "Then carry on." He turned to Gomez. "They're looking pretty good."

Gomez nodded back. "For a bunch of slack Earthworms, they're not bad." A chorus of mock groans arose from the ranks as Gomez grinned. "You heard the Sergeant. Carry on. And don't let any good words from him go to your heads."

The Squad broke ranks, heading for their individual assignments.

The give-and-take felt good, Stark thought, a sign morale was doing okay. Manning the front line wore soldiers out, sitting in a cramped bunker through weeks of inactivity punctuated by occasional spasms of fear and violence. He spoke quietly to Gomez. "We need to keep them busy, next couple of days, keep them from thinking too much about what might happen."

"Yeah, Sarge," Gomez agreed soberly. "You sure you should have told 'em?"

"Yeah, I'm sure. You don't keep your people in the dark, Anita. Treat them like you'd want to be treated in their place. This way they'll be ready, mentally and physically. That's important."

"Sure. Makes sense." Corporal Gomez rubbed her palms together, frowning into the distance. "I got a bad feeling about this one, Sarge. It's been a long time since headquarters screwed us. Might be our turn again."

"Might be. Worrying won't make it any better if it is."

"Si, Sargento. I'll make sure the Squad doesn't have time to get worked up. I'll keep them running so hard they won't even have time to think about Bunk Maneuvers."

"You figure out a way to get a grunt's mind off sex and I'll put you in for a medal." Stark gazed after his dispersing Squad. *What the hell? Isn't that . . . ? Nah. Of course not.* Sometimes he got startled, thinking he'd seen some soldier walking away who was no longer there, someone now dead or wounded too badly to ever fight again. Funny how he only got that feeling when he saw them going away from him. "See you later. I'm taking my walk."

"Enjoy." Gomez paused as she turned away. "Hopefully it won't be our turn in the barrel."

"Yeah. Hopefully."

Stark did a walk-through of the whole bunker, small as it was, every morning. Simple routine, to keep in touch and keep aware. He'd served under a Sergeant once who'd spent all day in his office. The Lost Sergeant, they'd called him, and gotten away with damn near anything out of sight of his doorway.

Troop living cubicles. Tight, four troops to a cube. Luxurious, some civ had called them, touring the excavation to stare sourly at raw lunar rock. He'd obviously been looking for another way to shave a few more bucks off of fighting a war, which was probably why headquarters had sent him to Stark's Squad. "Why three separate cubes instead of a single Squad cube for everyone?" the civ demanded.

Stark had extended one fist, slowly, while the civ's eyes widened appreciably. "People are trying to hurt us," Stark stated with exaggerated patience. "If they blow a hole through that rock, right there, I lose four soldiers. I'd hate that. But if this one room held my entire Squad, I'd lose twelve soldiers. I'd hate that a helluva lot worse."

The civ had squirmed under Stark's intense gaze, then rallied enough to speak again. "It's not very economical to build these extra sleeping cubes."

Stark nodded back, face unyielding. "It's cheaper than replacing twelve soldiers and a hole in the defensive line. Isn't it?" The civ had left hurriedly. Stark had never been told what the civ's report had said, but the bunkers had continued to be built with three sleeping bays, so headquarters had probably accomplished its dual goals of discouraging the intrusive civ and aggravating the notoriously difficult Sergeant Stark.

Chen occupied one of the cubes, bending under a bottom bunk to wield a hand-held vacuum against the fine dust that seemed to spontaneously generate out of the air in lunar living spaces. Since that fine dust could seriously screw up the fine electronic gear that kept humans alive up here, policing it regularly remained a tedious but necessary task.

"Hey, Sarge." Ghen looked up from his work with a tight grin.

"Hey, Chen. How's it going?"

Chen visibly hesitated before replying. "Fine, Sarge."

"The hell. What's bugging you?"

"Um . . ." Chen swung one hand to indicate the doorway to the cube. "We heard the doors got modified last time we were off-line, Sarge."

Stark stared dispassionately at the door edge where it poked out of the wall, a thick slab of metal necking down to a gleaming steel knife edge barely visible within its pocket. "Yeah," he acknowledged. "They boosted the explosive rams and modified the door edge to make sure the door can slam shut through any obstacle if there's decompression in the cube."

"What about the inhibit, Sarge?" Chen asked. "There's supposed to be an inhibit that'll keep the door from slamming shut if there's a grunt standing in the doorway."

"Yeah," Stark agreed again.

"But we were talking," Chen continued, "and it doesn't seem like the brass would risk losing a whole squad to decompression just because one grunt is in the wrong place at the wrong time. We figure there's not really an inhibit at all, and that door's going to cut in half anybody who's in the way. Is that true?"

Never lie to the troops. "I don't know that it's true and I don't know that it's not."

"So what should we do, Sarge? What should we do if at any moment there's a chance that door will slice in two any grunt who's standing in that doorway?"

"Don't stand in the damn doorway."

"Oh." Chen nodded vigorously. "Yeah. Okay, Sarge."

The stuff that passes for wisdom. If something's gonna hurt and you don't have to do it, don't do it. Stark nodded back to Chen before moving on.

On through the small rec cube, lined with resistance gear every soldier had to work at for a few hours every day to keep their muscles from going on lunar vacation. Then the adjacent kitchen, a tiny cell with access to the rations and minimal food prep facilities. End up in the main command room, biggest space in the bunker, not that it qualified as big under any other criteria. Walls lined with monitors and readouts, the sentry posted to one side. When they got attacked, which happened occasionally when the enemy felt like probing for weak spots, most of the Squad would head outside and fight from firing pits deployed around the bunker. The bunker's own firepower, chain guns and grenade auto-launchers in a handful of mounts scattered along the outside terrain, was controlled from seats here.

Similar bunkers, the products of years of carefully concealed construction, were strung at irregular intervals all along the American perimeter guarding the lunar colony city of New Plymouth. Facing the American line, a matching string of unseen enemy fortifications dotted the face of the Moon. The Great Wall of China on Earth, rumor claimed, could be seen from space, like a dragon sprawled across the land. Stark had never seen it, as even continents were sometimes hard to make out on the blue-white ball that dominated the sky, but he had watched a vid of the Great Wall once, and laughed. Too big to defend, all those kilometers of wall, and too easy to destroy, sitting out in the open. Mankind had learned a lot about killing since those ancient stones were laid. The lines of defensive works on the lunar surface lay hidden, deadly snakes ready to strike at anyone who stumbled too close to their lairs.

Several soldiers were sweating their way through training drills on the weapons stations under the alert and unforgiving eye of Corporal Gomez. Off to one side, Private Mendoza had the morning sentry detail, watching the outside through the eyes of the local sensor net. Mendoza, bored as every sentry since Adam fell asleep guarding the apple tree, jerked to an attentive posture in his seat as Stark entered. Stark nodded to him, wandering over to peer past Mendoza's shoulder at the situation readouts.

Screens displayed a wild array of pictures, depending on the sensors they accessed. Infrared painted an unreal scene of glowing blobs, fuzzy with radiated heat. Vibration sensors displayed sudden swelling pings on a sector map where rock contracted or expanded under sun's heat or shadow's cold, the events all assessed natural due to randomness by the sophisticated artificial intelligence monitoring everything that happened on this part of the line.

As always, the view from the visual monitor drew Stark's gaze. Black-on-white, harsh shadows scissored across the dead landscape. Incredibly old rocks and equally old dust. From this angle, no Earth lit the sky with its small reminder of color and life. He remembered clouds, white patches in unnumbered shapes, parading across blue skies, and water in great, unconfined bodies, thundering ashore as surf on the beaches not far from his boyhood home. Huge trees blocking the sky, like the choking vegetation in the handful of jungle countries where he'd fought before coming here. And grass, of course, its trampled green blades always splashed with red in his mind's eye. All far away now, and almost unimaginable in this world of rock and dust, black shadows and white light.

"Above, the stars still bravely shine."

Mendoza's words broke across his reverie. Stark gazed down at him, slightly angry at the interruption and slightly curious at the words. Curiosity won out. "What's that supposed to mean?"

Mendoza looked a little abashed, as if he'd inadvertently shared his own inward thoughts. "It's something from an old poem. From the early twentieth century, about a battlefield."

"That doesn't tell me much." *Anything to distract me from this dead world around us and the potential for extra-hazardous combat. Besides, Mendo doesn't open up much, but he's damn well educated. Oughta be an officer, from what I've seen in his files.* Not for the first time, Stark wondered why Mendoza had enlisted instead of becoming an officer. *Maybe I'll find out someday, though I can't imagine quiet, modest Mendo succeeding in the career-obsessed, political world our officers live in.* "So, tell me more. How'd the poem go original?"

Mendoza glanced around the bunker, where he'd become the center of attention from Gomez's group as well as Stark, then grimaced apologetically. "I don't remember all of it, Sergeant. It was about a place called Flanders. Flanders fields. The first verse said something about rows of crosses there, marking the graves of dead soldiers, and then something about larks still singing in the sky above them despite all the fighting. I thought, while looking out at the Moonscape just now, there aren't any larks here, so maybe the stars would do."

Murphy looked puzzled. "What's a lark?"

"It's a bird, stupid," Gomez snorted derisively. "What kind of Earthworm doesn't know what a bird is?"

"Hey, I know what a bird is. I just never heard of any lark." Murphy looked doubly insulted. "And I'm no Earthworm. I've been up here as long as you—"

Stark cut him off. "Fine, Murph, you're a rock-eater. Now shut up." He turned back to Mendoza. "Flanders, huh? A battlefield? What was that, some big show?"

Mendoza nodded. "Oh, yes, Sergeant, real big. Millions of soldiers, in the Belgium part of Euro. Brits, mostly, fighting Germans. They took hundreds of thousands of casualties in a few days crawling through mud to seize a few hundred yards of territory."

Gomez frowned. "Millions of soldiers? Hundreds of thousands killed and wounded? Where'd they get those kinds of numbers? And how'd they lose so many without their generals getting canned? The folks back home don't like too many body bags coming downrange."

"It was a different world back then, Corporal." Mendoza looked doubly uncomfortable at having to elaborate. "Most of the armies weren't volunteer, they were conscripted, made to serve, though the Brits I think all volunteered. They thought the survival of their state and their way of life and, well, everything depended on winning. So they joined their militaries, and back home people were willing to accept many casualties because they thought it was important, too."

The Squad members looked back at him with puzzled expressions. "Wars sure were different back then," Billings remarked. "They actually forced civs to join the mil and fight their wars themselves? How'd the civs ever vote for that?"

"I don't know," Mendoza admitted.

"Yeah, but didn't they get any vid of the fighting?" Gomez wondered. "Sure, they wouldn't have the almost real-time stuff like we got, but I know vid's been around a long time."

"Vid? Well, there wasn't any. Not like we know it. There's some old film, but it wasn't anything like today. You couldn't use the cameras on a battlefield, so hardly anyone knew how bad the slaughter was."

"But how'd they pay for it?" Murphy demanded, with a guilty glance toward Stark as he realized he'd spoken again. "I mean, with no vid? Where'd they get enough money for a big war?"

"Taxes." Mendoza left the single word hanging.

"Taxes?" Gomez bore the expression of a woman who thought she'd been made a fool. "Enough taxes to support a big war? Bull. Corporations cut deals and make sure the laws say they don't pay nothing. The civs don't pay, either. The politicians been telling them for so long that they can have everything they want without paying for it that they all believe it now. You know that. Back home they won't even pay for enough cops to keep the lowers from stealing their Social Security checks. Why the hell would they pay for a war that they were forced to fight in?"

Mendoza glared back, momentarily and uncharacteristically defiant. "Don't ask me. Civs were different back then. Maybe civs had a sense of duty in those days, like we do now. Maybe civs didn't know any better then, didn't know they could vote for someone else to do the dirty work and vote not to pay for it besides. Or maybe they really thought it was important, so they were willing to fight themselves and pay the taxes."

Stark shook his head in wonder. "What the hell war in what the hell world was this?" Probably something they'd covered in history back in Stark's high school, but maybe not. High school had been a long time ago, feeling as ancient as the old wars Mendoza spoke of. Stark had slept his way through most of the classes, but vaguely recalled wondering why the United States always seemed to be fighting somewhere right now even though their history classes never mentioned any wars in the past.

"Our world, Sergeant," Mendoza stated, "not that long ago. Early twentieth century, like I said. It was called World War One. Well, not at the time, because there hadn't been a Second World War yet. At the time, they called it the Great War."

"Doesn't sound so great to me," Gomez noted sourly.

"They meant 'great' as in 'big,' Corporal," Mendoza explained.

"No vid?" That was Hoxely, angrily gesturing toward the nearest monitor. "So it was the corporations, right? They made money off it, somehow, right?"

"I don't think so. Not like now. After the war, there was a lot of complaints about war profiteers, but I don't think that was the real reason."

"War profiteers?" Stark questioned. "That's some corporation that makes money out of selling weapons and stuff?"

"Yes, Sergeant."

"And the civs thought that was bad back then?"

"Yes, Sergeant. They thought their political leaders had sold out to the profiteers."

Around of bitter laughter erupted. "Good thing those civs ain't around now!" Billings hooted. "They'd be real unhappy."

"You serious, Mendo?" Hoxely wondered. "Civs paid major bucks for a war they had to fight in, they didn't want corporations making money off the mil contracts, and they worried about politicians selling out to the corporations like it wasn't routine? That's just too weird. The world never could've worked that way."

"Pyotr, I'm not putting you on." Mendoza looked unaccountably tired and spoke slowly. "That's the way they thought. A lot of them died because they believed in that. It didn't make sense then, just like it doesn't make sense now. Like here, but different. That's history, it's always like here, but different." A dark pause fell over the bunker at the sudden shift in the conversation, from the follies of ancient fighting to their own situation.

"Yeah, different." Gomez looked sharply toward Mendoza. "No birds here, right? Who cares? A bunch of civs died back on the World so long ago they didn't even have vid, and so what if they all got major screwed 'cause they were stupid? We're here now, protecting 'corporate assets' for the tycoons and their bought-and-paid-for politicians, our commanders would let us all get blown away if they could get promotions out of it, and the civs don't care how much we get screwed as long as we fight their battles and show them some entertainment on vid. Big surprise, Mendo. Nobody ever looks out for grunts but other grunts. Right, Sarge?"

"Right." Gomez had jumped in while Stark had still been thinking through his own answer. Normally that might irritate him for throwing his own thoughts off, but Gomez had nailed the issue to the wall better than he could have. Not a good idea to think too much, not when every day held the chance for sudden death, and every memory recalled friends they'd never see again this side of Heaven or Hell. Fate sucked, and the odds against every grunt sucked, and you had to know that to protect yourself, but you couldn't think about it too often. Otherwise you'd get sloppy and make mistakes, maybe fatal mistakes, or sometimes grunts would just put a round through their own heads to try to stop the fear.

"Right," Stark repeated aloud, giving extra force to the word. "That's all that counts out here. You know the score, and you know the only people you can count on are the people in this bunker and the other bunkers along the line. You rock apes look out for each other, or Gomez and I'll personally break heads. Nobody, *nobody,* is going to take you down while I'm in charge."

He hadn't meant to say the last, but it came out of somewhere deep and hung there, and it was right because he felt it was true, and the faces that had sagged a moment before tightened up to familiar patterns. *Poor bastards trust me. Hope to Christ I don't ever let them down.*

He turned back to Mendoza. "Don't think so much, Mendo. You'll never make Lieutenant if you keep it up."

Laughter from the bunker broke the remaining tension as Mendoza half smiled, nodded shyly, and turned back to his sentry watch, where all the screens looked at the world through different eyes, each displaying a different reality based on their vision of what mattered.

* * *

Stark had long ago learned there was usually a trade-off for knowledge. Ignorance makes it easy to be confident you know the truth about everything. Stark had watched the firm certainties of the world he'd once been sure of fall apart by bits and pieces over the years under the pressure of experience. Sometimes the pieces he lost were awfully large. A sizable chunk still lay on a grass-covered hill in a small country back on Earth, but other pieces had fallen away in less terrible moments.

A long time ago, maybe three weeks in the past, the unit had been on rest and recreation. That was the drill. One month on line, a week off for R&R, then refresher training and start over. But the first day of R&R was always the best. First beer, first semiopen spaces, first chance to relax tense muscles accustomed to always subconsciously expecting the worst. You could walk through corridors wider than a single arm span, drink a beer, or just be alone for a little while. Civs would never, Stark often thought, really appreciate how great those things could be.

For soldiers who wanted to seriously unwind, there was the Outer City, a rough circle of cheap bars, cheap hotels, and cheap hookers that spread out past the official borders of New Plymouth. Soldiers on leave who headed for off-base entertainment never made it as far as the clean, neat, and expensive city America's corporations had planted up here in expectation of huge profits down the line. Stark had been in the Out-City before, and would be there again, but this night he and Vic Reynolds had been unwinding together at a mil facility, without the high-pressure relaxation offered in the Out-City's rough pleasure spots.

Stark drank his first beer in one long gulp, shuddering as the cold liquid hit his gut. "Damn it."

Vic raised one eyebrow over the rim of her own beer. "Anything in particular?"

"Yeah." Stark ripped the top off a second beer and took another drink. "You know something? The only thing worse than being shot at is watching your friends get shot at and not being able to help."

"You got a point there." Vic's ironic chuckle came out as a humorless hiss. "Operation Offside probably looked brilliant on a big map at the Pentagon."

"Huh. Well, it was a disaster in practice."

"True. But then big disasters tend to attract big crowds.

I'm sure the ratings were great. Some general probably got a medal."

"Don't get me started." High-ranking officers cycled through Lunar Command so fast nobody bothered to learn their names, then headed home with shiny new medals pinned to their chests. Stark focused on the ribbons above Vic's left breast. "Speaking of medals, you ever gonna tell me how you earned that Silver Star?"

"Same way I earned the Purple Heart."

"I know it was before I met you."

"Duh, Ethan. If it had happened while we were serving together you'd know all about it, wouldn't you?" Vic shrugged, dropping her empty to grab another beer. "It's ancient history."

"Maybe it is, but I'm still curious."

"Fine. I'll make you a deal. You tell me about your past and I'll tell you about mine."

Stark glowered back. "No deal."

"Why not?" Vic questioned archly. "You brought up the subject."

"I don't wear my past on my chest for people to wonder about."

"No, you keep yours locked in your head except when it makes your mouth say the wrong things to officers." Vic took a long drink. "Or do something slightly crazy."

"I didn't ask for a psych eval. I just asked about your damn medal."

"What's the matter? You want one of your own? You can have this one." Vic picked at her left breast as if pulling the ribbon free.

"If I wanted medals I'd be an officer."

"That's it," Vic said with a laugh. "I got my medal when I was an officer, but they had to bust me to Sergeant when they found out I had a heart and a brain." She hoisted her beer. "And then they gave me booze so I'd have courage."

"Very funny," Stark observed. "Fine. Be that way." Reynolds chuckled again, this time with a trace of humor, as Stark stared around the Enlisted Club, an outlandishly large space that might have measured fifteen meters across. 3-D vids mounted on the rough rock walls created the impression of picture windows looking out on World scenes. That night they showed some sort of forest, maybe even in the Northwest, where he'd grown up. The natural-living-green wooded scenes clashed incongruously with the peeling and faded green-shades-painted rock walls around them. Supposed to be restful, the psychs said, but Stark always thought it just looked like green rock. Overhead, raw metal strung with glaring lights provided the usual ceiling for a lunar dwelling. Over that metal, Stark knew, a few meters of Moon gravel and dust lay as insulation and protection. Humans had spent thousands of years climbing out of caves and building technology so they could reach the Moon and live in caves again.

"So, why'd you join, Ethan?" Vic Reynolds's question caught him by surprise.

Stark frowned, trying to focus in on a past blurred by fourteen years' time and three recent beers. "That's another history question."

"So it is," Vic agreed, unabashed. "Why'd you join the mil?"

"Hell, I dunno. Why's anyone join? Temporary insanity."

Reynolds laughed obligingly. "Seriously. You just do the family tradition thing, or did you have some deeper reason? You never talk about growing up. Your old man was mil, right? What units?"

Stark laughed back at the absurdity of the suggestion. "Mil? My old man? Not even. Fish farmer in Washington State. He hated the mil. Thought I was some kind of idiot for joining."

"Really?" Reynolds peered closely at him. "So your mother was civ, too?"

"Absolutely. A clerk at one of those chain department stores." They were always at work, it seemed, something self-absorbed teenager Ethan Stark had actually resented even as he casually accepted the things their work paid for. "So what?"

"So what?" Vic repeated. "Ethan, nearly every grunt and every officer in the mil comes from a mil family living on a mil fort or base. You know that. I didn't even meet civs until I was a teenager. You're pretty damn unusual."

"Yeah. A lot of people tell me that."

"You know what I mean." Reynolds stared at Stark, shaking her head. "So why'd a dyed-in-the-wool civ join the mil?"

It was a very personal and complicated question, he realized, one he hadn't fully understood at the time and didn't even now. "I just did. Maybe it was the ultimate way to dis my old man. Didn't want to be a fish farmer, for damned sure."

"That the only reason?" Reynolds pressed, finishing her beer and looking for another. "If it was, you've changed a helluva lot."

"Well. . ." It had been a long time ago, but he remembered being alone. Community college had just been a large group of aimless teenagers looking for job skills and trying to postpone growing up for another two years. Grad night came, and he realized there wasn't a soul he felt really close to, a group he thought he belonged with. The mil seemed to offer that, though he couldn't remember now where he'd picked up the idea. Maybe in the real old war movies on the vid history channels, fighting on black-and-white battlefields where everyone seemed pretty sure of what they were doing and why.

Stark looked around as he thought, seeing the shabby club with a dozen other soldiers scattered at their own tables, outside its walls the dead Moon where every battle was still fought on black-and-white terrain, but out there was also his Squad and his Platoon and Company filled with people he knew who all followed the same rules and talked the same language. And who, if it came to that, would die alongside him. "Guess you could say I wanted to be part of something." He shrugged. "I found it, I guess."

"The mil?"

"Yeah. One big, happy family." He'd meant the words to come out tinged with sarcasm, but instead they fell out with flat sincerity.

Vic grinned. "A big family, anyway. Makes sense, Ethan. Most of us just come by that feeling naturally, because we're surrounded by it growing up in the mil, but I guess you had to look for it. I'm glad you found it."

"Thanks."

"But that's not the whole reason, is it?"

"Jeez, Vic, why you playing psych on me?" Stark grumbled.

"Because you do things that make me sure there's something else driving you."

Stark bit his lip, staring down at the battered tabletop. "I want to make a difference, Vic. I want it all to mean something."

"All what?" Vic demanded.

"Everything. Life. The universe. Getting up in the morning to get shot at. What the hell do you want?"

Vic shrugged. "At least you're ambitious. Gonna change the world all by yourself, huh?" Her beer came up in a mock toast. "Here's to heroes."

"I ain't no hero." Stark took another drink himself. "Don't aim to be one, don't intend getting myself killed being one, don't intend killing any of my people being one."

She nodded, grinning. "Good boy."

"Which part?"

"Not getting yourself killed, of course."

"Gee," Stark noted sarcastically, "I didn't know you cared."

Vic's grin widened. "Nah, I'm just selfish. Who would I get drunk with if you bought it?"

"You'd find some other stupid Sergeant."

"Probably," Vic agreed. She eyed her beer with a distasteful expression. "I guess the low bidder got the beer concession again."

Stark nodded. "Cheap beer that we pay primo prices for. Wouldn't be much sense in fighting if the corporations couldn't make enough money off the war. Of course, if the damn foreigners hadn't come up here in the first place we'd be fighting someplace where at least there's air."

"The foreigners had every right to come up here, Ethan."

"I know why they came," Stark protested. "All the stuff back on the World that's easy to get at is gone, and the U.S. of A. has got an effective monopoly on the tech that lets people get the hard-to-reach stuff, and we end up enforcing that damn monopoly in every country that tries to make a buck that our own corporations want in their own pockets."

"Good summation," Vic agreed.

"You remember what I said after we first landed. I'd probably have done the same thing they did. But we had these resources tied up, too. Not that I like the place, but what made the foreigners think they could just waltz up here and grab stuff?"

Vic shook her head. "You really don't know? It's because we *didn't* have the Moon's resources tied up."

"The hell," Stark objected. "We got here first. Back in, what was it, the 1940s or something?"

"Nineteen sixties," Vic corrected. "Whatever. We claimed it."

"No, we didn't." Vic smiled bitterly. "You're right, we got here first. But we didn't claim it, Ethan. I've been to the monument that's been built, out on the Trank Sea. It says we came 'for all mankind.' Something like that. Nothing about 'no trespassing.' "

"We planted a flag," Stark insisted stubbornly. "I've seen a picture. In my barracks, once, somewhere back on the World." A flag suspended stiffly, a figure in clumsy white space gear rendering a salute. The black and the white light, the barren rockscape, had been unfamiliar then.

Vic nodded wearily. "Yeah, we planted a flag. But not to claim it, at least not then, not for a long time." Her eyes grew distant, pulling up memories. "We stopped coming, Ethan. I don't know why. Maybe it was just too hard back then. Hell, when you own Earth, why bother with this hunk of dead rock? But eventually, other people came up here serious. Like you said, they needed the resources. So they planted colonies, built some bases, started low-g manufacturing and pulling out ore. Big bucks."

"So I hear." Stark brooded over his beer for a moment. "And it didn't belong to our own corporations already?"

"Nope. Told you, we'd never claimed it. It was supposed to be international or something, belong to everyone."

Stark snorted with derision. "Right. Belonged to everyone. Sounds like one of those brainless peace ops we got sent to enforce back on the World."

"I'm not saying it was a smart arrangement, but I guess it surprised our corporations when other countries took it serious." Vic used a finger to doodle idly in the wet rings left by the beers on their table. "So our business tycoons ran to their hip-pocket Congress and told them to pass a law that said the Moon was ours, back to when we landed."

"So we got ordered here. Nice."

"Not right away. The President said, 'Great idea, give me some money to enforce it.' Congress said—"

"Let me guess," Stark interrupted. "They said they wouldn't raise taxes to cover it."

"Bingo. The President was kinda stuck between a rock and a hard place. He didn't have the money to support a mil op to grab the Moon, but there was big public support for doing just that. After all, the law said Luna was ours, so we should kick off the foreigners, right? Made the civs feel real patriotic, not that they volunteered to come up here and do the job themselves."

"So what happened? Oh, hell," Stark added in disgust, "I know what happened."

"Sure, the mil got ordered up here and were told to do it without using any more money. Of course, the mil couldn't do it, couldn't find the money anywhere. Budgets had been too tight for too long, and all the surplus had gone to pay for more generals and for big, fancy weapons like those damned McClellan tanks."

"They're great tanks."

"Yeah, and each one costs so much they can't actually be risked in battle. Just like the F-38 Strato-Fighter. On second thought, at least the McClellans work, and from what I hear, the F-38 doesn't. Anyway, we can't afford to lose them, so we can't use them."

"You're preaching to the choir, Vic."

"I know." Vic glared at Stark, but her anger was focused elsewhere. "It looked like the brass would have to say 'Can't do it.' You know the brass hates to say 'Can't do it' to anyone who outranks them. So some unsung genius thought of another way to get money, maybe enough to cover starting the operation up here."

Stark nodded. "I thought that was where this was heading. You mean the vid programs, don't you? That's why they started showing us in combat for civ entertainment."

"Yeah." Vic spat it out. "The vid programs. We had all this great gear built in for command and control. Full-time comms and all-round vid so the officers could tell exactly what we were doing every minute and micromanage each and every grunt. It also provided great publicity footage after battles. Then somebody figured out they didn't have to give it away for free, that they could use it to make their own programs and sell the commercial time. Maybe even while the battles were still going on. Maybe even so close to real time that the civs would pay to watch."

Stark's face settled into grim lines of memory. Years ago, hitting the lunar surface for the first time and wondering why headquarters had been so worried about dramatic action. "Yeah. From all I hear, they were a real hit. Blood and guts live on vid. Somebody—Chen, I think—claims civ kids are tracking units and their wins and losses just like sports teams."

"I heard that, too. And you know what all the pro sports did, upping the violence in their own products to try to win back viewers. It must be a great time to be an adolescent back on the World, Ethan."

Stark laughed harshly. "Damn right. Old enough to get a kick out of blood but too damn young to think about how much it hurts the guy who's bleeding. But, hell, it worked, right? They made a lot of money, didn't they?"

"Worked great." Vic's bitter smile was back. "But it backfired."

"Let me guess."

"Yeah. You know this one, too, Ethan. Congress and the Pres figured out the mil had made a bundle from the ad revenue, so they cut the mil's budget. That made the mil dependent on the vid not just for start-up for this op, but also for day-to-day ops. It's been like that ever since." Vic shook her head in obvious disgust. "The bright kids at headquarters trapped themselves. Now they have to run ops to keep the ratings up, or the whole mil budget goes red. The bastards were just a little too clever, and they, or rather we, have been paying for it ever since."

Stark sat there, wondering what, if anything, to say. *They talk about ignorance being bliss, and I can see why. I don't know anyone who's any happier for knowing the answers to all this crap.* "You ever wonder, Vic, what would happen if we dropped it, if the mil finally said 'Can't do it'?"

That brought another sad smile from Vic. "You think our officers would ever do that?"

"No." Stark's teeth showed. "Congress won't take responsibility if things went to hell. They never do. Neither will the Pres. They tell us to guard their butts, and to go out to every bar fight in the world that threatens the profits of our all-American free-flippin'-enterprise corporations, and our officers say 'Yessir, yessir, three bags full,' because keeping the politicians happy is the path to four-star promotions and that seems to be all our officers care about anymore. Then we get told we don't need all the people and gear we've asked for, except the stuff that goes to buy mega-expensive weapons built by those same corporations and their civ workers who vote. And if the mil ever did cry that it's broke, the politicians and civs will just blame us for wasting money and having bad management, which has plenty enough truth to stick thanks to our officers who are too obsessed with sucking up to their bosses to ever try to fix problems themselves. Perfect world." Stark's teeth tightened, so that muscles stood out along his jaw. "As long as you happen to be in the White House, or Congress, or the Pentagon, and not up here."

"Congratulations." Vic hoisted another mock toast. "You are now educated."

"And ain't I the happy little bastard? If it wasn't for the damn oath . . ." Stark let his voice trail off.

"The oath?" Vic grimaced. "Yeah. The oath. 'I will support and defend the Constitution of the United States against all enemies, foreign and domestic,' etc., etc., etc. I guess we're all suckers, Ethan. We break our backs for that oath, I bleed into vacuum for that oath, all to defend corporate profits and a bunch of civs who think personal sacrifice means having to fetch your own beer instead of having it brought to you."

"That's not the only reason, Vic." Stark reached out to grip her hand hard for a moment. "That oath is also to each other, isn't it? Personally, I sometimes can't figure out who the real enemy is. But I know who my friends are. They're the grunts standing beside me."

Vic smiled ruefully. "Most of them, anyway. I talk too much, Ethan."

"Nah. You know too much." Stark slid another beer across the table, watching as it slid much farther under the Moon's minuscule gravity than the slight push should have managed, so that Vic had to grab it just short of the table edge.

"You trying to get me drunk, soldier?" Vic demanded.

"I thought that was a decent objective for both of us tonight."

"Sounds good to me." Another six-pack disappeared, while silence stretched out, broken only by the digitally recorded chirps of phantom birds in the branches of the vid-projected trees on the ugly rock walls. Finally Vic raised her right hand, then slowly ran her fingers across the Silver Star ribbon, her eyes somewhere far away. "Ethan, I got something to tell you."

Stark focused on her, frowning as his eyes followed the movements of her hand. "What?"

"I got this medal because I shot a Lieutenant."

"You're kidding."

"No. We were being hit pretty hard. Real heavy jamming, too, so we lost comms with our higher-ups, and our Lieutenant panicked. Tried to order us to retreat through an enemy kill zone. We would have lost most of the unit."

"Jesus, Vic."

"So I shot him." Her eyes came back, oddly emotionless, gazing into Stark's. "We held in place until relief arrived. I got a medal for leading the defense and saving the position."

"Which you had to do after you shot the Lieutenant."

"Yeah." One side of Vic's mouth quirked in a humorless half smile. "Funny, huh?"

"Yeah. Funny."

"You'd have done the same thing, right, Ethan?" It seemed less a question than a plea.

"Yeah." *Guess I'm not the only one carrying around baggage.* "I'd have done the same thing. What happened to the Lieutenant?"

Vic looked away. "Dead."

"I guess that's how it had to happen. Who else knows about it?"

"I think some of the people in my old unit suspected. That's why I transferred and ended up in the same unit with you. As to who knows for sure, that's me, you, now, and the Big Guy upstairs. I'll have to answer to Him someday."

"You did the right thing. You saved a lot of lives."

"Sure." One fingertip traced its way across the medal ribbon.

"Ethan, sometimes doing the right thing doesn't do a damn thing for your conscience."

"So why do you wear that damn ribbon?"

Her gaze speared him. "To remind myself that hard decisions carry a price, and knowing what's right isn't always easy, and that people pay with their lives when we do the wrong thing and sometimes even when we do the right thing." Vic's index finger leveled at Stark's chest like a pistol barrel. "And from now on I want it to remind you of the same damn things, Ethan Stark."

"Why do you think I need that?" Stark asked quietly.

"Because you've got a major demon inside and you're too damn devoted to duty and to your fellow soldiers and someday that's all going to come to a head and when that happens, Ethan Stark, you damn well better be sure you're ready to live with whatever you do or don't do."

"I will be," Stark vowed. "Why now? Why tell me all this? You think something big's coming?"

"I don't know," Vic whispered. "There're rumors, and rumors of rumors. Nothing definite, just that the corporations are tired of the stalemate because they want to grab more real estate up here, and the politicians are playing the 'Why can't you win?' game against each other in the elections, and our senior officers are worried sombody's finally going to ask why they can't do the jobs they claim to be best at. Does it mean anything? I don't know. If it does, there'll be major hell to pay."

Stark shook his head, confused and angry now. "I don't want to think about it anymore."

"You don't? What, is your demon drunk, too?"

"Not yet, but it will be." They split another six, the green-painted walls beginning to take on a nauseous tint as their vision blurred. "I think I've had enough," Stark finally announced, speaking with great care. He tried to stand, then let the Moon's gravity slowly haul him back into his seat. "Now I know I've had enough."

"Need a hand?" Vic offered, weaving upright, her own expression suddenly alarmed. "Oh, hell. I'll let you lean on me if I can lean on you."

"Deal." They headed for their cubes, temporary lodging fortunately not too far away, hanging on to each other for support as they moved down the faded green corridors in a cautious stagger made ridiculous by low gravity. Finally arriving at the entry to Stark's cube, he reached to hit the access pad, the panel whisking open in swift obedience. "Thanks for the comp'ny, Vic." He turned, looked straight into her eyes, and stopped moving, suddenly aware of her body, of her breast pressed close to his side and his hand resting firmly just above her hip. Vic gazed somberly back, the same awareness there. Stark took a quick breath, startled by the unexpected excitement, then hesitated unaccountably, just looking at her, his hands unmoving.

Vic spoke first. "You're a good friend, Ethan."

A moment's thought, good sense somehow surfacing through the alcohol haze in his mind. "Yeah, Vic, you, too. Too good a friend . . ."

"To risk ruining it?" she finished for him.

"Yeah," he agreed again. "Don't know what'd happen, but I know what we've got. Need you as my pal, Vic, that's what counts most." He paused, thoughts running sluggishly over their earlier conversation. "Government don't care, corporations sure as hell don't care, civs don't care, officers don't care, but grunts . . . we look out for each other. That's what keeps us going, isn't it?"

"Smart kid." Vic smiled fondly at him. "Yeah, we've got that, no matter what else they take."

They released each other, staggering at the attempt to balance independently. She had just started to turn away when Stark's hormones roused enough to kick his brain partially into action as caution took a momentary backseat. "But I bet you'd have been one hell of a partner in the sack."

She turned back, smiling languorously. "Damn right, Ethan. Best you'd have ever had. Dream about it." Her arm abruptly shoved him inside as she headed down the hall toward her own cube.

"Bitch!" he yelled, not meaning it, hearing her laughter float back down the hall. *Damn, I'm lucky she's in my unit. Kept me alive more than once. Maybe I'll return the favor. Someday.* Stark made a half motion to undress before saying to hell with it and falling in a slow-motion lunar sprawl onto his bunk to let sleep carry away the night's confusions.

Lieutenant Conroy cleared her throat, inadvertently emphasizing her youth to her three Sergeants linked in for the mission brief. "Second Platoon, Bravo Company has been selected to carry out a raid tonight on enemy forces occupying Sector Cowpens."

She sounds as if she thinks this is an honor. It hadn't been that long a wait for word, early afternoon of the artificial day humanity imposed on lunar life, just long enough for the enemy to find out about the ratings and get primed for action. *Typical,* Stark thought sourly. *Hope Kilroy survives enough of these 'honors' to get a clue.* Conroy began stepping through the brief point by point, as if she were reading off the briefing appendix from the *Platoon Leader's Handbook. Probably got a copy scrolling on her vid.* From her segment of the screen, Reynolds passed a meaningful look his way: She's new, Ethan, and at least she's trying, so give her a break. *Damn, sometimes seems Vic can read my mind.* Stark focused on the map vid as Conroy got to the meat of the mission. "Objective is the metals refinery centered at grid 44.10 151.72. We're to take it out with timed charges." The Sergeants all reacted involuntarily, Reynolds with a hiss of breath, Stark with a grunt, and Sanchez with a minor but uncharacteristic frown. The refinery was a *mojo* target, all right, but it was comfortably under the umbrella of the foreign troops defending that area. Worse, the 3-D contours of the map projection merely emphasized that the only feasible approach was across a dust plain where the platoon would stand out like silhouettes on a firing range.

"That's a very difficult approach, Lieutenant." Stark spoke mildly and with incredible understatement, but in a tone that conveyed volumes.

Conroy nodded slowly, then looked up with some irritation. "I know that, Sergeant." She glanced at Reynolds and Sanchez, reading the same concern in them that Stark had voiced. "It's not difficult, it's impossible, *unless* the enemy sensor net is blind to us."

Intriguing. Stark's estimation of the Lieutenant jumped slightly higher. She'd picked up enough tactics to see the obvious (which was far from a given with new officers), and she hadn't minded admitting the mission was tough instead of playing mindless cheerleader for the Brigade brass.

"Blind, sir?" Reynolds was clearly curious. Sensor nets were notoriously redundant in both scan gear and search capabilities. If they didn't see you on infrared, they'd look for image matches, or motion, or ground tremors, or what-all else. The countermeasure gear on the battle armor was incredibly good at hiding or confusing signatures, but moving to attack through a dust plain was like shining a spotlight on your head and singing the latest neoanarchist anthem on an all-frequency comm broadcast.

"Sort of." Conroy looked uncomfortable, then shook her head. "I can't tell you any more. Just accept that for mission planning purposes the enemy sensor net in that area will be blind."

Stark bit back an angry rebuttal, fighting to keep his expression composed. Sanchez, though, face now calm to the point of apparent boredom, cleared his throat, then began speaking in dispassionate tones that suggested that some other Platoon had been receiving the brief. "Lieutenant, a vital precept of mission planning is to ensure essential knowledge is shared among those most likely to need it. If something should happen to incapacitate the Lieutenant or even to disrupt her communications with the rest of the Platoon, the Squad leaders will need to be aware of tactical information that seriously impacts on their ability to successfully accomplish the mission."

Stark fought down a smile, wondering if Sanchez had long ago memorized a mission planning text just so he could use the words like this someday, or had simply kept a copy of the relevant verbiage scrolling across his own screen, ready to verbally download it if necessary. *I may never know what that guy is thinking, but he is one sharp grunt.*

Lieutenant Conroy started to reply, chewed her lip for a few moments, then nodded slowly. "I. . . guess that's right. You guys need to know this background if you're going to carry this op out."

A more experienced officer, one with more self-confidence in her job, would have told Sanchez to shut up and do his job anyway, but Conroy was new enough to be manipulated a bit. "About three months back," Conroy continued, "we managed to insert a new worm in the opposition sensor net in that sector. Since then, it's been laying low and monitoring activity to build up a bank of events. When it's activated, it'll block the real sensor readings for the area we're in and draw on the event bank to project a believable picture of what's going on there to the alert circuits."

"Clever," Sanchez noted approvingly, echoing Stark's thoughts on the matter. Worms had been around for years. Problem was, so had watchdogs, and the watchdogs had gotten very good indeed. A worm that simply blanked sensor readouts would be spotted and overridden in milliseconds. More sophisticated worms had mimicked the proper sensor picture to create the impression that all was well, but in a net monitoring every fall of gravel, the watchdogs had quickly learned to spot the faked inputs. Months of real readings, drawn on to build the bogus picture, would keep the watchdogs fooled for quite a while. One hoped.

"How did they find something good enough to do that?" Vic wondered out loud. "The only thing tougher than the enemy bunkers is the defenses they've got against information attacks."

"Urn . . ." Conroy looked even more uncomfortable, belatedly realizing that after disclosing the worm's existence she'd have to discuss other details. "I've been told it's a variation on the Mitchell Virus."

"Oh, hell!" Stark exclaimed. "Isn't that the junk that's been screwing up our own systems for the past several decades?"

"Right," Vic confirmed. "Developed by the Air Force as an information weapon, but it escaped during testing, contaminated friendly systems, and we've never been able to completely wipe it out because it was designed to mutate."

"It didn't escape, Sergeant Reynolds," Conroy corrected sternly. "It exceeded mission testing parameters."

Whatever you want to call it, Stark thought, *but it still adds up to the worst case of information fratricide anybody has ever heard of.* Which didn't mean there hadn't been worse cases, just that anything worse might have been kept quiet. "Well," he noted out loud, "anything that's given us so much trouble ought to screw up the enemy a bit, too."

"So it's supposed to blind the enemy sensors. How long will the worm hold and how much will it hide?" Reynolds demanded, focusing on the key issues while the rest of them were still absorbing the surface data.

Conroy looked even more uncomfortable. "They wouldn't say how long."

"Which means they don't know." Stark's statement earned a glare from the Lieutenant and a wry smile from Reynolds.

"Probably not," Conroy eventually admitted. "As to how much, there're limits. Too strong a signal will burn through. At that point the enemy information defenses will identify the false reporting problem and either kill the worm or bypass it." She indicated a point on the map on their side of the dust plain. "That's why we can't ride all the way in. Transport would put out too strong a signal to hide. The APCs will take us to here and then we have to walk in and back out."

Reynolds nodded. "That's why timed charges? To keep events down until we're clear?"

"Right, Sergeant." Conroy indicated a fortification symbol about a kilometer forward from the refinery. "With the dust plains around the site, the enemy hasn't worried much about surprise attacks. The only fixed defense is this bunker. Intelligence says it probably only holds three sentries, but it's got decent firepower and also controls two remote firing pits here and here." Heavy weapons symbols glowed brightly to the left and right of the fortification.

"Who's inside, Lieutenant?" Stark asked. "Pros or wannabes?" The position seemed both too small and too isolated to be part of the regular enemy defensive line, but there still could be well-trained defenders there. Despite the employment guaranteed by the apparently endless lunar war, several militaries were still hiring out units, often damned good units, but professional grunts were expensive as well as skilled. Hiring civilian mercenaries cost a lot less, which looked like a good deal to those who didn't realize that people don't put their lives on the line for paychecks. There had to be something more driving them, some higher sense of duty, something the mercs with their fancy uniforms and military playacting lacked.

"Mercenaries, Sergeant, hired by the foreign corporation that owns the refinery." Conroy suddenly smiled. "Intelligence reports they're from some outfit calling itself the Black Death Battalion."

The Sergeants laughed quietly. Professional soldiers had learned the more grandiose a merc unit's title, the less actual threat it presented.

The Lieutenant singled out Reynolds with a gesture. "First Squad goes in to take out that guardpost. It'll be blinded by the worm, but you'll have to move very carefully that close to enemy personnel."

Reynolds eyed the map, absorbing every detail even though it would be available in her Tactical throughout the mission. "And very quietly that close to implanted sensors."

The Lieutenant nodded back. "Yes, Sergeant. Very quietly. Second Squad, Sergeant Sanchez, will enter the refinery and place the charges in accordance with the orders in your Tactical. Sergeant Stark, your Third Squad will take up covering positions along this corridor." Symbols flashed on the map, detailing planned soldier positions and movements. "Just like in your Tactical," Conroy added with extra emphasis as she stared straight at Stark. "No deviations."

I guess Conroy got warned about me by the last Lieutenant. Or maybe the one before that. "Of course, Lieutenant," Stark agreed. "Subject to new tactical developments, of course, right?"

Lieutenant Conroy hesitated, obviously thinking through Stark's statement for implications and unable to come up with reasons not to agree with it. "Well, yes," she finally agreed reluctantly, as Vic Reynolds stifled a smile and shook her head at Stark in mock exasperation.

Stark studied the map carefully. "How big is the threat we're worried about covering against, Lieutenant?"

"Unfortunately," Conroy continued, picking up the thread of her brief again, "there's a professional military base a dozen kilometers north of the refinery. Normal manning is at least," she emphasized the last two words, "a reinforced mechanized company. It's the quick reaction force for their whole sector. They can get to the refinery area fast."

"So if they get alerted too early," Reynolds noted, "we're going to have a hot time trying to get away. Once the worm's been neutralized, they won't have much trouble tracking us."

Stark traced the Platoon's path across the plain. "Any support on the way back, Lieutenant? Any heavies going to move up?" APCs or tanks would be really nice to have on hand if a mech company happened to be snapping at their heels.

The Lieutenant frowned. "The raid is supposed to be carried out swiftly enough that we can exit the area before the enemy responds."

"Yes, sir," Sanchez interjected smoothly. "But if something should go amiss, heavy support could be crucial to successful egress."

Conroy spoke slowly, choosing her words with care. "We'll get additional support once we're under the perimeter defense umbrella. Brigade headquarters has indicated it doesn't want to risk heavy armor under . .. unfavorable circumstances."

Sanchez somehow kept his expression bland, but Reynolds was frowning now, too. Stark fought down a wave of anger. *She means the brass knows grunts are a lot cheaper than hardware. They aren't going to risk getting their expensive weapons systems trashed.* The viewing public didn't like watching their taxes go up in fireballs in almost real time on their vids, especially after having been told how invincible those expensive weapons would be in combat. More than one commander had been sacked following a few spectacular equipment losses, even if the result had been technically a victory.

"So," Reynolds spoke with equal care, "almost all of the way back we'll be on our own. If the enemy gets active fast, we're in for a long walk home."

Conroy bit her lip, then nodded once more. Stark studied the Platoon's withdrawal route again, the lunar dust plain sprawled across

the path like a sheet of ice back on the World, apparently an easy route but actually a possible death trap. *It could be a really long walk.*

Most of the mission details were downloaded to the squad bunkers after the face-to-face. Stark made a habit of screening the files sent to Corporal Gomez and the rest of his soldiers to make sure they got everything they needed. The brass often assumed the less the grunts knew, the better, but Stark figured they had the right and the need to know most details. If he got waxed or they got cut off, they'd require that information, and a tactical crisis was no time for headquarters to be downloading new mission data to a soldier. He abided by security on the worm, though. If that information got compromised, he didn't want to be on the receiving end of either enemy fire or "friendly" officers.

Technically, of course, you didn't need to brief the troops at all. They just had to follow the plan presented on their Tactical Displays: Go here now, do this now. Headquarters staff and their civ bosses back at the Pentagon were almost always complaining that mission preparation times were too long. Just download plans to the battle armor Tacs and go. Grunts in the field would have none of that. No one Stark knew depended solely on the Tac timeline, if for no other reason than the troops should know what the hell they were doing on the mission. Bad enough being on ops, without wondering what the next order from your Tac would be. Difficult enough being surprised by the enemy, without being surprised by your own plan.

Then came After. After you've got the mission brief and memorized your parts. After you've briefed your people in turn, and made sure the dense ones wouldn't screw up and the too-smart

ones wouldn't try anything they thought might be brilliant. After you've checked your gear and preinspected their gear. After all that, then there's not much left to do but wait. Stark hated After, the time when there was temporarily too much time.

Some grunts wrote letters during the lull, ticking carefully away on their palmtops, frowning over the unfamiliar effort of putting words into writing, or peering with feigned confidence into a cam port to record a vid message. *Dear Mom and Dad,* or *Dear Sweetheart,* or *Dear Darling and Kids.* What do you say when this might be the last letter, the last words they'd ever hear from you? Nothing could be good enough, so no one ever tried, instead talking of everyday matters or idle dreams of a future that might or might not be canceled this night.

Others played games, gambled, or read, whatever they'd learned would keep nerves in check. None of that worked for Stark. He'd long ago learned he wasn't any good at hiding his nerves while actually doing something. It didn't do to let the troops see their Sergeant getting jumpy. No, part of his job required showing confidence even when he lacked that inside. So the Squad liked to see him waiting along with them, looking cool and casual in that way that projects calm certainty of success no matter what uncertainties were churning away inside.

Stark had long ago worked out a routine to meet that need. He'd just sit back in the rec cell of the bunker, where everyone could see him, pretending to watch whatever vid entertainment had been officially approved for that day's viewing, while actually zoning out the world. Gomez had told him the Squad was impressed as all hell by the way he'd calmly watch anything on the vid prior to a

mission. Morale bonus for his coping mechanism. Go figure.

Private Hoxely pulled Stark out of his nonthinking reverie by jumping up and cursing to a couple of different deities. Frowning, Stark focused on Hoxe's group, three soldiers playing keno as if there were no tomorrow. Which, of course, there might not be for any of them. Craps was impossibly slow up here, dice taking leisurely tumbles for minutes at a time. Even poker played too slow for grunts keyed up for a mission, but you could lose big and fast bucking the tiger. Gomez stood up as well, quietly but fiercely read Hoxe the riot act, then left the chastened Private to watch his buddies split their winnings.

"Nerves." Gomez came up to Stark, speaking quietly. "With the vid ratings down, they know this op has to be high-risk to get the public tuned in again. There's a rumor the action will be seen on vid so close to real time the enemy will be able to target us from it."

"I doubt even our officers are that stupid." Stark raised his voice for the next statement, making sure the others in the room could hear. "If the action ain't a success, our commanders would get canned for losing too many grunts, so they'll keep the time lag long enough to make sure we can do the job." *I hope. Just because I know too short a time lag would be stupid doesn't mean our leaders will realize the same thing.*

"Makes sense," Gomez agreed. "That'll make the troops feel better."

Stark nodded. "They'll do okay if you and I stay frosty. Got to maintain the image. You handled Hoxe real well. Get him back in line, then leave him without shaking up anybody else. Good job."

Gomez looked away. "Thanks, Sarge."

Embarrassed, Stark realized with some surprise. He'd never gotten used to the fact that his opinion meant a lot to his soldiers. "Yeah. Just how I would've handled it. You'll make a good Sergeant someday."

A smile broke on Gomez's face. "Means a lot from you."

Stark fought down a sudden foreboding, recalling a similar conversation with another good Corporal years before. With some effort he smiled back, attempting an awkward joke. "Of course, that'll probably be ten or twenty years from now. Unless I buy it earlier."

Gomez's smile broadened at the banter. "That's not gonna happen, *Sargento.* You're, like, invincible. Like you're made out of rock."

"Sure," Stark snorted in derision, "me and the damn Moon. Two big ugly rocks."

"I mean it," Gomez insisted with a wink that denied the words. *"Gracias,* though. I try. I got a lot to live up to, and these guys, well, they ain't the best soldiers in the world, I guess, but they're pretty damn good."

"They're pretty damn good," Stark agreed, once again pitching his voice just high enough for the words to carry to the others in the cube.

Gomez grinned, noting the gesture. "Like that. Good trick." She looked around for an excuse to change the subject, focusing finally on the music playing over the vid. "You like these guys?" She squinted at the screen. " 'Jackson's Foot Cavalry?' Who the hell are they?"

Stark shrugged. He hadn't been paying much attention, but he'd heard the group several times recently. "Retro-Hill Rock, I think they call it, whatever that means. I heard these guys are really popular on the World these days. I guess the groups that were popular when we left are all gone now."

Gomez stared at the vid. "Yeah. It's different being out here, even with near-real-time comms. The World goes on and we stay where we were when we left."

"Always been that way." Stark found himself reminiscing about earlier deployments and campaigns, something he rarely did. "Even if you were deployed on the World. Home changed and we didn't. Funny." He waved Gomez to the chair next to his. She smiled in sudden delight at the invitation before sitting at a carefully gauged distance, Corporal to Sergeant. They talked for a while after that, about places they'd been and places they'd heard of in a thousand bull sessions in a score of barracks. Funny thing, each barracks was different, but also the same. You knew people, who also knew people, and everybody knew the places. Maybe his home had always been a bit bigger than he thought, scattered through bases around the World and up here. Or maybe not, maybe it all represented nothing beyond shared familiarity with a very widespread but very limited part of the World. Still, he felt at home in those places, with those people, and that was enough.

The group in the rec cell gradually thinned as individuals went to worry over their gear and start final preps. Gomez excused herself to don her own battle armor, one of her hands worrying finger-over-thumb that way she always did whenever action seemed imminent, as if she were manipulating invisible prayer beads. Stark stayed, having learned he hated standing around in armor even worse than sitting and waiting. Finally the clock worked its way to where it needed to be. Relieved to have purposeful action required once more, Stark rose, instantly becoming the center of attention. He swept the room with his eyes, announced, "All right, people, let's suit up," to the few remaining and headed for his own locker.

He put on his battle armor deliberately, double-checking each step. He'd found that process kept his mind from worrying itself throughout a mission over whether some minor detail had been overlooked. The readouts were supposed to tell you if anything had gone wrong or been missed, but vets learned not to trust 'trons any further than they had to. If something else could go bad, why couldn't the readouts also fail? Murphy's Law seemed particularly at home on the battlefield. Mendoza, in one of his talkative moods, had said once that some German claimed everything in war was easy, but all the easy stuff was really hard. Made sense out here, anyway.

The suit's diagnostics said everything go, matching the results of Stark's own painstaking inspection. *Just another mission, that's all. Keep the new Lieutenant from doing anything stupid. Meet the objective and get my people out safe.* Stark looked carefully around his cube, making sure everything sat neat and organized. Every grunt had their own fetish, a little ritual to give them luck on an op. For Stark, that ritual involved making sure nothing was out of place. Sort of a reverse fetish. He figured if you left something sloppy and undone, something you wouldn't want anyone else to see, you'd get nailed and everybody'd see when they came to pack your stuff up. Leave it all ready for inspection, and you'd come back. So far it'd worked every time.

"Sarge, the APC's coming in." Murphy, manning the watch

station, pointed to the armored personnel carrier image onscreen, enhanced to be visible. Bunker and APC systems exchanged cyber greetings, each deciding the other was friendly. Without IFF readings, the sizable armored vehicle would have been almost impossible to identify until it was right on top of them. Up close, the APC's rounded carapace made it resemble a huge insect, gliding with multiton delicacy over the jagged terrain.

"Thanks, Murph." He jerked his head toward the rest of the Squad. "Fall in."

Murphy jumped up, quickly sliding into his place where the Squad stood formed and waiting, Gomez at the head. Stark walked slowly down the lines, Gomez following close behind, visually checking each trooper while he flipped through their battle armor status scans on his HUD. As he passed Chen, a gaggle of red telltales suddenly popped up on scan.

"What the . . . ?" Gomez was startled into an exclamation. "Sarge, he was green when we suited up."

"Don't doubt it." Stark knew Gomez would never have let the armor through otherwise. He raised his own armored right fist and rapped sharply on the side of Chen's arm, just below the shoulder. The red telltales flickered, then went green all at once. *Damned Mark IV armor.* He gestured toward the suit. "This model gets false cascading failure indies once in every blue moon. Totally unpredictable. I've only seen it once or twice, but it's always like this."

Gomez's head nodded, her gaze riveted on the spot Stark had hit. She'd have it memorized before her eyes moved. "Nice to know. Any fix coming?"

Stark shook his head. "Not on this baby. The Mark V will fix everything, they promise."

A ripple of sardonic laughter ran through the Squad. New gear was always supposed to solve every problem. You soon learned it always brought a new set of faults to worry about along with its new capabilities and higher price tag. Besides, the Mark Vs had been "on the way" for the past couple of years. G-4 was probably trying to wear out the inventory of IVs before they issued any new suits, which made sense if you were in Supply and not getting shot at while wearing old gear.

"All right." Stark stood before them, a dozen opaque faceplates looking his way. Twelve outwardly identical suits of combat armor, but he knew each personality inside each one. *That's my job, and if I don't take it seriously, somebody else might pay the price.* "This is a tough one. No lie. Long way in, long way out. We've got some aces the brass are playing to make it easier, but I want nothing but the best from you. Anything goes critical, everyone will have to be sharp. Questions?"

There weren't any this time, even from the new recruits. A muffled clunk sounded as the APC grounded and mated to the bunker's main hatch. After a brief wait, the clatter of steps announced the arrival of the fire team that would man the bunker while Stark's Squad was out on the op. The fire team was from Alpha Company, faces known only in passing these days and names usually heard only on turnover briefs. The Corporal in charge singled out Stark. "We've got it, Sergeant. Good luck."

"Thanks." No sense in envying those who got to stay behind. Everybody went out on op eventually. "Take care of the place, and don't drink all the beer." Old joke. There never was any beer on the line, but rumor always claimed the other outfits had it stashed somewhere.

"We'll leave you a six." The Corporal waved one of his troops to the watch chair, then headed toward the command console to check in.

Stark pointed up the access way. "Go. By the numbers." The Squad headed out in predetermined order, Gomez first and Stark entering last. Last in, first out.

Even after years on Luna, living in spaces grudgingly hacked cubic meter by cubic meter out of the dead rock, the access to the APC still seemed tight. The other soldiers were seated and settling in as Stark came through and swung into the last vacant seat. He strapped down and then jacked in to the APC via the command relay. Secondary readings from the APC's auxiliary command circuit popped up on his HUD, and the internal comm net activated. "Third Squad ready."

"Roger." The APC commander sounded relaxed. One more transport run for him. "Good evening. Should be an easy ride."

For you, maybe. "Thanks. Get us there on time and there's a big tip in it for you." APC apes hated being compared to taxi drivers, which was why the grunts rarely lost an opportunity to do it.

"Yeah, right. Save your jokes for the enemy sentries, wise guy. Cycling up."

Stark rotated his thumb upward in a spiral to his watching Squad as a warning. A second later, the APC went off surface with a lurch and surged into forward. He called up the vid link to the APC's eyes, watching rock scroll rapidly past. Luxury to a grunt, to see where you were going and had been. The rest of the Squad had only the troop compartment and the armored figures of their Squadmates for scenery.

Inside the APC, two rows of armored figures rocked in their harnesses in time to the vehicle's turns, accelerations, and brakings. New soldiers tried to hold themselves still. Vets soon learned not to waste the energy, resting against their harnesses and rolling with each movement. In the small, darkened compartment they occupied, the soldiers resembled weirdly costumed worshipers, nodding in time to a ritual only they could hear.

Time dragged, as always on the run into a drop zone, but it seemed sudden when they arrived. The big rocks dropped away, revealing a long, flat sea of dust ahead. The two other APCs, holding First and Second Squads, were waiting, twin beetles perched on the edge of the dust plain.

Third Squad's APC braked hard, swinging in to nestle close to the other two. Parade ground routine, out of place here, where you didn't cluster targets close together. The APCs, great vehicles but like most of the heavy equipment too damned expensive, were so rarely employed in combat it wasn't surprising their drivers didn't think tactical. "Okay.

Sergeant. All out." No parting courtesies from the driver, probably still smarting from the taxi driver comparison.

Stark keyed his Squad circuit, running an eye over the now-rigid figures of his troops. "Let's go. Follow me, by the numbers." The APC hatch gapped wide, and Stark pulled himself through, lunging forward as soon as his feet hit to clear the space for the next soldier. There were still plenty of rocks here, but broken and interspersed with threads of dust. He did a quick Tac scan, noting the other APCs dropping their troops, the other Squads fanning rapidly out to form ragged lines facing toward the empty plain.

"Clear," Gomez advised laconically. She was last out, hurrying into position to Stark's left. With sudden, silent leaps the APCs sprang into life again, spinning around and gliding back toward their lines. They'd be back when the rendezvous time rolled around, but wouldn't sit out here vulnerable and relatively obvious waiting for the Platoon before then.

Stark checked the Tac scan again. All three Squads looked to be ready, each soldier's symbol lying on the position mandated by the op plan. The time readout in the upper left corner of Stark's scan glowed a happy green, meaning they were on the timeline. *Go here, do this.* He looked out across the open dust field to the ragged crater walls marking the far side, their broken peaks standing jagged against the eternal night sky. Those crater walls looked a long ways off. His gaze wandered higher, to where stars blazed against the black of endless space. Hidden among them rested the warships, American and enemy, orbiting far enough from the Moon to avoid lunar-based defenses, but close enough to menace those ships trying to run cargo and passengers to and from the lunar colonies. The enemy tried to blockade the Americans, the Americans tried to blockade the enemy, and sailors died in brief flashes of light against the dark. Sometimes the remnants of the battles fell where the soldiers could see them, pieces of wreckage that had once made up ships curving in to add their own impact craters to those formed by countless meteors.

Vic's voice on the Platoon command circuit brought him back

to this side of the plain. "First Squad ready." Stark quickly ran through his own Squad again, double-checking their status while Sergeant Sanchez reported in. "Second Squad ready."

Everybody looked good. "Third Squad ready."

The Lieutenant came on line, audibly nervous as her first combat op began. "Second Platoon, move out. Keep it quiet."

A very long time ago, a very big rock had wandered through the wrong patch of space, coming head-to-head with Earth's Moon. Where it hit, out somewhere far to the left of where the Platoon now moved, a huge crater had been gouged into the Moon's surface by the rock's death spasm. At the same time, probably breaking free from that big rock, a much smaller rock had hit up here, at the edge of the main event. Much smaller, but still plenty big enough to rearrange the landscape. That second rock had created an elongated smaller crater, with its own walls, forming a fingerlike extension off the big hole. Over time, dust filled the crater and its finger, forming lunar "seas" mockingly devoid of life. Multitudes of smaller craters formed cliffs and ridges radiating out from the seas, remnants of other times when rock flowed like water. Humans came, drawing up defensive lines, and saw the crater walls and dust plains here as fine natural defenses. So the unbelievably ancient legacy of natural violence became the stage for the most modern forms of violence humanity had devised.

Now the Platoon moved across the finger plain, thirty-nine men and women in three broken lines, plodding through the dust, heading toward a barely visible notch in the crater wall. Sometime, somehow, a pass had formed on that spot, a route through the worst of the ridges on that side of the plain. It was obvious as all hell as an attack corridor—so obvious no one in their right mind would assault toward it through the open plain. So the enemy had strung sensors out to watch the approaches and not worried about manning the site.

It felt strange, being out here. Stark knew the worm had to be working, or else they'd have been shelled by now. Normally you'd stay among the rocks, keep under cover. They called your suits battle armor, but they wouldn't stop most modern weapons. Only the really heavy stuff, junk an APC or tank could carry, would really protect you, and armored vehicles had their own threats to worry about. Smart soldiers, soldiers who wanted to live, stayed around things they could hide behind. Nobody in their right mind walked out onto a flat expanse of nothing. But sometimes doing something stupid worked, because nobody expected it. That was their only ace, that and the worm.

If for some reason soldiers found themselves advancing through an area without cover, they'd evade forward, half the Squad covering while the other half plunged ahead, dodging and weaving. But that'd be "noisy," lots of disparate movement, and no telling if it'd be too much for the worm to block. Instead the three Squads moved in route march, steadily eating the distance. Behind them, a strange fog hung low over the plain, fine dust stirred by their movement hanging just above the surface as Luna's weak gravity fought a feeble but unending struggle to tug the dust particles slowly back down to rest.

After a while Stark's mind shifted into neutral, automatically moving his feet, "waking up" only if something unusual happened. You could march that way almost forever, a lesson learned in boot camp and never really forgotten. Years of experience allowed him to monitor his Squad the same way, reacting only if something stood out as unusual. But the Squad and all their equipment gave no signs of trouble. Even Murphy, apparently unwilling to straggle behind on the open vista of the dust plain, kept pace without any threats or urgings.

It came as a surprise when Stark realized they'd reached the pass, cliff wall looming up black-on-black against the sky. First Squad went through slowly, carefully identifying sensor sites and placing command-detonation charges.

When they came back, the worm might very well be dead and they wouldn't want those enemy eyes active.

Second Squad followed, moving faster, almost treading on First Squad's heels as they cleared the pass. "Sanchez," Reynolds called over the Sergeant's private circuit, "keep your people back until we've located and mined all the sensors."

"Understood. I am holding them as far back as I can," Sergeant Sanchez replied. "The timeline is very tight here."

Too damn tight, Stark mentally agreed. *Officers sit back at headquarters and dream up timelines to match their plans instead of making the plans match reality on the ground. Good thing Vic won't be rushed on this job.* Something else bothered him for a moment, something that wasn't there. Then he grinned in relief. Normally there'd be multiple officers from up the chain of command jumping in to issue orders directly to the Platoon or the individual Squads or soldiers, but on this op the need to keep transmissions to a minimum had apparently kept that from happening. *Thank the Lord for not-so-small blessings.*

"Sergeant Reynolds, what's the holdup?" Lieutenant Conroy questioned.

"My Squad needs to do this task right, Lieutenant." Reynolds kept her tone even but unyielding.

"We're pushing timeline," Conroy complained.

"Lieutenant?" Stark hailed. "Do you want my Squad to deploy now and cover First Squad?"

"Deploy? Uh, wait one."

While Conroy was still considering the question, Reynolds called in again. "All sensors mined, Lieutenant. Continuing advance." Vic immediately switched to the Sergeant's circuit. "Thanks for keeping the Lieutenant off my back, Ethan."

"No problem. Making an officer think always buys you a few minutes."

Second Squad swung into motion as First Squad finally advanced, moving rapidly to catch up with the timeline. Minutes later, Third Squad cleared the pass in turn, their line bunching briefly through the notch and then spreading again on the other side. After that it was a forest of interwoven lesser crater walls, one after another, the Squad members weaving through rocks to find the easiest route. Stark felt himself relaxing, happy to be in broken terrain again, an absurd feeling for a grunt rapidly closing in on the objective.

An alarm beeped insistently, warning of a problem in the Squad, even as Private Kidd called in. "Sergeant, I'm losing one of my rebreather cartridges."

Stark checked his readout of Kidd's systems, scanning the whole display. "Got it. Looks like contamination die-off. Your other cartridges look good from here."

"Yes, Sergeant." She sounded a bit nervous, pretty new to lunar operations and one step closer to losing her oxygen supply on the surface of the Moon with friendly help a long ways off.

"You got two backup cartridges, Kidd. If one of those goes, too, I'll make sure Corporal Gomez is positioned next to you to do a rebreather link if you need it." Not good tactics, sitting two soldiers right next to each other, but the only practical thing to do. "You copy, Gomez?"

"*Sí, Sargento.* Keep it cool, Beth," Gomez added. "You're plenty small, like me. Not a big clod like some of the guys out here. You'll do fine on two cartridges. I've done okay on one, sometimes, for a while."

"Okay, Corporal. Thanks."

Stark's Squad was still in the last crater rim, so ancient as to be little more than a mild rise, when First Squad advanced into the relatively open area around the metals refinery, cautious once again, to take care of the merc bunker and its two weapons pits. Without the worm they'd probably just blow the bunker with a shoulder-fired antiarmor round. That'd be real noisy, though, certain death for the worm, so instead Vic's troops moved with precise care, emplacing charges on the bunker's exterior and on the remote weapons sites.

Stark momentarily shifted his scan to a remote view from Vic's suit, curious for a closer look at the fortification. From the First Squad leader's perspective, he saw that the bunker had been poorly maintained. Outside cover had been allowed to deteriorate, exposing patches of artificial material. Light, heat, and/or gases leaked from a half-dozen tiny ruptures. *Really sloppy. They might as well have hung a sign on the damn thing.* Inside the bunker, Stark knew, the mercs would be paying little attention to the outside, counting on their sensors to give them plenty of heads-up to anything unusual. Odds were, nothing unusual had ever happened here. Given that, and normal merc level of performance, the bunker's crew would probably be dead before they ever realized their sensors were lying to them.

First Squad took up covering positions around the bunker, ready to deal with it when the time came or if the mercs somehow figured out what was going down around them. The timeline showed green, everything hitting on schedule again, as Second Squad moved on, toward the metals refinery. After the deadness of the normal lunar environment, and the survivability-driven low signatures of military gear, the refinery stood out as a carnival of light and vibration. Heat blared from the complex, pulsing in time to the automated production sequence. Stark's gear adjusted frantically, dropping intensity scales to avoid burning out circuits. He stared, briefly, at an alien world, where life wasn't measured in the same ways he knew.

Don't know how the enemy sensor net could notice anything with that noise show going on, Stark thought, then reconsidered. *Yeah, but they're probably calibrated to recognize it and spot anything outside parameters. That merc bunker's probably there mainly to check out any alarms and make sure the mining company doesn't get nailed for false alerts.*

Second Squad came up to the refinery perimeter as Third Squad headed out to the left, individual members of Stark's unit moving to place mines on the access road leading in and then fall back to take up covering positions. This process, at least, had been immeasurably simplified by the soldiers' Tacs. *Put this mine here. Put that mine there.*

Piece of cake. Just follow the dots on the map on your HUD.

Stark moved directly to a position where he could overview the process, covering his troops as they placed and activated the mines. Watching state-of-the-art mines be activated had always fascinated Stark, focusing intently as each device scanned its immediate surroundings, then altered surface texture and color to blend in until he lost track of it visually. The mines could even extrude smooth or jagged edges to match nearby rocks. Fascinating, and really scary, because enemy mines could do the same things. If it weren't for the automatic disarming mechanisms that after a few days turned the mines into objects almost as inert as the rocks they resembled, Stark would have been afraid to take a step on the surface outside the American perimeter.

Mine emplacement had almost been completed, his soldiers scuttling back to drop into their own covering positions, when Stark noticed Sanchez's Squad sitting stalled on the perimeter of the refinery. "Vic, what's with Sanchez?"

"They found a secondary alarm net. Looks independent of the main security system." Vic sounded clipped and professional, keeping transmissions short.

"Why in hell would a metals refinery have a secondary independent alarm system?"

"Lieutenant Conroy guessed it's some insurance requirement."

"Insurance?"

"Yeah. Property insurance or something. Civ stuff." Vic let worry show through her voice, talking only to Stark. "Since it's independent of the sector sensor grid, our worm doesn't affect it. Sanchez thinks they can work a bypass on it fast, though."

Hope so. The time display numbers were changing shade, gradually lightening from bright green toward yellow. They were already behind schedule, working a timeline that, like every timeline developed by officers back at headquarters, required everything to work perfectly for it to be met. In this case that timeline had also been driven by concern the worm would fail and someone would come down the road Stark's Squad was guarding to find and trap them out here. Minutes dragged by, each seeming to stretch forever, and the yellow numbers on the timeline began to take on an orange tinge that threatened to shade to red. *Move it, Sanch.*

Abruptly, Second Squad's symbols did move, converging on a single point in the refinery perimeter and then fanning out rapidly through the complex. The ugly orange of the time display, deepening to red, held steady as Second Squad moved furiously to catch up with the timeline. Each soldier had charges and exact places to put them, some on equipment, some on structural members, some on the terminal for the mag-lev rail line running to the enemy industrial complex. More minutes crawled as the other two squad leaders waited, one eye on the areas they were covering and the other on the progress of Second Squad.

After a seeming eternity, Sanchez's people started moving back toward and through the rupture in the perimeter. Stark permitted himself a sigh of relief. *We may get away with this after all.*

Battle armor motion alert sensors suddenly pulsed, focusing on the point where the access road cut through a minor crater rim. "Vehicle inbound," Stark's suit calmly announced, "ID uncertain." Stark cursed briefly, then called the Lieutenant. "Sir—"

"Got it, Sergeant," Lieutenant Conroy cut him off, speaking

rapidly with a sharp edge of tension she couldn't hide. "What is it?"

Why ask me? The Lieutenant had access to everything Stark did, but it was natural for a new officer to lean on her Sergeants at a time like this. Within moments, visual and broad-spectrum observations from all the soldiers in Third Squad were correlated by Stark's Tac system, which checked the information against its database and came up with a guess. "Tentative ID," Stark's suit spoke again, "light armored car, probable Manta export variant."

More bad news. A civ car they might have been able to take down without too much fuss, but even a light armored vehicle would require some firepower to stop. *Damn.* "My Tac says it's probably a Manta armored car, Lieutenant. That model is merc equipment."

"What the hell are they doing here, Sergeant?" Conroy demanded.

You want me to ask them? "Sir, they're coming straight in, like they're not worried at all, so it's probably a routine patrol, maybe a relief crew for the bunker."

Seconds ticked by while the new Lieutenant dealt with her first real combat decision, the armored car closed the distance, and Second Squad's last member cleared the perimeter. On Stark's HUD, the timeline readout began to glow an angry red. If this had been a normal operation, half a dozen officers from headquarters would already have been issuing a barrage of orders to the Lieutenant as well as howling directly at the individual soldiers to get back on the damned timeline, target/don't target the Manta, and dig in/run away. This time, thanks to fears of uncloaking the worm with comm transmissions, headquarters was forced to remain silent. As he waited for the Lieutenant's reply, Stark had to fight down a sudden absurd impulse to laugh at a mental image of senior officers hopping around their headquarters communications terminals in wild frustration.

"Sergeant Stark"—Conroy paused, as if taking a breath—"destroy the armored car if it makes it through the mines you planted."

"Yes, sir." It was a lousy choice, guaranteed to announce their presence here in a way the worm couldn't hide, but it was also the only choice they really had. Stark passed the word to his Squad. "Fire on my command." Thirteen weapons lined up to track the oncoming vehicle as it neared the Squad's positions and the mines scattered across and around the road. Stark waited, double-checking the statistics on the armored car's defenses with grim satisfaction. Against the light armor the Manta carried, even the rifle rounds would punch through at this range, if it came to that.

It didn't. A third of the way through the minefield, the Manta suddenly hesitated, then lurched upward, propelled by a jet of high-velocity gas from the shaped charge in an antivehicle mine. The top of the armored car blew out, edges peeling upward, as a column of metal, gas, and other fragments vented overhead. The car sagged back down, slid sideways, then wedged itself into the surface halfway off the road. Its fountain of debris dwindled, gases rapidly dissipating while solids fell with dreamlike slowness back to the lunar soil.

Stark was jerked from watching the death of the armored car and its occupants by other detonation alerts on his scan. Behind, First Squad had triggered its charges, blowing in the merc bunker, disabling its weapons pits, and knocking out the enemy sensors covering their route back. The mercs in the bunker had probably still been open-mouthed with shock from the fate of the armored car when their own end came. Stark felt a momentary pity for them, playing soldier against professionals and probably never realizing how poorly prepared they were for the role. *Too bad, but it was you or us. Live stupid, die stupid.*

The universe seemed to pause to catch its breath, then shot back into motion. Stark's long-range scan showed enemy emergency sensor sats being lofted toward their location, trying to fill a sudden gap. *Guess that confirms the worm's dead.* Before they made their positions, the sats flared and went out, victims of waiting American antilunar orbital systems. That'd keep the enemy from targeting them right away, but the enemy already knew where they were, and it wouldn't take a genius to figure out where the Platoon had come from and which way it would be falling back. All of which meant it wouldn't be long before unwelcome company started coming down that road in armored vehicles that made the dead Manta look like a toy.

Lieutenant Conroy came on line, voice cracking with tension. "All Squads, Egress Plan Charlie. I say again, Egress Plan Charlie."

Egress Plan Charlie. Conroy's voice triggered the Tacs of each soldier in her Platoon to display that operation option, which was just a fancy name for Run Like Hell. Falling back by the numbers, with overwatch and careful movements, would be counterproductive now. If the Platoon got caught anywhere this side of the dust plain they were as dead as the mercs, with no cover or support of their own, doomed to be overwhelmed by superior firepower. Stark called his own troops, even though they'd heard the order at the same time he had and were already moving. "You heard the Lieutenant. Go! If anybody falls behind, I'll kick their asses up between their ears."

Even as he swung into motion, Stark watched on scan as First Squad moved quickly away from the ruined bunker site, a straight line toward the pass. Second Squad came right behind, all of its personnel clear of the refinery and converging on First Squad's route. Last, farthest out, were the soldiers of Third Squad, falling back swiftly to join the path of retreat somewhere beyond the bunker area. "Gomez," Stark commanded, "get up front and set the pace." With Gomez to keep up with and Stark dealing with laggards, Third Squad should continue moving rapidly.

As Stark passed the bunker area, its imploded shell off to his right now, Sergeant Sanchez broadcast a warning. "Heads up! Refinery's going." Stark braced himself, then felt tremors rolling through the rock beneath as Sanchez detonated his charges. Pebbles in place for uncounted centuries broke free to roll silently down as the shock waves from the charges rippled by. Stark stole a glance back, scan highlighting junk flying every which way, energy discharges flaring from shattered power lines and buildings slowly collapsing inward. *Helluva view, almost worth the ticket out here.*

"Keep moving!" he yelled into the Squad net, causing several halted figures to leap back into motion. No time to spare playing tourist, not with the mech infantry just down the road. They'd be limited to foot travel following the Platoon through rocks, but they'd get to the edge of the rough terrain fast in their APCs, especially with that damned Manta advertising the presence and location of the minefield. Once among the rocks, they'd move faster than the Platoon could, not worried about conserving strength for the run across the dust plain. You just had to hope they weren't too quick in responding to the alarm.

As Stark cleared the first rise, entering the rocks, his battle armor alarm sounded again. Far back on the road, a probable enemy vehicle symbol appeared, closing fast on the site of the ruined refinery.

This is gonna be one hell of a bad day. Stark dropped beneath the level of the rise, hiding from detection by the enemy but also cutting off his view of the oncoming vehicles. "Lieutenant, I spotted enemy armor coming up the road just before I made cover."

"Did they see you?" Conroy shot back, her voice still pitched too fast and too tense.

Stark fought down a sarcastic reply, recognizing the tension gnawing at his own judgment. "I don't know, Lieutenant. Probably not. They only had a moment, and one soldier in battle armor is a lot harder to spot than a moving tank."

"That's right." Conroy's relief was palpable. "Maybe that'll buy us some time."

"Maybe, Lieutenant," Stark temporized as he launched himself on a long arc down the slope. *Or maybe if they'd seen me the enemy would have thought we'd left a covering force behind and would advance a lot slower to avoid an ambush. Hell. No way of knowing, and too late to do anything different anyway.* He felt the force of events driving him hopelessly onward, just as his own movement dislodged rocks that could fall only as gravity and terrain dictated.

The rocks, slopes, and ridges that concealed the Platoon from the enemy hunting them also slowed down their own progress. Stark kept pushing his soldiers, snapping at their heels like a guard dog whenever one seemed to lag slightly, even as he studied the map on his HUD. How far could they go at this pace before tired soldiers began slowing? The battle armor could help, providing support and partial assistance to a walking soldier, but power supplies were limited. Push the soldiers too hard or push the suits too hard and the results would be the same, giving out short of safety. *And I only get one chance to get it right.*

Behind them, the symbology of their pursuers clustered, pulsing and shifting as updates and estimates jumped probable positions in a weird dance. The jerky motion of the enemy symbols always tended their way, though, closing with certainty on the one route through the crater wall ahead.

"Incoming supporting barrage," Stark's suit warned. *Best news I've had in a while.* Stark glanced up, instinctively and unnecessarily, since there was nothing to see and his Tac display was tracking the rounds. The incoming warheads burst and faded from display, too early and too far out. *Hell. We're too damned far inside enemy territory.* With the Platoon still under the enemy's defensive umbrella, their own artillery couldn't reach their pursuers. It was unlikely there'd be any more barrages. Shells cost, and the chances of one making it through were too small.

"Hey, Vic," he called.

"Here."

"Did the Lieutenant call in that artillery?"

"Yeah." Reynolds' reply held a mix of anger and resignation. "She's screaming for support, but that's all we're getting."

Stark checked his own back door into the command circuit, hearing Lieutenant Conroy's desperate calls for cover for the retreating Platoon being met by only occasional noncommittal acknowledgments. "How come headquarters is so quiet, Vic?" Stark wondered. "Why aren't they telling us what to do, like they usually do? The worm's dead, so they can micromanage everybody again."

Vic's laughter held no humor. "Ethan, we're in a lot of trouble right now, and unless a more senior officer tells her what to do, Conroy's the only person directly responsible if we get blown away before we reach safety."

Stark grimaced. "Sure. I forgot nobody high-ranking is ever at fault when something goes wrong. At least if it comes to that, we'll be able to die without some idiots back at headquarters ordering us to choose different targets or run in a different direction."

"That's looking at the bright side."

Stark checked his map again, measuring distances and movement rates, knowing what had to be done but delaying all the same. *Can't put if off much longer.*

"Sarge." Gomez called in on the Squad circuit, sounding calm but slightly breathless from the hurried pace.

"Yeah." *Answer the same way. Nice and calm. Don't let the others know how bad this is, how worried you are. Just another drill out here, people, keep your heads and you'll be okay.* He frowned, noticing Gomez's symbol beginning to drop back from its position at the head of the Squad. "You got a problem?"

"We got a problem." Like she was discussing a glitch in the sentry schedule. "Ain't gonna make it across that plain, Sarge. They're too close. They'll get to that big crater rim while we're still out there, and pick us off like roaches caught on the mess hall floor."

Tell me something I don't know. He'd reached the same conclusion several minutes ago. The Platoon was tired, worn from the long march out here and taking out the objective. They were feeling the effects of those long hours, while the enemy troops were fresh, rested, and mad as hell. Fear, training, and conditioning kept the Platoon ahead but couldn't open the distance. "So?"

"Is there gonna be anybody meeting us this side of the dust plain? Any support?"

"None that I know of."

"So we need a rear guard. I'm it."

"The hell." He should've guessed Gomez would make that move, and shouldn't have waited as long as he had to make his own. "You stay forward, got me? The Squad needs you out front."

"They need me watching their backs."

"No. Makes no damn sense for you to fall back this far. The troops will start to lose it if they see you dropping back. *¿Comprendo?*" Gomez's symbol had steadied, keeping up with the others while she argued with Stark. The other symbols were dragging slightly, trying to maintain their position relative to Gomez. "You're already slowing them down. Get back out front, now!"

A long pause, then Gomez's symbol surged ahead. "Okay, Sarge, but that don't solve the problem." From her tone, she was mad as hell and putting that emotion into her movement.

You had the right answer, Anita. Just the wrong person. Stark shifted to the command circuit. "Lieutenant? Stark here."

"Yes, Sergeant." Tired and worried. Scared, not that she didn't have every right to be. This wasn't the sort of tactical situation a new Lieutenant wanted to be trapped in.

"Lieutenant, we can't make it across the plain before they occupy the crater edge and blow us away. We'll be sitting ducks as soon as they get in position."

Several seconds ticked off as the pursuing symbology danced madly behind, continuing its slow closure on the Platoon. Finally the Lieutenant replied. "That's very likely, Sergeant. Do you have an idea?" Keeping it short, probably mad and frustrated, not seeing any way out, desperate enough to ask her senior enlisted personnel for advice even though everything officers were taught these days warned against that kind of display of fallibility. As if any enlisted ever believed their officers were infallible to begin with.

"We need a rear guard," Stark stated calmly. "Someone has to hold them long enough for the rest to get under our perimeter."

"No." The Lieutenant's answer came back immediately this time. "I'm not leaving your Squad behind. They'd be wiped out."

Good for you, Lieutenant, Stark thought with some surprise. *You care enough to reject that option, even though it'd guarantee you getting out safe.* "I agree, sir. But we don't need a whole Squad. One good soldier can hold them long enough." Say it professional, like it was a tactical problem during a simulation. "It's the only answer, Lieutenant. One casualty, maybe, and the rest of the Platoon gains time to get across the open area." Stark figured Vic Reynolds was still listening in to Conroy's command circuit. It wasn't too hard to imagine how she had to be feeling right now, because she'd surely already figured out who that one soldier had to be.

Lieutenant Conroy spoke slowly and reluctantly. "I can't order anyone to stay back alone."

"You don't have to, Lieutenant. I'm volunteering. Only logical choice. I'm farthest back, and I'm one of your most experienced soldiers." *Sell the Lieutenant on it, and sell myself. Make it make sense to both of us.* "I've got the combat experience to hold them long enough, and to get away clear after." *Hopefully, pray to God.* "I have no intention of buying any territory out here, Lieutenant, but the only way to save the rest of the Platoon is for me to hold off the pursuit for a little while."

Several more seconds. Odds were the Lieutenant was talking to Reynolds on the private conference switch, but for once Stark refrained from eavesdropping, even though he could easily imagine the conversation. *Is there any other way?* the Lieutenant would ask her, and *Can he get out?* The answers were easy enough, *no* and *maybe.* They wouldn't be easy for Vic to give, but she'd give them.

"Okay, Sergeant," Conroy finally agreed, relief warring with the shame of abandonment in her voice. "You . . . are to hold as long as . . . you feel necessary. Use your discretion on when to withdraw."

"Yes, sir."

"Sergeant Stark, once you move, the rest of the Platoon should be in position to cover your retreat. We'll cover you the minute you start to move. Don't try to hold too long. Okay?"

"Yes, sir." *By the time I start to move, you'll be too far out to cover me. You're too inexperienced and probably don't realize that yet, but I knew it when I volunteered. No other choice.* "I'm not bucking for a medal, Lieutenant. I'll be right behind you as soon as you're clear." *Maybe if I keep repeating that, I'll believe it.*

"Roger, Sergeant. We'll cover you, Stark. We'll cover you."

"Yes, sir." You could tell the Lieutenant was feeling guilty as sin. Good for her, again. It wasn't her fault, though, not her fault the war's vid ratings went low and her Platoon got picked to jack them back up. Not her fault the enemy had been faster and better than the officers in the rear had assumed. Not her fault the plan headquarters had dreamed up hadn't been quite as perfect as they'd hoped. "You did a pretty good job out here, Lieutenant." *Maybe Conroy can turn into a good officer, someday, if such things still exist.*

That brought another pause. "Thanks, Sergeant Stark. We'll see you on the other side."

"Yes, sir." Stark switched over to answer an incoming on the Sergeants' personal comm net. He knew it'd be Vic even before she spoke.

"Ethan, you be careful." No hysterics and no anger, not from her. She knew as well as he that he hadn't any real choice.

"Don't worry. I'm no hero, remember? See you back at R&R."

"'Don't worry,' he says. *Don't* be a hero, Ethan. Don't let the demon win this one. Don't hold too long. We'll be back." Reynolds' voice finally betrayed some of the concern she had been trying to hide.

"Never doubted it. But I won't let you or my Squad down, Vic. Whatever it takes. You make sure the Platoon gets back safe."

"I'll get them back safe. Don't you dare die for me, Ethan Stark."

"I've no intention of doing so. Take it easy, Vic."

"Yeah. You, too."

"Stark." That was Sanchez, calm even when breathing pretty heavily from the long retreat. "Good luck."

"Thanks. Look out for my Squad, okay?"

"Of course."

One more call, to Corporal Gomez. "Anita, I'm the rear guard." She tried to break into his call, but he overrode her signal. "Lieutenant's orders," he added, avoiding mention of his volunteering for those orders. "I'm farthest back and most experienced." He released the override.

"Dirty trick, Sarge. It was my idea."

"Nah, I'd already realized the same. Only option. You've got the Squad. Get them back safe."

"How long you staying?"

"As long as it takes and not one second longer. Don't worry about me. Worry about the Squad. I took care of them this far. Now it's your job."

After a long wait, her reply finally came. "Roger, *Sargento. Comprendo. Vaya con Dios*"

"Same." Nothing else seemed right at the moment. "Stark out."

He started carefully checking out the terrain ahead. First, good sites for the two mini-claymore mines he carried. They needed to be emplaced near where the pursuit would pass, ready to hurl their loads of shot horizontally into moving targets. Then, a good location for himself. That location had to have a decent field of fire that would allow Stark to see and shoot at enemy soldiers coming at him from almost any angle. It also needed some protection out front, and solid rock behind. He didn't want to be silhouetted against the horizon every time he moved. Overhead cover would be nice, too, but probably impossible. Usually, natural overhead meant a cave of some sort in a rock face, which meant you might be covered for a while, but you had no way out once the enemy zeroed in on the entrance. Not that he expected to find a cave here anyway, not on this airless, waterless wreck of a world.

Stark spotted a place that looked promising, up ahead just before the pass leading out onto the dust plain. The last of his Squad members were entering the pass as he placed his first claymore, covering the path along the direct route to the pass, then the second mine a hundred meters farther along. The way up to the position he'd chosen was a little steep, but that was good: He'd want to go back down fast when the time came.

The firing point proved to be a good one, with a fine field of fire out to where the enemy would come, a few meters of rock rearing up behind and a rock rim forming a low natural entrenchment out front. Stark settled, making sure he liked just where he was. On his display, the riotous movement of the pursuers' symbology was rapidly necking down toward the pass and toward Stark's position. Out on the plain, the Platoon's symbols headed outward, steadily opening the distance, still way too far from safety. Stark placed his grenades in front, ready to fire, rested his rifle beside himself, and waited, amid the rocks and stars, solid shadows and brilliant light. He couldn't recall ever having felt quite so lonely.

"You idiot." His father had been mad as hell. "You want to be a hero? Join the police, f'God's sake! At least then you could die in your hometown!"

Dad was still in his coveralls, wet and smelling of fish feed. Stark had stood before him, two months out of community college with a degree in inventory maintenance that qualified him to be a stock clerk in some big discount store owned and run by people who didn't really care about people like him. Twenty years old, unemployed-looking-for-a-job-that-didn't-doom-every-dream-once-dreamed, still dressing like the high-school kid he felt like inside. Nowhere to go, after wasting what educational chances he'd once had, until he ran across the recruiting spiel on vid during a break between old war movies. It had been a pretty forlorn recruiting spiel, as if even the actors used in it couldn't quite believe anyone would actually join the military. To Stark's own surprise, it hadn't taken much to convince him to join; no matter how bad it would be, it was somewhere else, one last chance to break away.

Stark, facing his father, fought to speak calmly, but his words had come out sounding like a kid caught coming in after curfew. "I thought you'd be proud." The hell he had. Like most of the people he knew, Dad had never hidden his contempt for the military, but it had sounded like a good potential reply when Stark had rehearsed the conversation beforehand.

"How could you have believed that?" Dad took a deep breath, looked around as if lost, then back directly at Stark. "Look, there're laws. You get to change your mind. You've got, what, seventy-two hours? Tell them you're not joining."

"Enlisting." Just knowing the term had somehow set him apart already. "And I'm not changing my mind." He had gotten mad, too, playing out another in the long series of fights for control, for independence. "I'm an adult. I can enlist if I want."

"You don't know what you're doing." His father looked half frantically toward the living room, hoping to see Stark's mother there, hoping for an ally, but she wasn't due off her shift at the store for another four hours. Stark had planned that, knowing he couldn't have faced both parents' pleas. "For once, just this once, listen to me. I don't know what they tell you, I don't know if they wave a slick uniform in your face, all I know is nobody cares about the military. Do you know anyone in the military? Of course not. They're not like us. They get sent to places no one wants to go, to kill people, and usually end up getting killed themselves. Is that what you want, for your mother and me to get a letter saying you died doing something worthless, fighting a war someplace no one cares about?"

Stark felt himself wavering. His father couldn't usually speak so well about important things, usually tongue-tied with anger or emotion, but this once at least he was managing to call up all the doubts Stark had earlier suppressed.

Then his father had gone one step too far and blown it. "Don't be a fool, like you always are! Don't waste your life!" Old words, words that provoked an old reaction in Stark.

"Waste *my* life? You know all about wasting a life, don't you? I may be a fool, but there's no way I'm spending my life feeding fish. I'm going somewhere, *anywhere,* just so's I don't end up here!" Stark had waved around the room, including his father's entire life in that last declaration.

His father had flushed red, then paled, then turned and walked away. They hadn't spoken since. Stark had left before his mother came home, unable to bear the thought of facing her. It would've been better to have said good-bye to her, he'd often thought since. His leaving like that must have hurt her something fierce. There'd been letters to and from home since then, not very often and always through his mother. Always regretting the last words he'd spoken to his father, Stark had increasingly thought about a way to apologize, to start over. Let his dad know he respected him, now, for the hard work and the hard choices. Let his dad know he'd accomplished some good things in the mil after all. Made a man of him, in ways that really counted.

Funny thing, as your third and fourth decades of life rolled by and over you, all the mistakes your father had made suddenly didn't look so dumb. Somewhere along the way, you realized how hard he'd tried, and how tough a job being a dad was. Being in charge of a Squad wasn't all that different, except you had twelve kids and both the enemy and your own officers kept trying their level best to kill them. He had a letter for his dad, back at the bunker, he'd been kind of working on for a year or so, but he'd never gotten the words right or the nerve to send it. Right now, he wished he had.

"Heavy jamming," Stark's suit announced in the same calm tones it would use to provide a routine status report. "Tactical picture lost." The symbology representing his own Platoon as well as that of the rapidly closing enemy froze and was overlaid with last-contact time ticks. The battle armor was compensating for the enemy jamming by boosting all its power to the command link, keeping audio and vid going to Stark's chain of command. So they could track him, know what was happening to him, and tell him exactly what to do. But not this time. Don't give the Sergeant any orders, and when he gets wasted it won't be your fault.

Stark had no doubt, though, that the brass was still feeding the command-and-control vid to the citizens clustered around their vid sets. *Your heroes on the Moon, featuring Stark's Last Stand in almost real time, brought to you by the makers of* . . . Funny to think, so many people probably watching what he could see right now. Hopefully, headquarters was putting a long enough time delay on it that the enemy couldn't use it tactically against him. Usually the brass did, but sometimes they fed it out too fast. Sometimes, when the story was too good, or the action too hot. *At least it may be the last time they screw me.*

A new symbol glowed brightly, outlining an object on the nearest crater wall. He sighted in, carefully, magnification swelling the object to an armored body scrambling over the crest, IFF on his HUD screaming red for enemy. Stark fired, a three-round burst. The figure froze, no doubt warned of incoming but with no time to react. It suddenly bounced back against the rock, once and twice under multiple impacts, then lay still, tiny streams of atmosphere venting from the new holes in its armor. The enemy would be more careful now, advance slowly, try to feel out how many soldiers were in the rear guard and where they were positioned. With any luck Stark could keep them guessing on both counts for a few more minutes.

A rush to the left. Several figures darted among the cover, evading forward. They were good, not leaving him any decent shots. Stark waited, until he was rewarded with another rush, slightly to his right. This group wasn't as good; one slipped in haste, hauled itself up to get under cover, then fell again as one of Stark's rounds hit it in the upper abdomen. Two down, but they were probably getting a good idea where he was by now. Stay, and they'd target you eventually. Move, and they'd see you right away. Stark stayed.

The figures on the chrono in his HUD cycled slowly. Stark no longer paid attention to the crimson digits of his timeline display, angrily proclaiming his failure to meet Tac objectives. Once again he marveled, briefly, at the lack of comms or interference from headquarters, realizing again that Vic had been right and no officer wanted to leave any fingerprints on what surely seemed a hopeless battle.

Stark's Tac had continued estimating the progress of the Platoon, three clusters of symbols tracking steadily across the dust plain but still too close to the ridge. Still too early for Stark to leave. *Maybe the APCs came out, picked them up. They could be safe now. No, I can't be sure that happened. Have to assume the worst. Have to hold the enemy a little longer, give the Platoon time to make it across the field. Not too long now.* A figure moved suddenly forward amid the rocks before him as a barrage of covering fire laid down around his position. The sight augmented brightly on the enhanced figure as Stark sighted and squeezed in one motion. His HUD tracked the round directly into the other suit's faceplate. A blossom of gas and metal erupted as the enemy trooper stiffened, then slowly dropped like a burned-out toy.

The enemy barrage hesitated as the attacking force picked up the loss, then redoubled in fury. *Damn. Mad as hell now, and they pretty much know where I am. Okay. Keep down. Let them shoot. Save your rounds.* Stark occupied his mind by carefully inventorying his remaining ammo as the storm of fire raged around and above him. *Can't get rattled. Can't get hit. Have to be ready to roll soon.* He rehearsed an escape plan in his mind, fretting over details. *Roll right, down the ridge. Got to go fast before they lock on. Then over the back, drop to the dust plain and run to the first rock cluster that offers any cover. Fire and fall back. Or just run and dodge. That'll throw up a lot of dust. Confuse their aim. Easy. I'll manage until the relief gets close enough to help me.*

Something suddenly erupted through the surface on his near left, the concussion blasting rocks into fragments that slammed into his side. *They fired an antiarmor round. Damn it!* His left arm wasn't working right, now. The battle armor med kit hummed as it automatically shoved and shock drugs into his system. The armor hadn't suffered a large rupture, thank God. A plume of gas would have pinpointed him in a heartbeat.

Okay. Going to be harder with one arm but still doable. Drugs will compensate, keep me hot. He hoped, anyway. Not a lot of experience with getting hit. He'd usually been lucky before. Maybe not anymore. Stark had been avoiding looking at the Tac's estimated position for the Platoon, but he glanced now. Not quite there yet, but the Platoon should be almost close enough to home now to get help. Then some relief could come out a ways, help cover him. Should be on the way real quick. Nice heroic rescue. Make real nice footage on the vid. Boost ratings and everybody happy. Not long now.

Except, a small voice wondered, *what if somebody figures a lone rear guard holding out to the end makes better footage? What if somebody figures a rescue column might take too many losses?* Dead heroes are good, noble examples who don't do any of the not-so-noble things living humans are prone to. Live heroes can be a pain in the ass, especially when they happen to be a Sergeant with a reputation for being just that already. So maybe the rescue group heads out just a little too late. Lots of suspense, but then damn shame. A hero, a safely dead hero who can be sanctimoniously elevated to near-sainthood, a hero who gave his all for his country and his buddies. Yeah, wonderful ratings. And everybody would get to see what a great thing the Sergeant did. *No,* Stark thought fiercely, *Vic won't let them. She, Gomez, even this Lieutenant, they'll come back.* Unless they couldn't make it back in time. Unless someone stalled, didn't tell them what was really going down.

The motion alert pulsed as more figures scrambled into motion, covered by the unrelenting fire. *Got a heavy-weapons unit here now, must be. Too damn much firepower for a bunch of foot troops.* He carefully gauged the angle, waited, then detonated one of the claymores as two figures neared its blast cone. One enemy was hurled back against nearby rocks to lie broken across them while the second spun suddenly to the side and fell, a slow-motion sprawl into the dust.

Okay. That'll slow them. Now they've got to screen for my mines. Another glance at the Tac. The Platoon had to be close to safety now. *Anytime. My Tac will estimate the Platoon's clear and I can pull out. Just roll right and down. Drop to the plain and run while they're still trying to decide if I'm really gone.*

System alarms pointed skyward as Stark watched the tracks of high-trajectory rounds arcing in from the enemy rear. *Damn it all!* Freeze and pray the suit camo works long enough and maybe they're short on shells. No top cover here. Not if he didn't want to be trapped. And he had to be ready to fall back. Anytime now.

Multiple rounds burst overhead, casting clustered warheads across the area. The suit's camo held, or Stark would have died instantly under the impacts of a dozen homing warheads. Failing to locate a target, the warheads dropped in random patterns, detonating in hopes of causing damage to hidden foes. A searing pain hit Stark's right leg as a warhead went off not far away. *Bad. Real bad.* He scanned the damage display. The suit had sealed the penetrations, but his leg had been badly messed up. The med kit hummed harder and the pain and dizziness dropped away, replaced with a false sense of well-being.

Not over yet. Tac check. Almost time. Relief column should be heading out.

I don't need both legs to roll. I can still get clear. He carefully checked his ammo again. Two grenades, one mine left out front. *Can't move yet. They'd lock in on me too fast. Pump out both grenades to distract, set the mine on autodetonate. Then I roll. Piece of cake.*

Down below and in front more figures moved, partially obscured in his sight by a ragged red rim around his vision. *Can't use grenades yet. Gotta save them for when I pull out.* He brought his weapon up one-handed, balancing it on the rocks before him, to aim and fire automatically, figures downrange dropping as they came under fire. No telling if there were any hits. Incoming fire around Stark was too intense, hazing his scan with concussions and energy bursts. He blinked furiously, wondering why he couldn't get the dancing red flecks obscuring his sight to go away. Torn grass blades seemed to wave among the red flecks, incongruous against the bare, dead rock all around.

A Devil's Foot slammed into the rock face above him and spat a flurry of arrowlike flechets downward. Two hit, piercing completely through Stark and his armor and on into the rock below. The suit instantly sealed the holes as the med kit hummed frantically, trying to overcome nature with a tidal wave of chemicals. *Oh, God. Not gonna make it, am I? Too late. Too late. Not going anywhere now. Just like all the grunts I left back on the knoll. Finally my turn.* For a moment, Stark felt an unnatural clarity, free of pain and loss. *But all the others got out this time, didn't they? Safe. Platoon's clear. My Squad's clear. Did my job. Didn't let them down.*

Pain hit hard through the thick haze of drugs. A roaring filled his ears. Somewhere in front the enemy must still be advancing, but Stark could no longer see, and something kept his fingers from clenching to fire his weapon. Against the fury of the enemy barrage, his battle armor continued calmly reciting its own damaged systems status, one more sound that merged into the chaos around him. Stark thought he heard his name being spoken or called, but the last traces of concentration dissolved into a jumble of broken sounds and images. The red haze grew to fill his vision, blotting out all traces of the phantom grass, and a black curtain fell across his mind, one with the rocks and the dust, the white light and the black shadows.

PART THREE

TELL THE SPARTANS

First, there was light, blurred into great, soft dollops of almost brightness. The dollops condensed slowly, forming bars of brilliance against light blue veined with cracks as if the sky were splitting into fragments and letting dead space spill through. Then eyes finally focused and the broken sky resolved into peeling, painted rock strung with fluorescent lights.

"I'm not dead." The words didn't quite come out, hanging up somewhere within a rusty throat.

"No, Ethan, you're not dead."

Stark turned his head with great care, until the face of Vic Reynolds swung into his field of vision.

"Then you're no angel."

"Not yet and probably never." Vic's face contorted with sudden anger as she jabbed a finger so close to Stark's nose that he flinched in reaction. "You idiot! Don't ever do something that goddamn stupid again!"

"You're welcome."

"You said you wouldn't stay too long. Well, guess what? You were about one second this side of a body bag when we came back over that ridge with a brace of tanks and four APCs behind us. If one of the APCs hadn't been rigged as a life-support field ambulance you wouldn't have lived long enough to reach friendly lines."

Stark managed a smile, wondering why his face felt so stiff, abruptly glad he couldn't see himself in a mirror. "I knew you'd come back with reinforcements."

Vic sat back, eyes aflame. "Then you were wrong. The tanks, the APCs, they were going to sit on their fat butts while you got shot to hell. First we pleaded, then we threatened, then we started back on our own. That's when they followed. Brigade couldn't afford to lose all of us. The civs would have been real unhappy with that many casualties and the General would've been sacked, great vid ratings for your heroic sacrifice notwithstanding. So we got back to you, rolled over a bunch of enemy infantry who thought they'd just won, picked up your damn-near-lifeless carcass and hightailed home with half the enemy expeditionary force snapping at our rears. Understand all that, Ethan? They would have left you." She leaned forward, staring into his eyes as if seeking answers there. "Why the hell did you do it, Ethan?"

"I had my reasons."

"I know." Vic ignored Stark's reaction, speaking crisply, her words clear and smooth in the hush of the hospital room. "Patterson's Knoll. You were there."

"How'd you find out?"

"I looked it up, on a hunch. Worst disaster in recent American military history. About a decade ago. Two companies of U.S. soldiers, trapped on an open hill and cut to pieces because no one could get to them in time. Only three soldiers managed to escape during the night before the position got overrun the next day. You were one of them, Ethan. Why didn't you ever tell me?"

Stark studied the white-painted wall before his face as if it held some special significance. "Never talk about it."

"So I noticed." Vic's hand reached out, turning Stark's head with carefully precise force to face her again. "So that's your demon. You never really left that hilltop, did you, Ethan? Part of you is still there, on that grassy knoll."

Stark tried to escape her eyes, but his head was held steady in Vic's grip. "I left a lot of friends up there, Vic. They died. I didn't."

"Fate works that way."

"There had to be a *reason*!" Stark insisted. "I survived for a reason, and maybe that reason was just to make sure it never happened to anybody else. Maybe I lived so I can make sure other soldiers don't have to die the same way."

"And maybe it was all chance. The luck of the draw."

"Dammit, Vic, it had to mean something!" Stark was trembling, he realized, as a hundred points of pain sprang into being where his body had been battered by projectiles meant to kill. The bedside med monitor hummed louder, as if disapproving, and began dosing more drugs into Stark's intravenous feeds. His pain fell away, along with the agitation, not really gone, but somewhere behind a wall where they could rage without hurting him. "It had to mean something," he repeated.

Vic stared down somberly. *"Now* do you want to talk about it?"

"I dunno."

"Ethan, I've been in nasty battles. Plenty of them."

"Not like that one."

"And it was a long time ago."

"No." Stark shook his head, eyes staring into the distance. "No. It's every night, Vic. Every night." He looked back at her, eyes slightly unfocused from the combination of medications and memories. "They hit us all day, raking us with small arms, dropping artillery and mortars on the knoll. Couldn't dig in 'cause there was rock right under the surface. Nothing to hide behind, nothing but the grass. Grass cut by shrapnel and spattered with blood and trampled into the dirt." He fell silent for a moment.

"Were you hit?" Vic prodded gently.

"Me?" Stark questioned, then shuddered. "No. Private Ethan Stark didn't get hit. I'll never know why. I was so damned young, and so damned scared and so damned tired I couldn't even hold my rifle anymore and I just hugged the dirt and stared at the damned grass and prayed. Finally it got dark. New Moon, thank God, so it really was dark. They couldn't see us anymore. And I couldn't see all the bodies around me. They were my friends, Vic."

"I know. Why didn't the enemy come up on the knoll and finish you off?"

"Scared of us. Even though they'd kicked our butts all day, they were still scared of going up against us in the dark. That's what Kate guessed."

"Kate?"

"Yeah. Corporal Kate Stein. Big sister, I called her. She called me little brother. Kept me alive, taught me how to fight smart." Stark blinked rapidly for a moment. "My armor had died already. Power supply exhausted. I pulled it off, went looking for anybody else still alive, and found her."

"She'd survived, too?"

"Sorta." Stark gulped at the memory. "Lost both legs. Only her suit's med kit had kept her alive until then." *Oh, Christ, Kate. I'll get you out. I promise. Carry you. Carry you all the way.*

No. Get out of here. You and anybody else who can still move.

I won't leave you. I won't. I'm staying with you and the other wounded.

No you ain't, little brother. Waste of your life. Mine's gone. Forget it. Save yours.

I'm not leaving you for them!

Won't be alive when they get here, bro. Got a grenade handy, though, just in case.

No. No. Look, there's got to be relief coming.

Relief? Her bitter cough had been weak and wet. *Get real. They've jammed our calls for help, they've got antiair enough to hold offevac assets, and all our stupid, worthless officers who hung us out to dry on this hill are dead. Any relief that's coming won't get here in time.*

There's got to be another way.

Sometimes the only other ways are worse. Get out of here, Ethan. I didn't teach you to fight so you could die for nothing, and staying here would be worse than useless.

I . . .

Go. You can't save me. Save someone else someday.

I will.

"Ethan?" Vic leaned close again, one hand on his cheek. "You there?"

"Yeah."

"What happened? To you and Stein?"

"She couldn't be helped. Couldn't be moved. She had a grenade, though." Vic nodded, face grim. "Told me to get the hell out of there." Stark smiled, so suddenly that Vic frowned in surprise. "You know what else she told me? To unload my weapon before I tried to sneak through the enemy line."

"Unload your weapon? Why?"

"'Cause if you've got a loaded weapon, and you get scared, you'll shoot," Stark explained. "And that would mean they'd be all over me. But if my weapon was empty, I'd hide instead and maybe save my butt."

Vic nodded again, this time judiciously. "Good advice. I take it you followed it."

"Uh-huh. We had a hard time getting down off the knoll into the vegetation, those of us who could still move. We made sure all the survivors who couldn't move had weapons first, though. The enemy spotted our movement, but some of us made it to the tree line. God, it was dark, Vic. Never seen anything so black, even up here. Couldn't see the enemy until you fell over them. Couldn't move without worrying about tripping over stuff you couldn't see. Longest night of my life."

"But they didn't spot you."

"Almost. Almost. Kate saved me, Vic. Twice, they were so close I tried to fire, but I couldn't because my weapon wasn't loaded. I was still cursing her each time when they turned away. Some other guys, I heard them open up. They died real fast." He paused. "It was almost morning when I heard heavy artillery again. They hit the knoll really hard. Then there was a lot of small-arms fire. Grenades. It didn't last long." Another pause. "I kept moving, fast as I could. A few hours later I sorta fell into the arms of an American patrol coming up the trail."

"A relief force? That close?"

"Not close enough and not strong enough." Stark closed his eyes briefly. "I told them what had happened. They didn't want to believe me, thought I was a deserter, but soon two other survivors got picked up by other patrols and told the same story. Thanks to the warning, that 'relief force' was able to retreat fast enough to save itself."

Vic leaned back, biting her lower lip. "At least we kicked butt later. I've talked to people who were in on the retaliatory strikes."

"Yeah, we kicked butt," Stark agreed, his tone acid. "But all the butt-kicking in the world couldn't bring the dead back, could it?"

"No," Vic nodded.

"Nothin' else I could do. Nothin' else anybody could do. Not by then."

"What else could you have done earlier, Ethan?"

"I could've stayed, Vic. Up on the knoll, with the ones who couldn't move."

"Until you all died together at dawn? Now *that* wouldn't have meant anything, Ethan. I'm glad you listened to Kate Stein."

Stark lay silent for a moment. "I'm still listening."

"Good. Save your sacrifices for when they matter."

"Like holding off the pursuit across the dust plain so our Platoon could escape, you mean?" Stark needled in sudden triumph.

Vic glared at him. "Dying in place wasn't the plan. You were supposed to delay them and then run."

"There wasn't any plan, and I had to hold them long enough to keep you safe."

"I don't need you playing hero to keep me safe! I want you alive and watching out for your Squad. You're a helluva lot more valuable to everyone that way. Remember that, and remember nobody was supposed to go back to haul your nearly lifeless carcass to safety."

Stark tried a shrug, wincing as a body cast halted the movement. "I knew *you'd* come back."

"Then you must think I'm as stupid as you are." Vic stood, shaking her head. "Ethan, we can't afford to lose you. I'm not telling you to forget the past, but don't let it rule you. Be more careful." She dug in one pocket, pulling forth a packet that she pitched onto Stark's chest in a dreamy low-gravity trajectory. "Your very own Silver Star, along with four Purple Hearts for our heroic Sergeant Stark. Got that, Ethan? Four Purple Hearts. You get one, you're lucky. You get two, you should be dead. You get three, you usually are dead. You got four, Ethan. Next time you're getting shot at, for Pete's sake, try to duck." Vic strode out, letting Stark's privacy curtain drop slowly shut, some of its creases holding their own against Luna's weak tug. Stark lay still, staring up at the cracked sky over his bed.

Sanchez stopped by later, a brief nod, the barest flicker of a smile turning up the edges of his mouth for a moment as he asked, "You okay?"

"Okay as can be expected."

Another brief nod. "Your Squad's fine. Gomez, she's keeping them in line. You got a good Corporal there."

"I know." Stark tried to reach out a hand, halting in frustration as his body cast limited the movement. "Thanks for keeping an eye on them, Sanch."

"Least I could do." Sanchez started to leave, pausing briefly on the way out. "Thanks for holding them off."

"No problem."

Sanchez might have quirked another smile as he left, but Stark couldn't be sure.

There weren't many other visitors as the days of healing turned into weeks. Even with the best medical technology, the human body required a certain amount of time to fix the sort of damage the best weapons technology could inflict. Stark knew only senior enlisted or officers were allowed to visit the medical wards, and both Vic and Sanch had their own Squads to watch over while the war continued its apparently endless course. One day, however, some unexpected visitors stopped by, bringing a fair share of confusion and concern in their wake.

The first person in the room carried what appeared to be a considerable chip on his shoulders along with a pair of Colonel's eagles. He nailed Stark with a disapproving glance, then lifted his sheet to check the body cast. "Is this as straight as you can lay?"

"Yes, sir."

The Colonel obviously didn't care for that answer, poking at the cast a couple of times. "Well, try to look military, for God's sake."

Stark kept his face expressionless and his mouth closed, though both took considerable effort. He was still cycling through replies he would have liked to have given when the curtain parted again to reveal another Colonel accompanying several men and women in civ clothes. *No. They* are *civs. What the hell?*

"This is Stark," the first Colonel announced coldly.

"That's *Sergeant* Stark, sir," Stark replied in equally frosty tones.

"Sergeant Stark," the Colonel grated out with a look that promised dire consequences. Stark simply gazed back until the Colonel looked away.

An awkward silence followed while Stark wondered what the purpose of the visit could be. "You were injured in battle?" one of the civilians finally asked.

Stark glanced toward the second Colonel, who nodded to indicate he could reply to the question, though her sour expression indicated she liked this even less than the first Colonel did. "That's right."

A female civ came closer, peering at his face. Not that Stark minded, since the woman had a nice face of her own and he could peer back to his heart's content. "You must have been hurt very badly," she finally offered.

"Yeah." Stark, never inclined to discuss physical ailments with anyone, found himself even more reticent than usual with these civs.

Her eyes strayed to the flat panel at the foot of the bed displaying Stark's vital signs. "You'll be all right? All your injuries will heal?"

"That's what they tell me."

The civ bit her lip, looking back toward the other civs in apparent uncertainty. Another civ, male and about Stark's age, nodded politely. "Can you tell us how it happened?"

The female Colonel stared ahead as if not willing to be involved in the conversation while she spoke in sharp tones. "Sergeant Stark conducted a delaying action against enemy forces while his Platoon retrograded to American lines following a successful operation against part of the enemy industrial complex."

The civs all looked puzzled, as if the Colonel had spoken in another tongue, while Stark fought down another urge to verbally abuse a high-ranking officer. *Retrograded? What the hell's wrong with calling it a retreat?* A momentary vision of bullets flaying the rock around his lonely outpost while he had held off the enemy flashed through his mind. *And why does this rear-area waste-of-human-flesh Colonel have to make the whole action sound like no big deal?* Stark tried to shrug, finding the habitual motion blocked by the cast he still wore. "I did my job. I guess you saw it on vid." The last almost came out as a harsh accusation, Stark catching the words as he issued to change them to a bland statement.

The civs all seemed surprised. "We don't see the military vid," the woman who'd spoken to Stark first explained. "It's not broadcast here."

"It's not?" Startled, Stark looked toward the Colonels for confirmation.

The male Colonel nodded once. "Security. We can't risk the enemy deriving information on current operations from the military vid."

Then why the hell do you show the mil vid on Earth where the enemy can watch it just as easily as the civs there can? A growing unease filled Stark, born of these unusual civ visitors, the clearly disapproving demeanor of the Colonels, and the feeling of having suddenly been dropped into the middle of some civ-mil issue he didn't understand and that seemed likely to cause him troubles he didn't need.

The civs exchanged glances but said nothing in reply to the Colonel, then nodded politely once more to Stark as they filed out. The female Colonel left last, pinning Stark with an all-purpose warning glare as she dropped the curtain behind her. *I don't suppose it'd do me any good to ask anyone what that was all about. God, I can't wait to get back to my unit.*

Eventually the body cast came off and the physical therapy ran its course. A tired-eyed medic checked Stark out, shaking her head as her laptop flipped through Stark's medical file. "I shouldn't let you go," the medic complained.

"Why?" Stark demanded. "Something still wrong?"

"Not with you." The medic sighed, keying a few entries before closing out the file. "Look, Sergeant, I'm like a technician who fixes the finest equipment in the world, and then gets to send it out for other people to try to destroy. It doesn't generate a lot of job satisfaction."

"If it makes you feel any better, I'll do my best not to be back here."

The medic grinned, though her eyes stayed tired. "You do that, Sergeant. Not too many decades ago the wounds you received would have killed you, or at least crippled you for life. So try not to let it happen again."

Stark grinned back. "It seems all the women I meet give me that advice."

"That's because it's good advice." The medic offered her hand for a shake. "Good luck, soldier. You're officially discharged to return to your unit."

"Thanks." Stark shook the proffered hand, standing to go.

"By the way," the medic added, "you've been eating about six full meals a day for a while. Your body doesn't need that anymore, but you're in the habit, so you'll have to make an effort not to overeat until you're back on a normal routine."

"Six meals a day? Why didn't I notice?"

The medic quirked another grin, which this time almost reached her eyes. "The miracle of modern medicine, Sergeant. We don't just watch the body's healing process, we turbocharge it. You've done the equivalent of more than six months' healing and recovery in about a month. Of course, that process speeds up a lot of your perceptions. We just keep patients on their own accelerated time schedule so they don't get disoriented. You're slowed down again, so don't worry about it unless you keep eating like you're on fast forward."

"Thanks." Stark left, walking down the white-painted corridors, stopping only to check on the date and time at a wall terminal. *I don't believe it. The medic was right. It's only been a month.* Memories he'd shied away from, of his body being torn by enemy fire, finally surfaced, so that Stark stared in wonder at his dim reflection in the terminal's screen. *Incredible. But the medic's right: They do all those miracles just so grunts like me can go out and get shot up again.*

He started to leave, paused, then punched in his unit identification to find out where his Squad had been billeted during R&R. *Only a month. Thought I'd be a stranger when I got back, but I guess not.*

Awkward. Stark hated what he knew was coming, knew he couldn't avoid it, and knew he'd be a lot happier when it was over—none of which made it any easier to walk through the doorway before him. Closing his eyes and gritting his teeth, Sergeant Ethan Stark walked through that doorway to face his Squad.

Corporal Gomez, it appeared, had been alerted to Stark's discharge from the hospital. She had the Squad drawn up in formation waiting for him, every soldier ramrod straight, every uniform sharp. Stark halted in midstride, balancing easily on one foot as all the lunar veterans could, then broke into an involuntary smile. "What the hell do you guys think you are, the Pentagon Color Guard?"

Gomez maintained a straight face, marching with precise movements to stand before him and render a perfect salute. "Ready for inspection, Sergeant."

Stark fought down the smile, returning Gomez's salute as crisply as still-slightly-stiff muscles would allow. The Squad hadn't moved, not even a twitch, putting on a far better show for him than they'd ever given to any high-ranking officer.

This ceremony was important to them, he suddenly realized, an unspoken way of saying thanks in the way his Squad thought would mean the most to him. He followed Gomez down the line, sternly eyeing each soldier in turn, finding only the tiniest variations from regulations on each uniform. The last individual inspected, Stark marched to face the entire Squad, allowing himself a small smile again. "Damn, you look good."

Gomez swung up another rigid salute, face professionally expressionless. "Thank you, Sergeant."

"No. Thank you." He trained an index finger down the line of soldiers. "This is how good you apes can be, how good I always knew you were. Thanks for letting me see it. Now fall them out, Corporal Gomez, before all their joints lock and they get stuck that way."

"*Sí Sargento*" Gomez finally grinned, big and sort of goofy on her usually intense face. "You heard the Sergeant," she addressed the Squad. "Fall out!"

Rigid military bearing dissolved magically into a clot of individuals milling about uncertainly. Finally, Murphy stepped forward with an anxious expression, saluted Stark, smiled, then stepped back. Mendoza followed suit, then Hoxely, then Billings, then the rest, one by one. Then it was over. There aren't any really adequate ways to thank someone for saving your life, Stark reflected, and even fewer adequate ways of accepting such thanks. "Okay, you apes. Our time off the line is almost over, I hear. I spent all of it so far in a hospital bed and rehab. Hope you guys made more productive use of the time."

A series of grins told him they'd had a fine time, indeed. "Too bad you missed it, Sarge."

"I had other commitments. How've they been doing on refresher training, Corporal?"

Gomez twisted her face in a vaguely dissatisfied way. "They been doing okay."

"We've been doing great!" Murphy protested. "Top scores, Sarge."

"Top scores? In what?"

"Across the board," Chen announced proudly. "We knew you were coming back, Sarge, and we wanted to be ready, so we've really been bearing down. Just like you'd want."

"Sure," Gomez noted derisively. "I never had to kick you guys' butts once, did I?" She turned back to Stark, permitting herself a smile this time. "They done good, *Sargento*. Real good."

"Outstanding. I'm proud of you. Now get out of those dress uniforms and get into working gear. I need to get into better shape pronto and I could use some workout partners."

The Squad scattered to their cubes to change as Stark beckoned Gomez to wait. "Anybody else know I'm back?"

"Just the rest of the Platoon."

"Just the rest of the Platoon? How'd you know I was coming?"

Gomez grinned. "I got my sources, Sarge."

"Great. You and Sergeant Reynolds. Everybody's got their sources but me."

"Hell, Sarge, you don't need sources. You got me and Sergeant Reynolds, ¿verdad?"

"I guess."

Vic Reynolds chose that moment to stick her head in the room, focusing on Stark. "Welcome back, soldier."

"Thanks. To what do I owe the honor of this visit? You inviting me to a welcoming-back parade?"

Reynolds shook her head in mock seriousness. "Sorry. No parade. We couldn't lay on any elephants and clowns. They were all busy at headquarters." She sobered, canting her head to indicate the direction back down the hall. "I came by to give you a heads-up. Captain Noble is headed your way."

"Captain who?"

"Noble." Vic shrugged. "Our new company commander. He rolled in while you were being put together again."

Stark sighed heavily. "Any assessment on him?"

Reynolds shrugged again. "Too new. Only been here a week. He hasn't done much damage yet, though."

"He hasn't had much time," Stark pointed out. "Is Lieutenant Conroy with him?"

"You didn't hear?" Vic looked uncomfortable.

"No, I didn't hear. I never hear anything unless you tell me, remember? What didn't I hear this time?"

"She got canned, essentially, while you were still in the hospital. Rotated out early to another assignment."

Stark frowned in puzzlement. "Why? The raid succeeded, right? She do something else?"

"Nah, she didn't do anything else, besides thinking she owed you an attempt at a rescue. We did something, Ethan. Going back to get you against orders and risking armor in the bargain. Generals don't like that. Conroy paid."

"Damn," Stark muttered. "Conroy didn't seem half bad. And she really wanted to come back for me?"

"Yeah. Didn't fuss too much when we started back, either."

Stark shook his head. "She'd probably have been a good officer someday."

Vic smiled sardonically. "Then she wouldn't have lasted anyway, right?" Then she was gone.

Stark became aware again of Gomez standing nearby. "Hey, Anita, how come you didn't tell me about Conroy?"

"Not my job."

"Then how about this Noble? Heard anything about him?"

"Just that his name don't have nothing to do with his character."

Stark grinned, then looked around the room as if searching for something. "Hey, I forgot to ask Sergeant Reynolds something. Who's Conroy's replacement?"

Gomez raised both shoulders in an I-don't-know gesture. "Nobody, yet."

"Nobody?" Stark's smile faded into a frown. "That's strange.

Usually there's a backlog of Lieutenants looking for a tour in charge of a Platoon."

"Well, there apparently ain't any backlog right now, *Sargento*. Noble seems to have come up with the last batch of officers, and there's no enlisted replacements coming in either."

"That's funny." Stark scratched one temple, frowning. "Almost sounds like they're winding down the war and getting ready to draw down forces up here."

Gomez shook her head emphatically. "That's definitely not the case, Sarge. Just before you got back we got dragooned into a work detail helping unload one huge shipment of munitions. Somebody's getting ready for serious combat action."

"Lots of bullets and no bodies. Doesn't match."

Whatever else Stark might have said went unspoken as Gomez yelled "Attention!" to announce the presence of an officer. He came to attention automatically, facing the door.

The Captain standing there nodded, waving one hand negligently. "Carry on. Are you Stark?"

Stark took a step forward, face carefully expressionless. "I'm Sergeant Stark, sir."

Captain Noble smiled in what he apparently believed to be a comradely fashion. "We're glad to have you back, Sergeant. We've got a great opportunity."

"Thank you, sir. That's nice, sir," Stark stated warily. In his experience, whenever officers said "we" it meant trouble. So did "great opportunity."

Noble gestured toward the empty suits of battle armor ranked along the walls for maintenance. "You know the biggest problem with those things?" Without waiting for Stark's reply, he held up one emphasizing finger. "Limited mobility."

"Captain," Stark began, "if I—"

"That's right. Limited mobility. It's amazing, isn't it? We're way into the twenty-first century and our infantry is still getting around the same way they did in the Dark Ages."

"Captain, the armor does do some of the work for us."

Noble shook his head firmly. "Walking work, Sergeant. That's not good enough. But here's the great opportunity, Sergeant. Combat Systems Development has it ready for field trials and they're looking for a squad good enough for the job. Your Squad is as good as they come, right, Sergeant?"

Stark tried to project simultaneous pride and discouragement, his disquiet growing with every word the Captain spoke. "Well, there's good and there's good."

"And there's great, Sergeant. Which is what this Squad will be while it combat-tests the new Enhanced Mobility Battle Armor. I'm sure a soldier with your record will be happy to volunteer for the chance."

Volunteer. In Stark's experience, that one word carried more danger than most weapons. Stark mentally backpedaled even faster, even as he wondered what the phrase "a soldier with your record" actually meant. "What exactly does 'enhanced mobility' entail, Captain?"

"A rocket-assist pack, Sergeant. Instead of walking, you'll be able to zoom—"

"Flight?" Stark demanded, ignoring the Captain's frown at the interruption. "They want to do that again? Captain, sir, with all due respect, survival on the battlefield is usually a matter of not being noticed. It's impossible not to be noticed when you're flying."

Captain Noble held up his hands in a calming gesture. "It's only limited flight, Sergeant, just for a few seconds at a time."

"Damn right it's limited to a few seconds. That's because the instant you get off the ground a half-dozen enemy systems will spot you and blow you into little pieces!"

"Sergeant, you need to give the enhanced mobility system a chance—"

"No, thank you, sir. No, thank you," Stark repeated. "Captain, I know our Combat Systems people are always trying to kill us with their bright new ideas and stuff that doesn't work in the field, but for God's sake, if they want us dead that bad it'd be a lot simpler for them just to design in illuminated targets to hang on our butts."

"I see." Captain Noble smiled crookedly. "I'll be sure to keep your opinion in mind, Sergeant."

"Sir, I respectfully request my Squad be removed from consideration for field-testing that new armor."

Noble smiled slightly again, his eyes avoiding Stark's, then turned and left. Stark glanced at Gomez, who had been following the conversation intently. "Did he agree to my request or not?"

"I dunno, Sarge. He didn't say anything."

"That's what worries me. You think maybe I laid it on too intense?"

"With him?" Gomez laughed. "No way, Sarge. Too bad the Captain didn't find time to tell you that you did a good job on the last op."

"Sure he did. He talked about my record."

"With a guy like that, that kinda statement could mean anything, good or bad, Sarge."

"I know. Ask me if I care."

Within a couple of days Stark felt as if he had never been gone, as if the last op and the hospitalization had been products of some unpleasant dream. Every time he stripped for a shower, though, he saw the scars still visible despite the medics' work. *Those are the scars that show, anyway. I don't know what's inside. Not sure I want to know.*

Just to further confuse life, the standard rotation policy was suddenly changed, leaving the current units either on the front line or in R&R for another few weeks. "How'd you swing that, Stark?" Sergeant Nguyen demanded from the bunker where Stark's Squad had been scheduled to relieve Nguyen's Squad.

"Not my work," Stark protested. "Sorry you're stuck out there."

"Who's work is it? What the hell's going on?"

"Either nobody knows or nobody's saying. Look, I'm heading to headquarters today to try to get some stuff done. I'll ask around."

Paperwork had stopped being paperwork decades before, but it still took up enormous amounts of time, primarily because many senior officers seemed addicted to the idea that accumulating huge quantities of data was the same thing as understanding what was going on. Stark stood before the counter at Division Administration, drumming his fingers on the worn surface and trying not to project the furious annoyance he suspected every admin clerk secretly sought to generate in their victims. "Ethan Stark? How's life, old buddy?"

Stark turned at the voice, frowning as he tried to tie it to a memory, then smiled as he saw the woman who'd spoken. "Sergeant Bev Manley. How come you haven't retired?"

She smiled back, yanking a thumb over her shoulder. "I'm still having too much fun, soldier. Come into my office for a private chat."

Manley's office could have doubled as a closet, which still made it a tremendous perk in lunar offices tunneled out of rock. She sat opposite Stark, then nodded toward her computer monitor. "Congratulations."

"Thanks. For what?"

"I've got correspondence here from Captain Noble saying you volunteered your Squad to field-test the new enhanced mobility combat armor."

"That damn little pissant."

Manley grinned. "You don't sound like a very enthusiastic volunteer."

"I'll kill him," Stark ground out. "I swear. Next time we're in combat together, assuming the little bastard ever goes near a battlefield, I'll put a round right between his beady little eyes."

"Don't waste the ammo," Manley advised. "I thought this didn't sound like something you'd do."

"Great. So what can I do about it?"

Her grin widened. "Ethan, stuff gets lost in the system all the time. Just kinda disappears." Manley reached over to punch a key. "Captain Noble's message just disappeared."

"Really?" Stark grinned back. "Is there any chance Captain No Balls will find out?"

"Not a one. He'll rotate out in a few months, fat, dumb, and happy, thinking he's done a major suck-up to some General in Combat Systems Development." Manley's grin took on an evil glint. "Me, I'd like to be a fly on the wall when he tries to call in a chit on the deal."

"What if the General tries to find out what happened? Won't your system leave fingerprints?"

Manley rolled her eyes. "Gawd, no. Mind you, when it was delivered we were told it was one hundred percent foolproof and maintained an unalterable track of every piece of correspondence that entered the system."

"How long did it take you to find a back door?"

"First day. We've found a lot more since then. Don't worry about me. There're no fingerprints."

Stark reached to shake her hand. "I owe you one, Bev. Big time."

"Nah, we're even. You saved my ass back on the World when those insurgents tried to overrun our base camp on Madagascar, remember?"

Stark scratched one temple. "Oh, yeah. Heck, I'd forgotten all about that."

"I haven't." Manley waved him out. "Watch out for yourself, you big ape."

"I'll try when I'm not busy protecting you rear-echelon jerks." Stark paused as he started to rise. "Hey, can you help me expedite this paperwork I'm stuck here trying to get processed?"

"What do you think I am, a miracle worker?" Manley demanded. "Ah, hand it over. I'll see what I can do." She frowned over the material displayed on Stark's palmtop. "What the hell is this?"

"I figured you'd know."

"Individual reliability assessments for every soldier in your Squad? Dates of last security reviews? Consolidated disciplinary report? Who the hell ordered this?"

Stark spread both hands. "No idea. My Captain said the report was required, not that I can trust a word he says. Supposed to go back up through him, but I can't get the guy to answer his calls, and he's never in his office, so I figured I could turn it in here."

"Huh." Manley turned to her terminal again, keying in data rapidly. "Security block? No access authorized for me? Fat chance. Just use a few skeleton keys . . . ah . . . there we go. Damn. They're asking for this stuff on every soldier in First Division. Why wasn't I told?" She glared at Stark. "This should have gone through me."

"Maybe you don't have a good reliability assessment," Stark joked.

"Maybe not," Manley grumbled, her fingers dancing over her input board. "Top brass ordered this. Hell, I could've put together all the security and disciplinary info from my database and saved everybody a lot of time. Something screwy's going on, Ethan."

"So what else is new?" Stark eyed her searchingly. "This has got you worried, doesn't it? So the brass went off on a wild tangent again. They always do that."

"They went outside channels, Ethan. They want reliability assessments for everyone and they went outside normal channels to get them. What does that tell you?"

"That they don't trust you, or me, or the guys who work for us."

"That's what I think, too." Manley shook her head, all levity fled. "We don't trust our officers and they don't trust us. Helluva way to run a military, Stark." She tapped her screen again lightly with one finger. "One more thing. You better be ready for some cramped quarters until you go back on the line."

"Why? I heard there're no replacements coming in."

"There aren't," Manley confirmed. "But there're orders here to prepare to double up all existing temporary barracks occupants."

"Why?" Stark repeated.

"I'll try to find out," Manley vowed.

"Thanks, but I think I know somebody else who might have the answer."

Half an hour and several kilometers later, Vic Reynolds stared back dispassionately from her chair as Stark took a seat nearby. "What's the word, Vic?" Stark jerked his thumb backward to indicate the barracks complex behind him. "Why the doubling-up?"

Vic pursed her lips. "How'd you hear that was coming down?"

"I got a source of my own. Amazing, isn't it?"

"Sure is."

"So what's going down?"

"There's no official word, Ethan."

"I know that. I didn't ask for official word. I want to know what's going on, and I know you know if anybody does."

This time Vic grinned tightly. "A reputation can be a terrible thing. Okay. You want to know why we're going to be doubling up here? To make room for reinforcements."

"No way." Stark squinted at Vic in a futile attempt to try to read any trace of mockery. "Reinforcements? Real honest-to-God reinforcements? Who's showing up next, Santa Claus?"

"If Santa does show up, you better be ready with some good explanations."

"I got plenty of those." Stark frowned, fixing his friend with a suspicious glance. "So why aren't you happy? Isn't this good?"

Reynolds avoided his gaze, expression still noncommittal. "Depends what you consider good."

"Okay, Vic. Stop playing games. What's going on? Why reinforcements, and why aren't you happy about it?"

The stars outside crawled millimetrically across the black sheet of endless night while Reynolds pondered her response. "Fair question. Ethan, aren't you wondering where these reinforcements will come from?"

"I hadn't gotten around to that yet." Stark scowled in frustration. "Where the hell do they come from? Second Division is supposed to be completely tied up with commitments back on the World."

"It is," Vic confirmed.

"So?"

"So they're sending Third Division up here. All of it."

Stark just stared, the words slowly entering his brain and hanging there, unable to progress because they wouldn't fit anywhere. "Third Division is the Strategic Reserve. The Continental Guard."

"Yes and yes," Vic confirmed dryly.

"They wouldn't send those pretty boys and girls up here. Who backs up the Armored Brigade if anything happens?"

"There's no more Armored Brigade to back up, Ethan. It's been disestablished, cannibalized to provide bodies to bring Third Division up to full strength."

Stark's eyes twitched as if of their own volition, focusing away from the face of Vic Reynolds and onto a nearby remote vid of the outside. Rocks. Dust. Black shadows and white light. People didn't belong here, didn't fit, and right now the things Vic was telling him didn't fit either. "Why?" he finally spat out.

"Big push. We're going to break the enemy perimeter, Ethan.

End the war with total victory." Vic stayed expressionless, reciting the words without emotion.

"Ah, sweet Jesus," Stark whispered, closing his eyes tightly for a few moments. "Tell me it's a joke, Vic. Tell me you made it all up."

"Sorry. No can do."

"They're sending our entire Strategic Reserve up here to try to break the stalemate?"

"That's right. They'll start disembarking within the next twenty-four hours. The whole force is supposed to be here by the end of the week."

"That's pretty damn fast. They must have crammed them awfully tight into the transports."

"The idea's to achieve surprise, Ethan."

"Well, they sure as hell surprised me. What are these fresh troops supposed to do, mop up after we miraculously walk through the enemy lines?"

"No, Ethan. They'll be the spearhead."

Stark's fist hit the wall, causing the image of the lunar landscape to jump in response. "That's too damn flippin' idiotic for even our brass to have dreamed up. Those new troops'll be green, totally unused to the environment up here. They'll be too busy learning to walk to think about fighting. They'll be—"

"Tell it to someone who doesn't know all that, Ethan," Vic interrupted coldly. "They didn't ask us, and they won't ask us, and they won't listen if we try to tell them."

"I know that." Stark stared from his hands back to Reynolds. "Why them in the spearhead? I sure as hell don't want to do it, but why them?"

Vic smiled in self-mockery. "Because we lack fighting spirit, Ethan. They say we're burned out."

"No kidding. War does that. Someone finally noticed?"

Vic ignored Stark's gibe. "Third Division, on the other hand, has great morale."

"Sure they do. They probably think they can catch bullets with their teeth, but that's 'cause they ain't been shot at in, what—fifteen or twenty years?"

"So," Vic plowed on, "their fighting spirit will enable them to overcome the enemy. Then we mop up in their victorious wake."

Stark glared at the outside remote view again, anger and futility warring within him. "Just how many millimeters of protection does 'fighting spirit' add to battle armor?"

"It's not my idea, Ethan."

"If it was I'd personally blow your head off."

"Tell that to General Meecham."

"Who?"

"General Meecham." Vic's mouth twisted in a bitter half smile. "Our greatest strategic and tactical thinker."

"I've done quite a bit of tactical stuff in the past few years and I've never heard of him."

"You will. He's coming up here to implement his, uh, 'revolutionary force-multiplication' concepts. Something called Synergy Warfare."

Stark rolled his eyes in mockery. "Be still, my heart."

"Yeah. Anyway, we'll get lectures on the whole framework for the offensive before the attack goes down."

"They're going to give us the whole plan in advance?"

Stark questioned, not trying to hide his surprise. "That's not bad."

Vic laughed as if the effort pained her. "I didn't say a lecture on the plan, Ethan. Lectures on the framework, the theoretical basis for, um"—Vic's eyes closed as she dredged up a memory—"'overwhelming the enemy mass with our fighting spirit and superior idea paradigm.'"

Stark's jaw dropped. "What the hell.. . ?"

"Don't ask me. Just be glad we won't be leading this attack."

By the time Stark got back to his quarters, a notice awaited, ordering his Squad to vacate half the quarters they'd been occupying. His soldiers were still grumbling when the first members of Third Division arrived, staring around like hick tourists visiting the big city as they stumbled, bumped, and bounced about in the unfamiliar gravity. Mostly, they stared at rock. Rock hallways and rooms tunneled out of the lunar soil. Rock floors left fairly rough to provide traction in a place where gravity didn't help nearly enough. Overhead, mostly raw metal sealing in the little things humans needed, things such as air and heat and moisture.

Stark had seen the city from the outside, staring down at it from some of the heights where American troops held positions. Sometimes it made him think of a spread-out anthill, with big and little humps scattered around to mark high ceilings, and raised strips over subsurface corridors. Here and there, higher towers and clusters of low buildings rose, heavy masonry walls formed from lunar rock pulled out of the subsurface excavations. Not heavy because gravity required it, but because heavy helped keep in that air and heat, and keep out falling rocks and radiation. Nothing like the fairy-tale towers rising under transparent domes in the really old pictures guessing at mankind's future. Fairy tales, after all, are nice to look at, but hideously expensive to build in a place where everything was already really expensive, and far too vulnerable to the threats posed by nature even if other humans hadn't been targeting weapons there as well. No, for fairy towers you had to look at some of the industrial complexes, open to the lunar environment, lights flashing amid skeletal frames rising what seemed far too high for their light structure. Mankind's future, where the fairies had been sent to build and labor in factories on the lifeless rock of the Moon.

The new soldiers, Stark noticed, tended to cluster in the courtyards, small rooms with thick windows set in the ceilings or walls to offer direct views of the outside. Apparently none of them noticed the airtight emergency doors ready to slam shut if one of the windows failed. Stark, like most of the veterans, preferred remote views over standing near a window with vacuum on the other side.

"You guys need any help?" Murphy offered as a Third Division Squad moved into part of his old quarters.

"Not from you," one of the new Privates cracked, drawing laughs from his comrades.

"What the hell's that mean?" Murphy demanded.

Stark stepped in before the Third Division personnel could answer, staring them down with a steely gaze. "It didn't mean anything, right?"

The new soldiers exchanged uncertain glances before one answered. "No, Sergeant."

"'No, Sergeant' what?"

"Uh, no, Sergeant, it didn't mean anything."

"Good. You'd be well advised to accept any help lunar vets can give." Stark turned to Murphy. "Why don't you and the rest of the Squad take the night off? Go out and have a good time. Probably be your last chance for a while."

Murphy shot a now hostile look at the Third Division soldiers, then nodded. "Okay, Sarge. You coming along?"

"Nah. I need a drink right now." The All-Ranks Club down the hall no longer felt large, not with the floor cluttered with gear belonging to the new troops and most of the chairs occupied by the same. Stark tried to ignore the eyes that followed him as he headed for the bar, suddenly aware again of how easily he could move in the low gravity compared to the stumbling, uncertain efforts of the recent arrivals.

"Stark? Ethan Stark?"

Stark turned, already smiling as he did so. "Rash Puratnam? Where'd you come from? I haven't seen you since—"

"Since I transferred over to Third Division?"

"Yeah. Why the hell did you do that, anyway?"

"My kid sister got sent to that outfit and I wanted to kinda watch over her." Puratnam grinned. "Now she's tough as nails. She's the one who watches over me." He gestured toward the nearby wall unit. "You want some coffee, tough guy?"

"Sure you don't want a beer?"

"Nah. On duty. Got to get back to my unit soon." They sat at a small table, nursing their steaming cups, while Puratnam stared into his drink morosely, as if oblivious to the crowd around them.

"You sure you're in Third Division?" Stark finally teased. "You don't seem all rah-rah, like the rest of them."

Puratnam didn't smile. "That's because I saw combat up until I transferred in. The rest of these guys . . . hell, they're trained real good, Ethan. Maybe overtrained. But they're not veterans. They've been the Continental Reserve so long they've never seen action." Puratnam grimaced as if in pain. "They don't know. They think being ready to kick butt means you will kick butt."

"That's part of it," Stark offered. "Yeah, you need combat time to really learn the ropes, but if your morale ain't high enough, you can't win."

"Morale alone won't do it, Ethan. I saw you walk in here, and I saw how the guys in my unit are trying to walk. There ain't no comparison."

Stark waved depreciatingly. "I been practicing for a few years."

"That's the point. We've been told to be ready for offensive action within a week. A week! They gave us more time than that to acclimate to jungle countries back on Earth."

"Yeah." Stark gazed into his own drink for a moment.

"What do you want me to say, Rash? That you're gonna suffer a lot of casualties just because your people can't move up here? If it was up to me this wouldn't be happening."

"Sergeants don't run the army," Puratnam noted.

"No, they don't. What can I do? You tell me, and I'll do my damnedest."

Puratnam grinned suddenly. "You would. Of course, when any officer heard Sergeant Stark wanted to talk to them they'd just run the other way."

Stark laughed back. "You saying I got a reputation in Third Division, too?"

"Let's see, how'd the Colonel put it? He said, 'I don't want to see any wise-ass senior enlisted in this unit. I expect you people to follow your orders and keep your mouths shut.'"

"I follow orders. Usually."

"Hah." Puratnam grinned again before turning serious. "Thanks for the offer, but I think we've got to fight this battle."

"Rash—"

"No. Please. Don't offer anything you can't hope to deliver." Sergeant Puratnam turned his coffee cup slowly, first in one direction, then the other. "You ever been to Greece, Ethan?"

"That's in Euro, right? I don't think so."

"I have." Puratnam bit his lower lip. "A border-protection op, I think it was. Or maybe something else. Anyway, there's this place where a bunch of guys died a long time ago. I forget what they called it, but these soldiers were named Spartans."

"Never heard of 'em."

"Like I said, it was a real long time ago. About a hundred of these Spartans were ordered to hold a pass against an army, a real big army, and they did for a while. They were like the very best troops around in those days. Then they got overrun and all died right there. They wouldn't retreat or surrender." Puratnam nodded to himself, confirming the memory. "There's a monument at the pass. Kinda nice. It says something like 'go tell the Spartans we're still here just like they ordered.' "

"Huh. What made you think of that?"

"I was wondering. Those Spartans stayed and fought just because they were ordered to. I mean, the Greeks with us told me their home was a long ways from this pass. Would we do the same thing, stand and die like that?" Puratnam suddenly looked embarrassed. "Oh, hell, I know you would, Ethan."

"Knock it off. I did my job."

"No," Puratnam corrected. "You did something you thought you should, and you did it to save your unit, right? The soldiers you fight with. But suppose some Colonel or General had ordered you to do that? Ordered you to hold alone and die right there?"

Stark's laughter rang out harshly. "Hell, they'd just be trying to cover up something they'd screwed up, and make me the fall guy."

"See what I mean? We don't trust the people who give us orders. We do our job, do our duty, but would we do that Spartan stuff? Or would we fight our damnedest for a while and then fall back because we can't assume what we've been told to do is really important?"

Stark thought about it for a long moment, then for another long moment. "I dunno," he finally admitted. "I wouldn't let down anybody who was depending on me. You know, just surrender and leave the grunts on either side hanging or let the apes in the rear get overrun. I'd hold the line."

"Yeah. Me, too. But I get the feeling there's another line out there somewhere. A line I might cross someday. I never even thought about that line when I first enlisted, but now I know it's out there." He sat silent for almost a minute while Stark waited patiently. "It's kinda weird. Charging into the attack is pretty easy. You don't have time to think. You just do it. But holding is hard. You've got to sit there and take it. They're going to order us to attack, Ethan, and we're going to do it. Can you guys hold if need be?"

Stark glared back. "Why the hell are you asking me that?

Damn right First Division will hold. There's not a grunt in the unit who would let you guys down."

"Sorry. Sorry. Didn't mean it to sound that way. We've been fed a lot of crap about you guys being worn out and unreliable."

"Tell that to the enemy soldiers who get real bloody noses every time they try to push us."

"Good point. I didn't believe it, not really, not about you guys, but I know what years of combat can do to even the best units." Puratnam drained his cup, rising from his chair and wobbling as he did, so that he had to grab for balance. "Nice seeing you, Ethan, but I got to get back to my unit. Get them settled in. We're supposed to start low-gravity training tonight."

"Headquarters going to let you guys sleep anytime?"

Instead of laughing, Puratnam looked weary. "Probably not. Full press, you know, hit the ground running, keep the momentum going."

"Slogans don't stop bullets, Rash."

"I know that. You got any advice?"

"None that'd help," Stark stated flatly. "Getting prepped to conduct ops on the Moon takes time and practice. A lot of practice. Moving around up here has gotta be almost reflexive. You make a mistake, push off too hard or too high, and you're a target, a slow-moving target. We survived long enough to learn how to move up here because the other side had to learn the same lessons, but now they're vets, just like us. You're not, and you're not gonna learn how to be vets in a week or two."

Puratnam turned red, squeezing his empty cup so hard it crumpled into a small cylinder as his fingers quivered. "I know," he finally whispered. "I told 'em, my officers. They don't care. We got our orders, and we're going to follow them, come hell or high water."

"There's no water on the Moon, Rash."

"Then that only leaves the other alternative, doesn't it? See you around, Ethan."

"Yeah. Take care of yourself."

Puratnam shook his head. "I got a lot of other people to take care of first, Ethan, just like you do." He moved out of the room, staggering from table to table, bumping into other Third Division soldiers, who were bumping into him at the same time.

Stark lowered his head to the table and closed his eyes, trying to see only the darkness, trying not to think. After a while he rose and walked out, once again ignoring the curious/disdainful eyes of the Third Division soldiers. *I've got to get out of here. How many of these fools are going to be dead within a few weeks?* He headed on out of the barracks area, his feet carrying him down raw stone corridors toward the Out-City bars.

The bars presented uniform faces to the world, usually a one-window/one-door facade formed from local materials, their only distinguishing features the small signs that hung outside, some illuminated by weak spotlights and others buzzing erratically in neon colors. Stark paused before a half-dozen entrances, hesitating at the sounds of loud voices that could only be those of the new Third Division personnel, then headed on again. Finally he stopped at one that seemed relatively quieter than the others. Glancing inside, he saw why.

The bar, as cramped inside as the other "establishments" in the Out-City, held four small tables. Two of them had been pushed together to form a larger focus for a squad from Third Division, while the other two served the same role for several members of Stark's Squad. *Oh, yeah. I told them to head out and have a good time. That might have been a mistake.* Stark hesitated again, watching from just outside the doorway for a moment.

Billings stole a sidelong glance toward the noisy celebrants from Third Division. "Kinda loud, aren't they?"

Gomez shrugged. "They're just off the transports, Nance. And they're green. Give them time to blow off steam."

A voice rose above the buzz from the other table. "Hey, First Division, you guys need any help getting home safe tonight?"

Murphy, flushing, started to reply but was restrained by Gomez's hand on his shoulder. "The Sergeant wouldn't like it," she cautioned, then turned to face the other group. "Take it easy, you guys. The low gravity and the canned air make you a little disoriented at first."

"I feel fine," one of the new soldiers stated. "Ready to win this damn war."

"That's a big job. How about we buy you guys a round to welcome you up here?"

"I don't need advice or beer from gutless wonders," someone muttered.

Gomez jerked, lips in a snarl, eyes tracking for a target. "Now you're getting personal. Which one of you Earthworms said that?" Silence and smirks answered her. "So you can talk but not fight, eh? I'd heard that about Third Division."

Feet hit the floor, soldiers rising at both tables. A big Sergeant came over from the Third Division table, moving carefully but still making slightly ridiculous bobbles as he walked, until he stood looming over Gomez. "What did you say?"

Gomez stayed seated, denying her foe the chance to compare heights directly. "I said fighting the enemy is hard enough. We don't need to be slamming each other."

"That's not what I heard."

Gomez shrugged, pretending indifference. "That's what I meant, *compadre.*"

The big Sergeant leaned forward, one blunt finger hovering near Gomez's chest. "I guess you've been up here too long to remember military courtesy. I'm not your damn *compadre.* I'm a Sergeant. Remember that."

Gomez's eyes flicked from the offending finger to the angry visage of the Sergeant. "Get your hand out of my face . . . *compadre.*"

"I said I'm a Sergeant—" the Third Division man began ominously.

"So am I." Stark strode into the bar and over to the table. The other Sergeant had perhaps an inch advantage in height, but Stark somehow overtopped him in presence. "What the hell's going on here?"

"Your Corporal—" the Third Division man started.

"He's an asshole," Gomez interrupted casually.

The strange Sergeant's face darkened to match the lunar sky as his fingers closed into a fist. Stark raised his own hand, flat palm interposed like a wall between his Corporal and the Third Division noncom. "That's enough. Gomez, you're out of line."

"But—"

"But nothing. You know what to do."

Gomez's own face darkened, but she came to her feet, facing the Third Division Sergeant. "I apologize for my lack of respect,

Sergeant. It won't happen again."

Stark switched his attention to the Third Division soldier. "Satisfied?" he challenged.

The other Sergeant shook his head like an angry bull facing a red cloth. "She——"

"I asked if you were satisfied by Corporal Gomez's apology," Stark stated forcefully.

Something about Stark's tone penetrated the anger of the other man. He began to speak again, then caught sight of the decorations on Stark's blouse. His eyes shifted, reading the name tag on the other breast. "Stark? Oh. Okay." Biting his lip, the Third Division Sergeant nodded sharply. "Yeah. If *you* say so." Turning, he stomped back to his table, or attempted to do so. Unaccustomed to the low g, his heavy steps only resulted in propelling the Sergeant into high, slow arcs, as if he were skipping across the distance. "Come on," he announced loudly to his companions. "Let's find another place." The Third Division contingent filed out, trying to look tough as they went.

Gomez followed their progress with eyes like lasers targeting sights. "Why'd you make me apologize to that big, fat——"

Stark held up his hand again, palm out toward Gomez but still commanding. "You don't insult a noncom in front of his troops. Period. "*¿Comprendo?*"

The fire faded abruptly from Gomez. "Ah, hell." She sat, avoiding Stark's gaze. "Sorry, Sarge. I oughta know better."

"Yeah, you oughta. You're just lucky he backed down instead of making a case out of it."

"Hell, Sarge," Murphy offered, "he backed down because he recognized your name."

"I doubt that. I don't know him."

"He knows you, Sarge," Chen stated. "Everybody does. You've got a reputation."

"The hell I do," Stark noted sarcastically. "I'm just a Sergeant."

"You're the Sergeant who saved the line years ago after the enemy counter invasion," Billings corrected softly. "You're the Sergeant who stayed behind so the rest of his Platoon could escape. Everybody knows, even these idiots from Third Division. Those who weren't there saw it on vid."

"So what?" Stark demanded. "I did my job. That's all."

"You did more than your job," Murphy insisted. "Sarge, if we're in a bar and other soldiers find out we're in your Squad they want to buy us drinks and stuff just so we'll talk about you."

"You've gotta be kidding."

"No, Sarge." Murphy bent his head, trying to hide an uncharacteristic blush of embarrassment. "Heck, I'm really proud to tell other guys I'm in your Squad. You're sort of a hero."

"Oh, hell." Stark looked around, trying to project disgust. "You apes ought to know better than that. A hero is just a bum who happened to be in the right place at the right time."

"And did the right thing?" Gomez suggested.

"Okay, I guess I did the right thing. So what?"

"So if you hadn't," Chen pointed out, "we'd all be dead."

"Maybe. Maybe not. You guys said your thanks a while back. I appreciated that. But let it drop."

"Okay, Sarge," Billings agreed. "But everyone else is still gonna remember."

"I guess that'll be my cross to bear." Stark looked around, then focused back on his Squad members. "I probably shouldn't have told you guys to go to the Out-City tonight. There're too many new troops around."

"Yeah," Murphy agreed. "And they're looking for a fight, Sarge! Guess they never been in combat."

"They haven't." Stark felt his face harden. "They're going to be. They're going to get the worst fight of their lives if what I hear is true. So just stay clear of them. They've got a real bad shock coming up."

"Maybe we oughta just go back to the barracks," Billings offered. "It's pretty crowded, now, though," she added. "I'm sleeping on the floor."

"You can share my bunk," Chen suggested.

"In your dreams, Earthworm."

Stark leaned toward Gomez as the others bantered. "Anita, you know where Mendo is?"

"Yeah, Sarge. He headed into the Patton Bar on the way here. I guess he and the guy who owns the place like to debate philosophy or something."

"Thanks." Stark tilted his head to indicate the rest of the Squad. "You need help getting these guys back safe?"

"No, *Sargento*. We're already there."

Stark headed back out into the street, sparing a rare glance upward as he did so. *Never look up anymore. Why bother? Nothing but rock or an ugly metal ceiling inside, and nothing but stars, a sun you can't look at, and an Earth you can see but not get to outside. HUDs tell us if anything is going to fall on us. Funny how life up here changes things in ways you never even think about most of the time.* He turned left, heading back toward the outer edge of the Out-City.

A few minutes later, in the sort of wide underground corridor that marked the main drag in this part of the Out-City, Stark stood under the small, flickering red, white, and blue neon sign that marked the Patton Bar, its multiple colors casting dim illumination onto the poorly lit central area where people and an occasional electric cart passed in a spasmodic stream. *No sense in wasting light fixtures, and the power to light them, in a place where the civs hardly ever went,* Stark reflected. He leaned against the stamped metal sheet that made up the facade of the bar, watching the neon colors shift as he waited, until the soldier he'd been waiting for stepped out of the doorway a short distance away. "Mendoza."

The Private jerked in surprise at Stark's call, then came to stand near him under the garish neon light. "Yes, Sergeant?"

"There's been something I've wanted to know for a long time. Why the hell aren't you an officer?"

Mendoza hesitated, staring first at Stark, then into the dimmer areas beyond the light. "My father was an officer, Sergeant."

"The hell." Stark felt suddenly awkward, wondering what fate might have consigned an officer's son to enlisted ranks. "Look, I—"

"That is all right, Sergeant." Mendoza brushed aside Stark's half-formed apology. "My father left the active service as a Lieutenant. He could rise no higher, because he was a man of honor who refused to treat officer rank as a political prize. He advised me that unless I could forgo honor myself, I could have no future among the officer corps which rules our military in this day."

"That's tough advice."

"Yes, Sergeant, but true. The enlisted personnel"—Mendoza

smiled sadly—"they are not angels, but they are at least true to each other. Why did you ask me your question now, Sergeant? I have been in your Squad for years now."

"Because we need good officers, Mendoza. The things I've been hearing latcly have made that need a lot more obvious. Couldn't you change things, try to make the system better?" Even as Stark spoke, he knew the words were wrong, the sort of thing someone with no experience in getting run over and crushed by the real world would suggest.

Once again, though, Mendoza failed to take offense, instead shaking his head and speaking with earnest seriousness. "Sergeant, it is not so easy. There are always some bad officers, obsessed with their own careers to the exclusion of the tasks they swear to carry out. It has always been that way. But when an officer corps begins to go bad, when too many of the good officers leave in disgust and too many of the poor ones stay on to play political games, it is something that can happen fairly quickly and yet take a very long time to correct. Because now the self-obsessed careerists control the promotions and the job assignments, and thus they can eliminate anyone who does not play the game their way."

Stark nodded somberly. "So anybody who tells the General his idea is screwy gets canned, while the ass-kissers who tell him he's a genius get promoted."

"This is so," Mendoza agreed sadly. "The corruption worsened during the long draw-down after the twentieth century's Cold War, when so many officers were discharged in just a few decades, and of course it was the political ones who survived because they cared more for their own survival than for the people they commanded and the missions those people were ordered to carry out."

"So you're saying there's nothing we can do? The mil is just stuck like this?"

Mendoza hesitated. "Usually, in history, such a corrupted military would eventually fall in the course of a war, but the United States is too powerful, Sergeant. We hold an unmatched strategic arsenal, of which nuclear weapons are just a part. No one may threaten the United States itself, and so the military never really faces crucial, total defeat. I do not know how this can end. A losing war would purge enough of the bad officers to help rebuild a decent officer corps again, but how can such a thing ever happen? How, now, can enough officers be removed at once to allow good men and women to prevail?"

Stark frowned, eyes hooded under the glare of the bar sign. "Something about the way you said that sounded scary, Mendoza."

"I meant nothing frightening, Sergeant," Mendoza advised hastily. "I am afraid I think too much inside. Sometimes, when I speak, the inside thoughts come out too easily."

"Huh. You think good, usually, Mendo. You're wasted as a Private, but I can't tell you to become an officer, not after your own father told you different and not when I know you're right about the officers who run things these days, but I hope you're wrong about one other thing. This can't last. We can only hold the mil together for so long if the people in charge are worried about everything but their people and their jobs."

"Is something about to happen, Sergeant? All these new soldiers are arriving, and they seem very sure of themselves."

"Yeah, that they do." Stark exchanged brief glances with a

group from Third Division as it passed with wobbling footsteps. "You know a lot about history, Mendo. How much do you know about corporations?"

Mendoza made a face. "Some, Sergeant."

"What motivates them? I mean, they want to make a lot of money, right? Is that all?"

"Not entirely. A lot of money is nice, but they also always want to make more. No matter how big the profit is, they want it to be bigger."

"Always? They're never satisfied?"

"No, Sergeant, they are never satisfied. Every year they must grow larger, and have larger profits, or the corporation is seen as failing. It is strange. A corporation could gain total control of every market in the world, but then it would be a failure because it could no longer keep growing. I have never understood it, but then I was raised military." Mendoza looked puzzled. "Does this have something to do with the arrival of the new soldiers?"

"It might. The enemy holding us inside this perimeter are certainly keeping the corporations from growing here on the Moon. But I don't know for sure. Thanks, Mendo. The rest of the Squad's heading back to the barracks. You probably ought to do the same." Stark gripped Mendoza's shoulder in a brief gesture that brought a sudden smile to the Private's usually anxious face, then left, walking toward the barracks on his own. *Not sure what's happening. Not sure why it's happening. Life in the army. I bet Mendo would say it's always been that way.* His steps quickened, as if faster movement on his part would somehow make the next several days pass more quickly.

Mail call. A very old name for a very important thing. The form of the mail had changed over time, from rice paper with a few precious words scribbled in smeared ink, to archaic computer discs with a little magnetic memory precariously balanced in their guts, to the current almost indestructible coins that provided vid playback when popped into any convenient reader. The ancient cliché had it that strong men wept if they left mail call empty-handed. Not anymore, of course. Now you'd have to say strong men and women wept.

Except Stark. With his mil "family" around him at all times and a consistent dearth of long-term girlfriends he'd never expected mail, never been disappointed by empty hands when the last coin had been tossed to an eager receiver. But now he stood, not just one but two coins in hand, wondering what they could mean and who could have written.

At least he didn't have to hunt down privacy, like most of the rest of the soldiers in the barracks. Stark slid his cube door shut, then popped the first coin in. "Greetings, Ethan Stark." A woman. A civ. Looking bright and precise in good clothes and one of those nice gravity-defying lunar hairstyles that the civ women favored. He knew her, from a hospital visit whose purpose he never had figured out. "My name is Robin. Robin Masood. I need to talk to you on your next visit to New Plymouth. My number is enclosed. Please use it. I'd really like to see you again." The screen blanked as the brief message ran its course.

"The hell," Stark muttered, rubbing his chin warily. A civ, a good-looking civ with presumably her pick of civ men, wanting to see a mil noncom. Not that he minded the implied compliment, but this Robin Masood seemed out of his league. He could see her, maybe, on some officer's arm, but not his. She didn't look like a beer-and-then-another-beer kind of woman, and whatever virtues Stark believed he had, he knew he was that kind of man. "What's she want?" he wondered aloud. *Guess I can go into town tomorrow. Beats hanging around the barracks staring down Third Division Earthworms. But she won't be living in the Out-City. Not a high-class civ like her. Maybe I shouldn't . . . ah, hell, Stark, what are you afraid of? If some civ cops give me a hard time, I'll take them apart.* He keyed the attachment on Robin Masood's letter to call up her number, then downloaded it into his palmtop before reaching for the next coin.

The second coin slid in smoothly. Stark frowned in momentary puzzlement as a man appeared, some sort of distorted and older version of himself, like the fake aging mirrors played back in cheap funhouses. "Ethan?" the older, different version of himself faltered, and as it did, realization flooded in. He'd had it backward, for Stark was the younger version of the man on the screen.

"Dad." Ethan only had time for the single word before the old man began speaking again, face twisting as if words were unaccustomed to it.

"Ethan," his father repeated. "I, I got your mail. I, uh, I. . . ah, hell. Thanks. Maybe you were ten kinds of fool to get into the military, but I'm glad you're still alive. I didn't understand a lot of what you said, what all you do, but I guess you've got a lot of responsibility now. People depend on you. That's . . . well, that's really important. Me, I was never good enough for that. Just a fish farmer, like you always said. Only things that depended on me were the damn fish. And you and your mother, I guess. And I thought I'd let you down. For a long time. Only one kid, one chance, and I screwed it up."

Stark's father looked down, mouth working in remembered anguish. "But maybe not. Your friend, I guess she is, somebody named Reynolds, she sent us a copy of some award you got." Suddenly his father's eyes shone with something Stark had never seen there. No, two somethings. Not just tears, but also something more. "You were going to give your life for your friends. Almost did. After we got that letter from your friend Reynolds we called up a copy of the vid broadcast and watched. How did you do it? All those people trying to kill you, all those bullets, and you stayed because you believed you should."

His father glanced up, as if looking Stark in the eye, shaking his head in wonderment. "My son. Here I thought you'd never be half the man I'd been and instead you're twice what I ever was. Three times what I was. I don't care about that hero crap, but I sure care that you protected those people. You don't ever let them down, Ethan. I know I let you down, but you're more than me now, and I'm proud of that. Don't let them down, because they need you, and maybe you need them."

His father looked frantically to the side, as if searching for a forgotten text. "I, uh, I. . . I'm glad you wrote. Good to know you're okay. If you, um, ever get down here, please, um, stop in. Wear your, uh, uniform if you like. I'm sure you look real good in it. It's . . . been a long time." Screen static replaced his father's aged face; then the coin popped out, ready for replay or reuse.

Stark took the coin carefully in his hand, weighing it like a talisman. "You didn't let me down, Dad," he finally told it. "Not really. And thanks. Don't worry. I won't let these apes down." He pulled out a fresh coin, inserted it, then laboriously began recording a reply, trying to ignore the way his halting delivery mimicked that of his father.

Stark fidgeted outside the door to Robin's apartment, wondering anew just why the civ woman had called him, and feeling extremely out of place in uniform amid the civ furnishings, decorations, and people who filled this portion of New Plymouth. He stood stiffly as a police officer paused nearby, then walked over. *I'm not a kid anymore. If this guy tries to ride me, I'll*—

"Excuse me." The officer spoke politely, not trying to hide his curiosity but without any obvious hostility. "Can I help you?"

"No. Thank you."

"If you need directions—"

"This is where I want to be," Stark interrupted, with a sharp gesture toward the door.

"All right. If there's anything you need, you let me know."

Stark finally turned his head, frowning at the officer. "Sure. Mind telling me why you're being nice to me?"

"I don't understand."

"Neither do I. I'm a soldier, right? I'm in a civ neighborhood. That doesn't bother you?"

The officer frowned back. "I've seen very few military people here, so naturally I'm curious. It's my job to look out for this area, just like you look out for the colony."

Stark paused in mid-reply as the officer finished his sentence. "You're not worried about me?"

"Most of us worry about the soldiers on the perimeter."

"That's not . . . never mind. Thanks. I'm okay." He watched the officer walk on down the corridor, well lighted here, with actual living plants growing in occasional planters set along the walls. *What was that about? Damn strange. Maybe I should have listened to Vic.*

"Ethan," Vic had offered in tones of utter seriousness after he'd discussed his plans for the evening, "you want me to come along?"

"Two women on one date?" Stark joked. "That'd sure boost my reputation."

Vic hadn't smiled. "Ethan, you know mil, like me. You don't know civs, and you sure don't know women. I just want to keep you out of trouble."

"Thanks, Mom. But I think I can handle this alone."

"Famous last words." Vic had let him go, watching with worried eyes.

Robin's door finally slid open to reveal the civ woman smiling in welcome. "Thanks for coming by. It's important."

"Mind if I ask why?" Stark wondered, standing rigidly in the small room that made up the apartment's living room/bedroom/office.

"I've a friend who needs to talk to you." Robin gestured toward the kitchenette. Another woman stood there, middle-aged with streaks of gray along each temple, a woman who radiated the kind of confidence that comes with high rank in any profession. Stark had to fight down a sudden urge to salute as the woman walked up to him and extended a hand.

Stark shook it, sitting awkwardly in an offered seat as the two women sat opposite him. "Would you like something to eat or drink?" Robin offered.

"No, that's okay." On a small shelf nearby stood a short, fat figurine, a silly grin plastered on its comical face. Stark smiled in sudden memory. "This yours?" he asked, indicating the toy.

Robin half smiled back, as if embarrassed. "Yes. My mother gave it to me when I left Earth. It was hers. She thought it would remind me of home."

"Does it?"

"Yes. Why do you ask?"

He touched the figurine's face gently with one fingertip. "My mom has one, too. Back home. Guess all the women that age bought 'em, huh?"

"Many did," the other woman admitted. "It was quite a fad. Where is your home?"

"You mean, where did I grow up?" Stark smiled at the silly figurine again. "Seattle Area."

"Really?" Robin asked. "I'm originally from the Portland Area. I didn't know there was a fort in the Seattle Area."

"There isn't. My parents weren't mil. Military. I grew up just like you did, I guess."

"That's fairly unusual, isn't it?"

"Yeah, well, that's me. Fairly unusual." Stark felt himself relaxing, as if the ridiculous figurine were a talisman summoning memories of his life as a civilian. "Funny, you from the Pacific Northwest, too, and having the same whatchamacallit."

"Pacas. They're called pacas. I don't know why. Did you ever go to the beaches?"

"Sure. Everybody did."

"I miss the beaches," Robin remarked wistfully. "I wish the Moon had an ocean."

"It's got seas," Stark joked.

"That doesn't count," she laughed in reply.

A momentary silence settled. "What's this about?" Stark finally questioned. Nothing about the encounter seemed social, despite the relaxing atmosphere, sparking reminders of Vic's worried attitude.

"Mr. Stark," the older woman began.

"Sergeant."

"I beg your pardon?" The woman seemed genuinely bewildered.

"Sergeant," Stark repeated. "That's my title. In the mil. The military. It's what I do."

"I see." The older woman nodded in apparent understanding. "Well, Sergeant Stark, I'm Cheryl Sarafina. My title is executive director to Colony Manager Campbell. Do you know who that is?"

"Sounds like the head civ."

"That's right. James Campbell is the senior elected civilian official in New Plymouth, which means he's the top elected civilian on the entire Moon, though his actual power is severely limited as long as we're under martial law." Sarafina paused, then stared grimly at Stark. "Mr.—I'm sorry—Sergeant Stark, I'd very much like to ask you some questions about the military."

"I can't divulge any operational stuff to you, ma'am, not without clearance from my chain of command."

"Ma'am?" Sarafina seemed amused by the title. "Don't worry. I don't want to know anything you can't tell me. No, I'd just like to know your opinion on some issues."

"My opinion?" Stark laughed. "I'm a Sergeant. Nobody cares what I think, except the grunts in my Squad."

"I care." Sarafina leaned forward, eyes intense. "Sergeant Stark, would you regard a negotiated peace settlement here on the Moon as a betrayal?"

"Huh?" Stark scratched his head, glancing at Robin and then the paca on the nearby shelf. "Why would I do that?"

"Because of all your comrades who have died up here. All the fighting you've done to achieve victory."

"Ma'am, most of the fighting I've done was to achieve my personal survival. As for my comrades, yeah, I've lost too many, here and a lot of other places. And let me tell you, one is too many. But it happens, and nobody cares all that much except us."

Sarafina frowned in puzzlement. "Surely your officers care."

"A few do, most don't. A lot of them, the higher-ranking ones in particular, seem to think of us as nothing more than spare parts sometimes."

"I don't understand."

Stark shrugged. "Neither do I, ma'am. Why are you asking me this?"

"Because," Robin chimed in, "we, the civilians here in New Plymouth, would like the war to end. Everything we want to accomplish on Luna is being limited and stymied by the need to fight, by the resources we're forced to send back to Earth as what we're told is our share of the war's cost, by the partial blockades that make getting people and materials up here harder than it needs to be. And, of course, the heavy taxes on anything and everything up here."

"Taxes?" Stark questioned. "I thought civs could elect people who wouldn't make them pay a lot of taxes. Has that changed since I enlisted?"

Robin Masood smiled bitterly. "It's not that we don't expect to help pay for the military forces that protect us, but we seem to be taxed beyond that, certainly much, much higher than our counterparts on Earth. And there's nothing we can do about it. We can't exercise the same rights to self-government that Americans back on Earth can, because as long as the war lasts, we'll remain under martial law. We're not even allowed to vote for representatives in Washington."

"In addition," Sarafina noted, "the corporations that sent us up here invested heavily, and as a result continue to demand ever larger output from our mines, labs, and factories. Yet we cannot meet those output goals as long as the war demands resources from us and limits our ability to expand."

"So you're between a rock and a hard place. You saying your bosses don't listen to you either?"

Sarafina smiled grimly. "Sergeant Stark, are you familiar with the term 'chattel labor'?"

"Can't say I am."

"It refers to workers who are so indebted to their employers that they must continue working. Workers who have no say in their own fates. Workers who are effectively little more than slaves. We are tired of living such lives, Sergeant Stark, yet there is no hope of improvement as long as the war continues. Therefore we want to negotiate a settlement."

Stark shrugged again. "So negotiate it. That issue's way above my pay grade."

Sarafina speared Stark with another intense gaze. "Sergeant, as I noted, we've been told by your officers, the most senior ones, that any attempt to negotiate a settlement would be regarded as a betrayal by the enlisted personnel. We've been told you would never stand for it."

"Nobody ever asked me." Stark screwed up his face in puzzlement. "Hell, I've been in more than a dozen campaigns. They all ended, and a lot of them didn't end the way we wanted. Nobody asked me if I cared or liked it then, and nobody's asked me up here."

"Are you saying you'd actually like a negotiated settlement?"

"Ma'am, I generally like it when people stop shooting at me."

The two women exchanged glances. "It appears your officers may be lying to us," Sarafina noted.

"They lie to us all the time," Stark agreed, then frowned in sudden concern. *Damn. Shouldn't have said that. Way too relaxed. So what if Robin's from Portland Area and her mom had one of those dumb smiley things, too. They're civs.* "I probably shouldn't be that blunt with you. I'm sure my officers would be real unhappy if they heard what I've been telling you, even if it is just my opinion."

"Sergeant, I swear anything you have or will tell us will remain confidential," Sarafina promised. "Your officers will not be told you ever spoke to us."

Can I trust that? Hell, I don't know. They seem nice, but . . . Vic's right. I'm out of my depth here. "Suppose I asked you not to tell anyone else."

"No one?" Sarafina didn't seem pleased at the prospect.

"Right."

"Please reconsider. I believe this information is very important to Mr. Campbell, and therefore to all the inhabitants of New Plymouth."

If she was lying to me, she'd just promise anything to keep me talking. Yeah. No question. "That's okay. You can tell Campbell. Just keep it quiet beyond him. I talk too much for my own good sometimes."

Sarafina didn't try to hide her relief. "Certainly. You have my word, Sergeant Stark."

"Thanks. Look, I can't help you on this negotiation issue. I don't have any power outside the twelve soldiers I command. And my officers have made it plenty clear they don't want to hear my opinions on any subject."

Sarafina smiled. "On the contrary, Sergeant Stark, you have helped us. Understanding your opponent is important in politics. I assume it is the same in military matters, isn't it?"

"That's right."

"In the same way, knowing what motivates your senior officers will help us in our dealings with them."

"Good luck." Stark looked around to mask another wave of uncertainty. "Uh, Robin, I guess that's the whole point of this? Nothing social? Not that I expected anything," Stark added hastily.

She flushed slightly. "I'm very sorry. You probably expected something else when I sent you that letter, didn't you?"

"You didn't promise anything."

"No, but. . . I am sorry for implied expectations. It's nothing personal."

Stark found himself grinning. "It never is. Don't worry about it." He nudged the paca again. "Nice to see this thing. My mom's used to embarrass the hell out of me. But that was a long time ago. You ever get back to the Portland Area?"

"I can't afford it. Like most of the workers up here, I seem to get deeper in debt by the day. Have you been to the Seattle Area lately?"

"I've been up here longer than you. So, is there anything else I can do for you ladies? We're pretty busy these days. I probably ought to be getting back."

Sarafina glanced away, seeming somehow embarrassed to Stark. "There is one more thing, Sergeant. Is there anything we, the civilians in New Plymouth, can do for you?"

"For me?" Stark shook his head. "I don't need anything special."

"No, not just you personally. Anyone, everyone in the military. What can we do?"

Sometimes things happened that simply didn't fit. Lately that sort of thing had been happening often. First the cop, then this. Stark rubbed his neck, puzzled. "Why are you asking?" he finally wondered.

Robin answered, pointing off toward the spaceport. "We see them all the time, sometimes just a few, sometimes more. The . . . the . . . containers for the dead."

"The body bags." Stark nodded. "Yeah, I know they're not bags anymore, but that's still what they're called."

"You're dying for us," Robin continued, eyes suddenly reddened. "We know that. You keep us safe at enormous risk to yourselves. That's one of the reasons we insisted on visiting the hospital where we saw you, so we could gain a better understanding of your sacrifices for us."

"One of the reasons?" Stark asked.

Sarafina smiled tightly. "We also wanted a chance to speak to some military personnel for their candid opinions. However, if you recall, no such chance presented itself. The officers who escorted us made it clear we shouldn't ask too many questions and they effectively intimidated anyone who might have given us the answers we sought anyway."

"So you set up this meeting. Good; now I understand."

"It makes you happy to know this?"

"I like knowing what's going on and why it's going on," Stark confirmed. "It's one of the things that helps keep me alive. As for what you can do for the mil, I've got no idea. You've got no control over our officers, and you say you can't vote, so none of the politicians will listen to you, and the corporations that seem to be driving a lot of this mess are driving you, too. So I don't know. Maybe just be nice when you see one of us."

"We hardly ever see any military personnel," Sarafina noted. "They pass through the spaceport and on out to your restricted areas." She paused, suddenly pensive. "There seem to have been a very large number of them arriving lately."

Stark glanced downward. "That's something I can't talk about."

"There's a lot of talk about a big offensive," Robin chimed in. "The newscasts are full of it."

"The newscasts." Stark simply stared back.

"There was an interview with one of your, um, Generals? the other day. He talked a lot about winning the war and applying some new way of fighting."

"A General? Some guy named Meecham?"

"I think so. He seemed very confident."

Stark choked down a reply. *Confident. I guess it's easy to be confident when you have no idea what the hell reality is. Just like those poor, ignorant bastards in Third Division. The difference is they'll bleed and die and that General will sit back at headquarters and watch it happen.* He shook his head. "I'm sorry. Can't talk about it. Don't want to talk about it."

Robin began to say something else, but Sarafina forestalled her with a raised hand. "Certainly, Sergeant. We respect your wishes."

"Thanks." Stark stood, feeling awkward again. "I ought to be going."

"Of course." Sarafina rose as well, extending her hand once more. "Thank you, Sergeant Stark. Good luck and Godspeed."

"Sure." Stark shook her hand. "But don't wish luck to me, wish it to all those new arrivals. Robin, hope you get to visit Portland Area soon." He left, standing once again in the civ corridor of the civ building, where civs stopped to stare as he walked by, a uniform where uniforms did not belong. For the first time in a very long while, Stark stared back briefly, surprised to see more of curiosity in the civ eyes than fear and hostility. *Some mil are different from other mil, like the Third Division apes are different from us. Maybe some civs are different from other civs, too.* The thought disturbed him on some level where the way the world worked sat engraved in his mind. *Is it possible the mil up here could have something in common with the civs up here? I guess stranger things have happened.*

The corridor leading to Stark's cubicle in the temporary barracks ran by a small lounge area that was basically just another cubicle with no door, a few more chairs, a drink dispenser, and no bed. As he passed the lounge, Stark spotted Vic sitting in a chair that gave her a view out the door. "Hey. What're you doing around here?"

Vic twisted up one corner of her mouth in a noncommittal expression. "Nothing much. Just taking a break."

"Funny place to take a break. You weren't waiting up for me, were you?"

"Why would I bother with that?" she noted carelessly. "You're a big boy."

"Sure." Stark came in, sitting opposite her. "You gonna ask?"

"No."

"Okay. All she wanted was to talk to me, her and this friend of hers who's some high-ranking civ."

Vic raised one eyebrow. "They just wanted to talk? Ethan, you're not exactly the greatest conversationalist."

"I know, but it wasn't that kind of talk. They had a bunch of questions they wanted to ask me."

"Questions?" Vic frowned, leaning forward slightly. "What kind of questions?"

Stark waved one hand in a dismissive gesture. "Nothing operational or anything. No secrets. Get this, Vic: The civs have been told by our officers that the reason the war's still going on is because we, enlisted like you and me, insist on fighting until we win."

Vic chuckled, shaking her head. "Come on."

"I mean it. They were serious as hell, and really surprised when I told them nobody cared what we thought and we didn't particularly want any war to go on any longer than necessary." Stark paused, noting the expression on Vic's face. "What's wrong with that?"

"Ethan," Vic stated with more than a trace of anger, "what do you think our officers are going to do when some high-ranking civs tell them you said our officers are lying?"

"I wouldn't want to guess," Stark declared indignantly. "But it won't happen. The civs promised they wouldn't tell any officers they'd talked to me."

"And you believed them?"

"Yeah. Not at first. But they convinced me."

"They're civs, Ethan!" Vic's face tightened as her anger flared. "They think we're some kind of gladiators who die for their entertainment! They won't vote for enough money to support us properly! They don't care about you or any of us."

"Vic, these civs don't watch the mil vid, they aren't allowed to vote, and, believe it or not, they seem to care about us."

"Bull. Ethan, you are such a sucker for a pretty face—"

"Listen to me! I may not be the smartest guy in the world, or up here for that matter, but I do know when someone's trying to work a scam on me. They didn't ask for anything, Vic."

"Sure," Vic grumped. "And next time she calls you she'll have the vid waiting to take down every word you say. Either that or she'll scream 'rape!' and get her own vid time."

"I know she's a civ, but. . ." Stark hesitated, trying to find the right words and failing. "She, and the other civ, they didn't act like I was mil and they were civ. It was different, Vic."

"Just what does 'different' mean?"

"I don't know." The admission seemed to mollify Vic somewhat. "Just something wasn't the same as it usually is. Hell, Vic, on the way back through the civ areas I swear a couple of them smiled at me, like they wanted to be friendly. And this civ cop, he acted nice, Vic."

"Stranger things have happened, I suppose"—Vic sighed in unconscious mimicry of Stark's own thoughts—"though I don't know what. Still, Ethan, you probably shouldn't see that woman again."

Stark grinned. "What, are you jealous?"

"Oh, please!" Vic looked incredulous.

"Well, we do spend a lot of time together."

She shook her head and rolled her eyes simultaneously. "Ethan, that's because we're friends. Friends, Ethan. Even if we weren't, I'd still feel obligated to hang around you so I could warn off any other female who saw you and suffered a momentary lapse of judgment by thinking you'd be a good catch."

"Thanks. I really like you, too." Stark stared at his hands for a moment. "They told me something else, Vic. Seems our General Meecham has been on the newscasts talking about the offensive."

"I'd heard that."

"Why didn't you tell me?"

"Because I couldn't quite believe it. The civs saw it, though, huh?"

"That's what they said. Guess that program got censored from the stuff we get to see." Stark clenched one fist. "Keep us from seeing what a General says on security grounds but let every civ and foreign viewer watch it all. That makes a helluva lot of sense. Vic, why do I feel like somebody watching a train wreck happening in slow motion?"

"Probably for the same reason I do." Vic held up her palmtop so Stark could see the screen. "Get ready to watch some more. There's a lecture tomorrow morning by Meecham's staff. All Sergeants in First Division who aren't on the line are required to attend personally. Sergeants on the line will be linked in."

"Oh, man." Stark narrowed his eyes to read Vic's screen. "Why do I think this is gonna be real ugly?"

Whether the lecture proved to be ugly or not, the lead-up to the talking heads on Meecham's staff developed in the tortuous fashion common to most major briefings. Only the military, Stark thought sourly, could design chairs capable of being highly uncomfortable even under the gentle tug of lunar gravity. He shifted position for perhaps the tenth time since taking a seat, then turned his head questioningly in response to a tap on one shoulder. "Yeah?"

"Hey, Stark, what're you doin' here? I thought you knew everything about fighting wars."

Stark smirked in exaggerated comradeship. "Sergeant Yurivan. I thought you were locked up in the stockade again, Stacey."

"Me?" Yurivan mimicked Stark's expression. "Nah. Me, I'm innocent as can be."

"Sure," Reynolds chimed in from her seat. "Does that mean you destroyed all the evidence, Stace?"

"Every piece." Sergeant Yurivan waved grandly toward the stage that dominated the front of the hall. "Now I'm trying to learn all the secrets Stark here has been keeping from the rest of us."

"What makes you think I know any secrets?" Stark wondered.

"You're alive," Yurivan pointed out, "and you ought to be dead several times over. There's usually a limit on how many dumb things a grunt can do without getting taps played over his or her heroic funeral, but you, Stark, you just keep on rolling. You're either very, very smart, or very, very lucky."

Sanchez tilted his head just enough to take part in the conversation. "Maybe he's just very, very dumb."

"Could be," Yurivan agreed cheerfully. "How come you guys look so glum?"

"Because," Stark stated with forced solemnity, "we are here to be lectured on some General's theories for revolutionizing warfare. I'd rather be shot at."

Yurivan beamed happily. "Me, I love it."

Reynolds raised one skeptical eyebrow. "You got a concussion, Stace? Or are you just trying for a mental discharge?"

"Neither," Sergeant Yurivan insisted. "I just love the concept this General dreamed up. 'Sin energetically.' What a great idea!"

Stark stifled a laugh. "Stacey, it's synergy, not sin energetically."

"You fight your way, I'll fight mine." Yurivan sat back with the self-satisfied grin of a class clown who'd scored a joke while circles of smiles and guffaws radiated out from her position as surrounding soldiers repeated the gag to their neighbors.

"Attention!" The Sergeants leaped to their feet, standing rigid as a full Colonel in a faultlessly tailored and creased uniform strode onto the stage, an entrance flawed by the Colonel's staggering attempts to move in low gravity.

"Seats," the Colonel commanded with an air of great dignity. "I am Colonel Penter, Lunar Expeditionary Force Joint Command Headquarters staff. I have the pleasure and duty of providing you with an overview of the brilliant revolution in operational military activity that has been developed by General Meecham." Fumbling beneath the center-mounted podium, the Colonel finally located the switch he'd been seeking, causing the heavy curtains behind the stage to roll apart with slow majesty. The opening revealed a large briefing screen that now dominated the stage behind Colonel Penter, displaying a sector of the front in ultrahigh-resolution, color-coded, 3-D-terrain-enhanced, integrated-data elemental glory. "As you can see, we've assembled a perfect picture of the total environment and now have an unparalleled grasp of the military situation on the lunar front."

Stark leaned slightly to whisper in Vic's ear. "Since when do collecting and displaying data elements equal understanding things?"

"They don't," she muttered back.

"As General Meecham had the insight to state," the Colonel lectured in the tones of an elementary-school teacher, "understanding the enemy is the first prerequisite to defeating the enemy."

"Excuse me, sir," a Sergeant somewhere far to the right side of the briefing room called, "but didn't Sun Tzu say that a couple of thousand years ago?"

The Colonel paused, his mouth a thin line. "Comments are neither required nor desired. I expect silence and full attention while presenting this information. Now, as I was saying, understanding of the enemy requires an exhaustive analysis of mind-set parameters fused with historical biases toward action and inaction within discrete decision matrices. These matrices are in turn heavily influenced by enemy perceptions of our own projected, expected, and traditional force employment options."

Smiling confidently, Colonel Penter raised a dramatic finger for emphasis. "Synergy Warfare is based upon careful calculation of the correlation of forces taking into account every physical condition and weighing the subsequent results against the critical nonphysical conditions to produce a definitive course of action with a finitely determinable outcome. For example, in a sample limited-force engagement this correlation is partially determined by measuring relevant combat-impacting factors as they relate to force employment considerations. Application of variables regarding terrain effects is achieved using exhaustive analysis of available data as processed through applicable force-movement and deployment models. Logistics requirements are based on historical-use data streams that reflect current trends in depletion of consumable stockpiles during periods of high-stress activity. Naturally, some approximations must be used in all cases to smooth out jagged anomalies in curve rates of projected applied analyses."

"Naturally," Sanchez whispered softly.

"The proper force application vectors," Colonel Penter droned on, "are determined by high-level secondary and tertiary branch analysis with a heavy emphasis on decision-linkage theory and high-tempo crisis management tools." He paused, raising a finger on the other hand for additional emphasis, so that the raised digits framed the wall of medal ribbons covering most of his chest. "I might add that this particular facet of Synergy Warfare received special praise when General Meecham briefed the Joint Staff."

Goody for him. Stark felt his mind fuzzing as the relentless stream of jargon continued unabated. *This would be sort of funny, in a sick way, if so many lives weren't riding on this verbal pile of garbage.*

"These paradigms are essentially self-evident operational/ strategic vectors impacting on each other in an eminently predictable fashion. General Meecham's special contribution to the modern art of war is the recognition that clustering of operational paradigms into highly focused yet diverse grand tactical applications produces an uber paradigm capable of overcoming standard resistance models with multiplication factors dependent only on special considerations and the mental discipline of relevant commanders at all levels." The Colonel produced a laser pointer, holding it like a sword of triumph as he swung toward the display screen at his back. "This presentation represents a typical nonexceptional situation on a discrete portion of the lunar front. Individuals without a grounding in Synergy Warfare concepts would conclude that attacking forces would require a significant material advantage in order to overcome resistance from defenders employing commonly established defensive measures applied by inherent traditional warfare mind-sets as modified by current transitional trends within physical force employment constraints. This, of course, is not actually the case."

"What the *hell* is he talking about?" Stark whispered fiercely to Vic.

"I doubt if even he knows," she breathed back. "As Napoleon once stated, the moral is to the material as three is to one." Colonel Penter swung his laser pointer triumphantly, outlining a portion of the display with quick slashes. "In this area, application of Synergy Warfare in its most rudimentary form would allow concentration of our forces to achieve a three-to-one material superiority. By applying the higher-level paradigm clustering inherent in properly focused Synergy Warfare, we re-create and enhance the basis for Napoleon's greatest victories. In short, with this material advantage magnified by employment in accordance with Synergy Warfare, we automatically enjoy the equivalent of a nine-to-one advantage!"

An audible murmur ran around the room as one Sergeant stood to speak. "Excuse me, sir, but are you saying three soldiers equal nine soldiers in your planning?"

The Colonel nodded with obvious satisfaction. "That is correct, if highly simplified, as far as it goes. Of course, when other superiority-enhancing paradigms are applied and multiplied by our own technological superiority, conservative estimates indicate an effective virtual superiority in the range of twelve to one."

"Three soldiers equal twelve soldiers?"

"No, no, no! One soldier equals twelve soldiers!" Colonel Penter gestured grandly. "This is, as I said, a conservative estimate that does not even factor in the obvious huge advantage granted our forces by our overwhelming superiority in leadership by our senior officers."

Oh, God. Stark stared, speechless for a moment. *They based their plans on the assumption they're playing with twelve times as many people as they've actually got? And they're congratulating themselves on how brilliant they are to do that?* Before he could muster any response, another Sergeant stood.

"Begging the Colonel's pardon, sir, but is that display meant to portray the actual situation in that sector of the front?"

"That is correct, Sergeant. This is, I assure you, a definitive display."

"Colonel, I'm sorry, but that's not a complete picture, sir. There's a number of enemy fortifications missing."

Penter nodded sharply. "Of course. Those extra fortifications were carefully evaluated and assessed to be either abandoned or the product of deliberate deception operations."

"Sir?" The Sergeant's dismay was plain to see. "Colonel, sir, I've led patrols along that front. A lot of them. Those fortifications are there."

"No, Sergeant, they are not. We are well aware that, shall we say, exaggerated estimates of enemy capabilities have been used to justify a long-term lack of results, but—"

"Colonel," the Sergeant broke in, clearly furious at the implied insult, "you can't achieve material superiority by wishing away some of the enemy forces."

"I told you," Penter declared in icy tones, "that this picture of enemy capabilities was developed by careful analysis of all available intelligence."

"Colonel, nobody asked me or anyone else at the front about those capabilities, so I don't know where you got this 'intelligence.'"

Penter didn't so much grin as bare his teeth. "I seriously doubt that General Meecham or his planners require the input of a disrespectful Sergeant in order to reach the necessary conclusions about enemy capabilities."

White with anger, the Sergeant sat abruptly, even as Stark muttered in Vic's ear. "He gave himself away. 'Necessary' conclusions about enemy capabilities, the Colonel says. If they didn't decide the enemy forces were weak enough there, Meecham's plan couldn't work even with this moral superiority nonsense."

"Right," Reynolds agreed. "They did wish away enemy capabilities they didn't want to deal with. Easy to do when you're not gonna have to face them personally."

"*If* I may have everyone's full attention," Penter announced over the rising buzz of conversation, "I will continue telling you what you need to know." The laser pointer swung again, moving in great, sweeping arcs. "The enemy mind is his weakest point, and that is where Synergy Warfare concentrates its efforts. By employing multiple diversions across a wide area, the enemy's attention is distracted. By then striking with a carefully sequenced succession of heavy, closely coordinated attacks against several sectors, the enemy is unable to reinforce threatened areas and will exhaust his reserves by rushing them from place to place. Adhering to a precise timeline is, of course, critical to achieving this goal. The enemy will be unable to determine the most critical point as our forces strike at him repeatedly. Most importantly, by employing our forces in a visually intimidating and aggressive posture, we ensure the enemy defenders are overawed. Their firepower will avail them nothing if their fingers freeze from fear on their triggers." Penter smiled triumphantly. "That last sentence is a direct quote from General Meecham."

Stark stood, despite a frantic but futile grab by Vic to keep him in his chair, drawing the attention of the room as he did so. "Colonel, given your intentions to employ Third Division in this assault, I submit it would be wise to either provide them more training in movement under Lunar conditions—"

"Impossible. We will not dither away our opportunity for victory."

"—or build enough flexibility into your precise timeline to account for the difficulty Third Division personnel will have moving under unfamiliar conditions through unfamiliar and difficult terrain."

"Impossible," Penter repeated. "General Meecham's theory of Synergy Warfare demands *the precise* coordination of all elements in order to generate a quantum magnification of force on narrowly focused areas."

"Colonel, you can't have a precise timeline if your planning doesn't reflect real-world constraints."

"Our planning reflects our doctrine, Sergeant," Penter insisted, nostrils flaring.

Sometimes it's a good idea to think instead of quoting doctrine. "Colonel," Stark continued out loud, "the Third Division troops can't make a precise timeline over lunar terrain. At best, they'll either sacrifice formation integrity, or any attempts at maintaining a covered advance. That's not theory. That's fact. Any rock-eater can tell you that."

"Rock-eater." The Colonel shook his head in disapproval. "I assume you mean a lunar veteran. Unfortunately, Sergeant, you lunar veterans need to be remotivated. Staff planners are certain good troops will make that timeline."

"SUAFO," Reynolds muttered, the soldier's acronym for Shut Up And Follow Orders.

"With all due respect," Stark stated flatly, "is the Colonel saying we are not good troops?"

"My words speak for themselves, especially since good troops wouldn't be questioning every word I say up here! The next individual to comment from the floor will be charged with insubordination. Am I clear?"

Stark stood for several seconds more, his eyes fixed on the Colonel, then finally sat with enough deliberation to earn another glare from Penter. The Colonel swung his laser pointer some more, reciting Meecham's theories with the apparent enthusiasm of a recent religious convert while the enlisted personnel sat watching in a silence so complete that it began to draw annoyed glances from the officer. Finally he shut off the pointer, resheathed it in his pocket with all the dignity of a warrior putting away his weapon, and glowered at the assembled Sergeants. "It's obvious anything else I might say would be wasted. This briefing is over." He walked off the stage with another staggering attempt at dignity.

"Somebody forgot to yell 'Attention!' " Sanchez observed.

"I don't think forgetting had anything to do with it," Stark suggested. "Let's get the hell out of here."

Stacey Yurivan stalked by, glowering, as she also headed for the exit. "I've just about had enough of this crap," she declared to no one in particular, then focused on Ethan. "Hey, Stark. You gonna let them get away with this?"

"Sure, Stace, I'm gonna walk into the General's office, tell him he's an idiot, and plant my boot in his backside."

"Really?" Yurivan asked, brightening.

"Hell, no. You think I'm crazy enough to do that?"

"Oh." Yurivan managed to look disappointed. "If anybody's crazy enough, it's you, Stark."

"Thanks," Stark replied with all the sarcasm he could project. "I bet afterward you'd feel bad about serving on my firing squad."

"Real bad," Yurivan said with a grin. She reached to grab his arm as Stark began to move away, leaning close. "You ever do decide to do something, you let me know, Ethan."

"What are you talking about?"

"Maybe nothing. See you around, Stark." Yurivan vanished into the crowd.

"Is there something else going on that I don't know about?" Stark complained.

"Not that I know," Vic stated with a hard look. "Is there?"

"Don't you go weird on me, too. Hey, just a sec." Stark strode over to a comm panel they were passing, keying in the number for his Squad's quarters. Sure enough, Mendoza sat there, studying a vid screen of his own intently. "Hey, Mendo."

Mendoza looked up, startled, before focusing on the comm panel. "Yes, Sergeant?"

"You ever hear of some guy named Napoleon?"

"Napoleon Bonaparte?"

"Yeah, I guess so. Some big-time General."

Mendoza nodded vigorously. "Yes, Sergeant. A very big General some centuries ago."

"He win any battles?" Stark wondered.

"Oh, yes, many battles. He was a genius at land warfare for his time."

"Huh."

"Of course," Mendoza added thoughtfully, "Napoleon's armies also suffered terrible losses, especially when he ordered attacks against strong defensive positions. Then there was the invasion of Russia."

"He invaded Russia?" Vic asked.

"Yes, Sergeant Reynolds." Mendoza made a sorrowful face. "He lost practically the entire invasion force, about a million men."

"A million?" Stark questioned. "You sure about that?"

"Yes, Sergeant. It was a military disaster of almost un-equaled scale."

"Thanks, Mendo. See you later." Stark killed the comm connection, staring sourly at his companions. "Great. Our brass admires some guy who lost a million soldiers in one op."

"They're taking advice from him, anyway," Vic agreed.

"We have seen the future of warfare," Stark deadpanned, "and it sucks."

"You're just upset because you didn't think of Synergy Warfare first," Vic observed dryly.

"Nah. I'm upset because I still don't know what the hell Synergy Warfare is."

"Simple." Sergeant Sanchez grunted. "Synergy Warfare is how you win battles without enough firepower or ground troops."

Stark nodded, all levity gone. "Yeah. You think Synergy Warfare is going to impress the enemy as much as it does our officers?"

"No," Sanchez replied calmly.

"You think it's going to work?"

"No."

"So what do you think will happen to this grand offensive of General Meecham's?"

For the first time in Stark's memory, Sergeant Sanchez's imperturbable expression cracked slightly, eyes haunted by foreboding. "What do I think? I think we're going to get our butts kicked. I think we're going to lose a lot of soldiers. I think the angels are going to cry when they watch it happen." His face closed down once more, emotionless.

"I've got a real nasty feeling that you're right, Sanch," Stark noted after a long moment of silence. "Anybody else feel like getting drunk?" His comm unit buzzed before either Reynolds or Sanchez could reply. "Stark here."

"Sergeant, you have been ordered to report to Major Fernandez at Division Headquarters as soon as possible."

"Major Fernandez? Who's he? What's this about?"

"I don't know the answer to either question, Sergeant."

"Great. Thanks." Stark raised his hands, palms up, in a rueful gesture. "Guess my afternoon schedule just got filled. See you guys back at the barracks."

Vic nodded. "Have fun, Ethan. And try to stay out of trouble."

"Trust me." Stark walked toward the headquarters complex

while Reynolds and Sanchez headed for the relative sanctuary of the barracks.

Headquarters. Big corridors with walls carefully smoothed so they felt like something back on the World. Lots of officers, most looking like they were doing The Most Important Thing Ever, but still with enough free time to shoot long, questioning glances at a lowly Sergeant cluttering up their halls. One Major speared Stark with a rigid finger as he walked past her. "Get those ribbons replaced," she ordered, indicating the row of decorations on the Sergeant's left chest. "They're frayed."

"Yessir." No sense in arguing. Stark knew, and the Major knew, that replacement ribbons couldn't be had on the Moon for love or money, but the order wasn't really about ribbons. The order was about him being a Sergeant and her being a Major and rubbing it in.

He walked on, past a Colonel who issued another variation on the "new ribbons" order, until he reached a door with "Fernandez" on it in gilt lettering. Stark hesitated before knocking, remembering how often officers changed assignments and therefore offices, which meant those letters represented no end of labor and expense. His knuckles landed directly on the lettering, unfortunately inflicting no damage that Stark could see.

"Come in." Stark entered, seeing a more spacious version of the glorified closets that passed for private offices in the underground warrens of Luna. Major Fernandez smiled in welcome, waving the Sergeant to the office's single chair, then leaned back, eyeing Stark appraisingly. "I suppose you're wondering why you are here, Sergeant."

Stark twitched his brow in a fraction of a frown. "Frankly, yes, sir. I am."

"You've been involved in combat on the Moon for quite a while, haven't you, Sergeant?" Fernandez didn't wait for an answer before continuing. "That's very strenuous, very hard on a soldier."

"I haven't done anything a lot of other soldiers haven't done, sir."

"But how do *you feel* about it, Sergeant?"

"I beg the Major's pardon?"

Fernandez smiled gently. "Just between you and me, Sergeant. Do you hate your officers?"

You've got to be kidding. Just between him and me ? "No," Stark stated flatly. *Hate's a useless emotion.*

The Major glanced toward his desk surface, then lost his smile in favor of a slight frown. "You don't? No hatred? No desire for revenge?"

"Revenge for what, sir?"

"Your friends. You have had friends die in combat, haven't you, Sergeant?"

Stark nodded. "Everybody has."

"Don't you want to avenge them?"

"With all due respect, sir, I don't know what you're driving at."

Major Fernandez waved a hand in the air. "How about killing the officers who order you into battle? Don't you ever want to do that?"

"No. Sir."

Fernandez's gaze flicked to his desktop once more, and his frown deepened. "Deep down inside, don't you want to call the shots, Sergeant? Be in charge?"

"No, sir, I do not."

This time the Major's gaze lingered on his desk for a moment, then he jerked a thumb toward the door, all pretense of friendliness vanished. "Very well. You may leave."

"Thank you, sir." Stark walked back down the big corridors, trying to reach the limits of the headquarters complex as soon as possible.

"Stark?"

The voice wasn't familiar, but Ethan turned at the sound of his name, hoping it wasn't another Major or Colonel. "That's me."

The Sergeant who'd spoken smiled hugely. "Don't know me?"

"Afraid not." Stark's brow furrowed in thought. "You used to be with First Battalion, didn't you?"

"That's right." She nodded in evident pleasure. "I'm stuck here at headquarters doing penance for my sins, while guys like you earn their pay. What are you doing here, anyway?"

"I haven't figured that out yet," Stark admitted. "Major Fernandez called me in for a meeting."

The headquarters Sergeant's eyebrows rose. "Major Fernandez? He wanted to meet you?"

"Yeah, but he didn't really say anything. Just asked me some dumb questions, got mad, and then told me to leave."

"At least you're not under arrest." She shook her head, looking around. "There're too many ears in headquarters, Stark. Can't talk much, but Fernandez is our security mole."

"Are you saying I just got a security screen?" Stark demanded, feeling his face flush with heat.

"You sit in his chair?"

"Yeah."

"It's rigged with a remote polygraph. Any answer you gave he was screening for truthfulness."

"Damn." Stark shook his head angrily. "So that's why he kept looking at his desk. Am I going to be locked up now?"

"You said he got mad?" the other Sergeant pressed. "He didn't like your answers?"

"No, he kept asking me if I'd like to kill officers or something and I kept saying 'no.' I don't like killing anyone. Just because it's part of my job doesn't mean I enjoy it."

"Hah." She chuckled softly. "Congratulations. You passed. By dumb luck, maybe, if he asked you the wrong questions. If you'd failed, Fernandez would have had you arrested right outside his office."

"Thanks. Any idea why I was called in?"

She shrugged. "They're doing random pulls. Allegedly random, anyway. Always have, but there's a lot more showing up lately. Guess they're worried about something."

"They oughta be worried about the enemy, not their own troops."

"You're right." The Sergeant waved farewell. "Hell of a note, ain't it?"

Stark thought about it, all the way back to the barracks. Thought about trying to figure out who the real enemy was, about civs who didn't act like civs always did, about a lot of soldiers who were going to be thrown into a major assault with little chance of success, about senior officers who didn't think it strange to send grunts out to die so the vid ratings would stay high, about corporations that could never be satisfied no matter how much they acquired, and about officers who were maneuvering against their own enlisted personnel on the eve of a major battle. He thought about it until he didn't want to think anymore.

Several of his Squad members were lounging about the barracks, making disparaging cracks about the attempts of the Third Division soldiers to walk without bumping into walls or each other. "Hey, Gomez," Stark called with a beckoning gesture. "Gotta talk."

She rose and came over quickly, not trying to hide her concern. "Something wrong, Sarge?"

"No. I want to ask you to get something for me."

"No problem, Sarge. Whatdaya need?"

"This isn't an order," Stark cautioned. "It's personal. You don't have to do it."

"Okay," Gomez agreed just as rapidly, though puzzlement entered her eyes. "What is it?"

"Anita, I need a special system file." Stark outlined his requirements as Gomez listened, her eyes narrowing in thought. "Can you get me that?" he finished.

"Sure. You think you're gonna need that, Sarge?"

"I dunno. Maybe. Never thought I'd say that, but maybe. I just want to be prepared."

"You will be," Gomez promised. "I'll have it for you by this evening."

"You don't have to," Stark advised again. "You don't need to be involved in this at all."

"*Sargento,* you think maybe you might need this file, so I think maybe I ought to get it for you."

"Thanks. Oh, I need to make sure the system watchdogs can't spot it."

Gomez looked indignant. "I know that, Sarge. Trust me. The watchdogs'll never know it's there." She moved away with the speed and assurance of a soldier carrying out an easily executed and important task.

Stark watched her go, trying to fight down his misgivings. *I can't believe I'm doing this. But I might need it. I wish to hell I knew where right and wrong lay in this mess.*

Two more briefings. Three more days. Six morning and evening roll calls. Nine scheduled meal periods in the mess hall. The Third Division soldiers slowly began to learn to move without falling all over each other and any nearby furnishings. Simultaneously, their confident expressions grew haggard as simulator runs followed weapons practice followed familiarization drills followed exercise periods followed briefings followed more simulator runs.

Stark and the other Sergeants of First Division kept their troops away from the Third Division personnel. "How come, Sarge?" Chen complained. "I want to get out of these damn barracks and do something, but we're stuck in our crowded quarters or this rinky-dink lounge. We might as well be on the line."

"Yeah," Murphy chimed in, "we can't even get sim time because all the training stuff is full of Third Division guys."

"You volunteering for extra training, Murph?" Stark demanded.

"Well, no, but. . ."

"That's what I thought. Look, you apes, there's nothing I can do about this, but it won't last much longer. Just hang in there. I'm going to need you guys sharp."

"Okay, Sarge. You saying there'll be more room in the barracks soon, too?"

"Yeah." Stark turned away, his expression grim. "I'm afraid there's gonna be a lot more room in the barracks soon."

Everywhere he walked, Stark encountered signs of Third Division troops and their ongoing training. He prowled the corridors for a while, hoping for another glimpse of Rash Puratnam, but saw only unfamiliar faces. His own cubicle felt too tight this evening, a claustrophobic cabinet in which sleep refused to pay a visit, so Stark finally headed for the lounge in vague hopes of finding company.

Even before he reached the darkened room Stark saw the flickering lights that meant the vid was on, even though no sound could be heard. He peered in, seeing one figure slouched in a chair facing the vid screen. "Vic?"

Reynolds responded with a halfhearted wave. "Hey, Ethan. What are you still doing up?"

"I can't sleep." Stark slumped into the seat next to her, staring moodily at the silent images leaping across the vid screen. "Why are you awake?"

"Same reason. Feels like a storm's about to hit."

"Yeah. Big storm."

"Ethan, promise me something."

"Sure. What?"

"Just—"

A harsh buzzing interrupted Reynolds. Both Sergeants froze, then tabbed their individual comm units to hear the same message announced in a professional monotone. "Prepare your units for action. Assembly areas are specified in battle armor Tactical Displays. All personnel are to be ready for combat by 0200."

"Looks like the storm just broke," Stark observed. "What were you saying, Vic?"

"Nothing. Let's go. It's going to be a long day, Ethan."

Stark's Squad rested in two adjacent, crowded cubes. He hit the access pads for both, then slapped the lighting controls on. "All right, ladies and gents. Everybody up and into their armor. We got orders."

"Ah, hell, Sarge," Billings complained, "I only got two hours' sleep."

"Then you're two hours ahead of me. Move it, you apes!"

The assembly area for Stark's Platoon lay out on the lunar plain, behind the front but within easy marching distance for veteran troops. APCs shuttled the squads out, then left to ferry more units into position. Stark scanned his Squad restlessly, checking every soldier repeatedly for any problems. *Damn. I'm scared. Is it because I got hurt so bad on my last op? No, I don't think so. Something else.* He glanced toward the front, and beyond it to the too-near-horizon line where enemy fortifications lay hidden. *No, I'm not afraid of them. Not any more than usual, anyway.* With sudden determination he strode over to First Squad, aiming for Vic Reynolds' position.

"Vic. I got a real bad feeling. Anything special bothering you?"

"I'm not sure what you mean, Ethan." Her face shield turned toward him, blank, the nonreflective surface revealing nothing, not the brilliant pinpoints of countless stars in the blackness overhead, not the barren lunar landscape around them, not even Stark's own image.

"Vic, dammit, we're going into action. If there's anything else you know that I ought to know, too, then tell me."

"The enemy's expecting us."

Her words came so quickly, and so lacking in apparent emotion, that Stark had to think a moment to absorb the meaning. "How do you know that?"

"A friend in Intelligence. I checked with him after what you told me about the civs seeing our General on vid. The enemy's been watching Meecham and a lot of other big shots, political and military, shoot their mouths off on vid newscasts. They know a big offensive is coming soon, they know Meecham is going to base it on his theories, and they've been digging in deeper and reinforcing their lines."

"If Intelligence knows this, why haven't our plans changed?"

"Because the officers in Intelligence won't tell the General anything he doesn't want to hear. Everything has either been ignored or explained away."

"I see. Thanks. Good luck."

Another suited figure approached, moving with such care that Stark wondered if a Third Division soldier hadn't wandered into their area. He checked his scan for the figure's identity. *Captain Noble. Now my cup runneth over, indeed.*

"Bravo Company," Noble announced. "You are to, um, advance in accordance with your Tactical Displays and carry out the ordered actions. I will. .. occupy a position where I can provide oversight of the Company's movements."

"A rousing speech," Sanchez observed over the Sergeants' circuit. "Our new Captain has a flair for inspiring the troops."

"Just as long as he stays out of the way," Stark grumbled.

"Since this Platoon lacks a commanding officer," Noble continued in tones that betrayed no enthusiasm, "I will, ah, exercise personal control."

"Don't say it, Ethan," Vic warned.

"I'll try." Tactical displays suddenly glowed with orders. Stark trotted back to his Squad, making sure they all hit their start markers. "Everybody stay sharp," he cautioned.

"What's going down, Sarge?" Gomez asked.

"Probably the big offensive. I don't know what our role will be. Just follow your Tacs."

"Okay, Sarge."

Timelines ran down, triggering a new set of commands. "Let's go, Third Squad." The path laid out on the Tacs led fairly straight-line toward the enemy. Stark checked his back door to the command-level scan, seeing similar advances all around the American perimeter. *I don't know if they're confusing the enemy or not, but right now I sure as hell don't know what's going on.*

The Squad passed through the front line, muscles tensing as they advanced into the kill zone between the opposing forces. No enemy fire responded however. The high ground to the Squad's front was brooding and silent, as if the terrain held no more life than most piles of rock on the lunar surface. Stark and his soldiers halted on their new markers, taking cover, weapons canted toward the silent ridge ahead.

"You there. Get your people on their markers."

Stark checked the ID on the transmission to confirm that it had been sent to him from someone in headquarters. "Sir, my people are all within a meter of their markers. They have only adjusted position as necessary to protect themselves from enemy fire."

"No adjustments are authorized! Get those soldiers on their markers!"

Stark counted to ten slowly. *Might as well save my fights for anything more serious down the line, and I'm sure there'll be something worse coming later.* "Okay, everybody. On your markers. Exact position."

"But Sarge—"

"Just do it." Stark held his breath as several soldiers shifted position, ready to shout a command to get back under cover if the enemy responded to the sight of apparently easy targets, but the unnatural silence from the enemy fortifications continued.

More time passed, another timeline running down until it hit zero. Additional commands sprang to life. Advance along planned route. Engage enemy front-line positions. Stark studied the routes laid out on his Tac, puzzled. *We're not attacking. Not like this. Firing from those locations won't accomplish anything. A diversion? Gotta be. But the enemy would have been firing at us already if they were worried about us. Maybe they're just waiting for us to get closer.*

"Let's move it. Real careful." Stark advanced cautiously, rock to rock, one eye on the terrain that could mask his movements and the other on his Squad members as they followed his lead. "Chen, keep your head down. Kidd, keep your rushes shorter."

"Okay, Sarge."

"Yes, Sarge."

Stark reached the position ordered by his Tac, crouched behind a low rise, rifle at ready. As his Squad dropped into their own places, Stark raised his weapon, aiming carefully toward enemy lines. As the timeline ticked down to zero, his Tac ordered Stark to begin shooting. "Open fire," Stark ordered, and the Squad's weapons spat fire toward the seemingly empty ridges ahead. One clip expended, Stark reloaded, firing at the aiming points dictated by his Tac, since he lacked any real targets. A few enemy weapons fired back—scattered, harassing shots that fell around the Squad's position without doing damage. Stark switched to command level scan for a moment, seeing that squads and platoons all around the perimeter were engaged in similar light probes, then returned to watching his own Squad closely.

Another timeline reached its end, triggering the next order: "Fall back." Stark retreated just as carefully as he'd advanced, taking a slightly different route just in case the enemy had tracked his earlier movements, until he and the rest of the Squad reached their starting positions once more. "Action completed," Stark reported.

"Okay." Captain Noble sounded genial but distant, as if he hadn't been paying much attention.

"Captain," Stark pressed, "if that was intended as a diversionary action, it failed. The enemy did not respond in a manner that indicated any concern about our actions."

"Thank you, Sergeant."

"Captain, my assessment is that this action did not fulfill its intended purpose."

"Sergeant," Noble stated in a noticeably less genial tone, "the purpose of the action is not your concern."

"Captain, we did not draw any significant enemy fire."

"That's enough, Stark. Just follow your Tac."

You lay on the rock, more rock stretching away as far as the eye could see, which even after years of viewing, your mind still insisted wasn't far enough because the horizon was just too damn close. The dust never seemed to settle completely anymore, as humans tossed it up by movement, by digging, and by explosions and impacts of various sorts. No matter how the Moon tugged in a stubborn, tireless effort to bring its dead components back to the rest they'd known until humans came to disturb things, disturb them humans did. "Moon fog," the veterans called it, a slight haze hanging everywhere people fought and labored here, a form of air pollution in a place without air.

He began to feel some cold seeping through the suit's insulation despite its efficiency. One foot began tingling slightly in that way that foretold a limb falling asleep. Stark moved as best he could without moving, trying to generate both warmth and circulation with minor tremors. Phantom pains started sprouting where enemy weaponry had wounded him in the past, as if his cells remembered the damage and were broadcasting it now in reminder of what could come.

Stark could only concentrate on himself for so long, even while scanning his Squad for any problems or carelessness. He finally called up the back door into the command scan, seeing what every officer could see, despite his misgivings.

On the highest level of command scan, Stark could finally discern the outline of the attack plan. The three brigades of Third Division had been positioned at roughly even intervals around the American perimeter, one of those brigades behind Stark's own unit. As he watched, that closest brigade jumped off, advancing to pass through the forward positions.

"Vic, you watching the command scan?"

"Yeah."

"They've got armor in with the ground apes. They're actually sending tanks forward as part of an assault."

"I noticed." Vic sounded far away, as if she'd detached herself from what was about to happen.

"Dammit, you don't send armor up against an unshaken defensive line. They'll die faster than the infantry."

"I know, Ethan."

Stark's eyes were locked on his scan, oblivious for the moment to the ravaged lunar terrain, seeing the massed symbols sweep forward until they had nearly reached his own position, waiting for something else, something he finally recognized by its absence. "Vic, where's the artillery? Why hasn't any artillery opened up to screen this advance?"

"There won't be any artillery. Remember? They want the enemy to have their heads up, to see what's coming and be overawed."

It made an insane kind of sense, in the sort of world Generals inhabited. Stark stared at the display, mesmerized by a sight he'd never imagined seeing outside of a simulator. A full brigade of soldiers advancing in skirmish formation, heading for a single point on the enemy line, a hammer aiming to smash its way through entrenched defensive positions by the force of its will and the strength of the individual bodies that made it up. Studded throughout the formation like mobile fortresses, the tanks slid forward without apparent effort, black shells studded with weapons canted toward the still-silent enemy positions.

It's beautiful, in a way. Or maybe magnificent is the word. Watch it. Fix it in the brain. Before it all ends and you never see the like again. Stark said a quick prayer for the brigade moving to attack, knowing as he did so that prayers were poor substitutes for common sense.

The Third Division brigade moved through the forward

American positions, some of the ranks passing Stark's own Squad where it lay in gape-jawed amazement. "Sarge?" Billings whispered. "Are they gonna—?"

"Shut up. Everybody shut up."

Up ahead now, the assaulting units began to lose their carefully knit formations as the soldiers displayed more difficulty moving in the unfamiliar gravity and terrain. The enemy line stayed dormant as the leading units came farther within range, the objective ridge looming dark and apparently vacant while the brigade surged farther forward at a more rapid clip, most soldiers abandoning any attempt at keeping to cover as they sought to maintain the formations dictated by their Tacs.

Maybe it'll work, Stark thought desperately. *Maybe the enemy'll be scared senseless, pull back. Maybe, maybe, oh, please God—*

His HUD screamed. Tied into the command circuit, alarms cried frantically from every vector as the ridge erupted with enemy fire so intense it seemed a sunrise had sprung to life from the muzzles of their weapons. Incoming rounds swelled into life, threat symbology dense enough to obscure the view ahead. The limited defensive umbrella the assault troops carried was swamped in milliseconds; then the fire hit and rolled over the attackers like a wave.

As Stark watched in horror, entire formations vanished, their green symbols flickering into the fixed markers of death or simply disappearing as suit systems were destroyed. On the left flank, an advancing platoon froze in its tracks, every soldier dead in moments, their symbology glowing eerily, still in almost perfect alignment. Tanks burst into ragged fireballs as flurries of antiarmor weapons slammed home, their now-useless armor ɔnverted into clouds of shrapnel flaying their own infantry.

The formations dissolved, some symbols going to ground, others falling back in various degrees of order and disorder, and incredibly, many still advancing, moving forward into a gale of fire that nothing living could front for long. Comm circuits, overloaded beyond capacity and stressed by enemy jamming, broke up into a thousand fragmentary messages.

"—where's it coming from?"

"C'mon, let's—"

"Medic! Med—!"

"—enemy strongpoint on the right—"

"—not on Tacs—"

"—Sarge? Lieutenant? Anybody?"

"—take it under fire—"

"—get—"

"—down! He's down!"

"—where? Where?"

"Keep going—"

Suddenly the wild stream of broken conversations shrank into near-silence. Stark checked his command tap, confirming his suspicion. *They're filtering out unauthorized comms at the relays. Everybody's shouting into silence now.* Calls for help, reports to other units, last words from those who had time to say them, all consigned to nothingness.

Many of the survivors of the Third Division brigade surged onward, shedding newly dead and wounded as they went like a stream of water evaporating as it rolled across a hot griddle. Somehow a few made it to the enemy positions, scattered clusters of two or three friendly symbols clawing their way up the ridge in the teeth of the enemy fusillade. They made it up, onto the top of the ridge, and then they died, isolated among defensive positions that poured fire into them from every angle.

The wave retreated, survivors of the assault falling back, losing more soldiers as they came. Stark watched, his Tac silent and unchanging. "Captain," he finally demanded, "are we going to cover them?"

"You'll see any orders on your Tactical, Sergeant."

"Captain, they're being slaughtered out there and we're just lying here!"

"I don't want to hear another word out of you, Stark."

Stark felt himself trembling, but he stayed silent, checking his command scan to see that new orders had at last gone out to the attacking units. The remnants of the Third Division brigade reached an area about one hundred meters short of the First Division positions, then halted, somehow maintaining enough discipline to take cover rather than continuing to retreat.

The enemy barrage finally lessened, dropping in intensity as it shifted to precision fire, trying to take out every American soldier spotted forward of the line. *Okay, you had your damned assault,* Stark seethed inwardly. *Now call a ceasefire so we can get medical aid to the wounded out there.*

Instead, Stark watched in amazement at the command scan as another Third Division brigade, about one-third of the perimeter away, jumped off for an attack similar to that which had just occurred to his front. He screwed his eyes shut, unwilling to watch, until he heard the alarms sound again and knew another couple of thousand soldiers were being butchered. The futile attack lasted, if anything, a little longer than the first had. *Stop. Now. It's not working, dammit. Your 'sequenced assaults' and 'focused application of force' aren't accomplishing anything but wiping out your own soldiers.*

But the third brigade jumped off in turn, and died in turn. Stark lay, almost physically stunned by the events he'd been forced to witness, then stared in shock again as new orders came through to the surviving Third Division troops, not only those to his front but also at the locations of the other two attacks.

"General advance. Assault your objectives."

In blind obedience to duty, the soldiers came to their feet, unit by unit, trying to advance a little smarter this time, trying to take advantage of cover, but usually failing because of their unfamiliarity with moving under lunar conditions. The enemy fire doubled, then redoubled, raking the advancing troops. The assault stumbled, as if the soldiers had hit a wall they couldn't breast, then ground to another halt.

Stark's back door into the command circuit came to life again as headquarters began hurling individual Third Division units forward, one by one. "Bravo Company. Assault and seize Objective Yorktown. Acknowledge."

Bravo Company of First Battalion of First Brigade of Third Division. Stark's Squad belonged to one of the Bravo companies in First Division. He felt an extra, irrational bond with those foolish, inexperienced soldiers who were being cut to pieces out in front, a bond formed of shared identities built around one letter of a phonetic alphabet. Another Bravo Company dying under unrelenting enemy fire, and that somehow made it a little worse to bear.

After a long moment, a reply came, the words slightly ragge
as if their speaker were having difficulty stringing them in
sequence. "This is Lieutenant McMasters, acting Bravo Company
commander. I have twenty-five effectives left in my unit. Did not
copy your last. Say again."

"Bravo Company, assault and seize Objective Yorktown."

Another prolonged moment passed while Stark lay in the dust,
watching weird lights flash up ahead where soldiers were fighting
and dying in violence rendered unreal by its silence. Scattered
in broken patterns around the terrain, the shattered hulks of
armored vehicles burned like ancient funeral pyres, their fuel and
explosives providing the means for self-contained fires on a world
too dead to supply any support for the brilliant death-flares.
Finally, another answer came, slower, the words spaced for effect.
"I say again, I have only twenty-five soldiers left. We are under
heavy fire and cannot advance."

"Lieutenant McMasters, this is Division headquarters. You are
ordered to assault Objective Yorktown in accordance with the plan
spelled out in your Tactical Display. Carry out your orders or you
will be relieved of command. Acknowledge."

Stark stared at the lights, his eyes flickering to his HUD, where
symbols crawled in wild patterns to mark the tracks of threats and
defenses. It was all too easy to put himself in McMasters' place,
to feel the frustration and hopeless anger, and to know what the
inevitable reply would be. "This is Bravo Company. Acknowledged.
Assaulting Objective Yorktown."

Stark breathed another silent prayer, understanding even as he
did so that it was futile. All he could do, all anyone could do, was lie

the dust and wait, listening in on the chaos of a battle that had long since spun out of control.

Perhaps ten minutes later, as a welter of communications marked hopeless attacks by a multitude of shattered units, Stark's ears keyed on another specific message. "This is Bravo Company." The voice was thin with exhaustion and drained of emotion.

"We have heavy jamming interfering with your signal. Lieutenant McMasters?"

"This is Corporal Cozek, acting Bravo Company commander. Lieutenant McMasters is dead. Bravo Company is down to maybe ten personnel, myself included."

"Continue your assault, Bravo Company."

Cozek's voice would have been unrecognizable this time if Stark's suit hadn't tagged it with Bravo Company's ID. "Brigade, goddammit, most of us are wounded. We're pinned down. We can't move. Get us out of here."

Stark checked his HUD grimly. Bravo's symbols lay in a staggered crescent about three hundred meters forward of the front line, farther forward than any other surviving Third Division unit. Threat symbols converged on Bravo's crescent in an almost continuous stream, every disappearing symbol marking another explosion, another shell, another burst of death.

"Bravo Company, continue your attack. That is an order."

"We can't," Cozek screamed. "We are pinned down under heavy fire. Position untenable, less than ten effectives left. Jesus, help us."

"Corporal Cozek is relieved as acting commanding officer. The next senior soldier is to assume command and continue the attack. Acknowledge."

No reply came, whether out of defiance, or because it had been blocked by enemy jamming, or perhaps because there was no longer anyone left in Bravo Company able to respond. Stark studied his HUD, trying to bury himself in an analysis of the battle, anything other than think of the soldiers trapped in front of friendly lines. The situation gradually came clear, even through the enemy jamming and the partial picture Stark could derive from his back door into the overloaded command net. Headquarters had been dealing with the disaster by throwing the least damaged units into already failed assaults, and now they'd run out of even those units and were using whatever was left, reinforcing failure in a panicked fixation on the original plan. Everything was coming apart, the brass didn't know what to do, and they were sacrificing more and more of the front-line soldiers rather than admit failure. For the first time in his career, Stark truly hated the faceless minds directing a battle. *Hate accomplishes nothing,* he tried to remind himself. *But these deaths aren't accomplishing anything, either.*

"For God's sake, get us out of here!" someone pleaded, the words partially obscured by the thunder of almost continuous concussions transmitted through the lunar rock into armor clinging to that rock in desperate search for safety.

Stark lay still, an ache in his belly building as if fire and acid warred there in match to the violence outside. Thoughts ricocheted through his head, cascading memories and visions. Corporal Pablo Desoto, dying instantly in the hellfire of a heavy shell. His father's voice: *Don't ever let them down, they depend on you.* Lying alone on another ridge, trying to hold off pursuers and pretending help would come when he knew his chain of command didn't give a damn what happened to him or any other soldier as long as the officers could sit in the rear and play their promotion games. And long ago and far away, another set of friends, dying one by one amid grass slick with their blood. It had happened before. It was happening again. It wasn't supposed to. It was never supposed to happen again. *Kate, goddammit, I promised you.*

Nothing you can do, little brother. Save yourself.

No! I promised.

Save yourself.

The hell. Not this time.

Stark lay on the frigid lunar rock as the fire inside grew, pressure building through his chest and throat, hands trembling slightly, eyes unfocused. The pressure built to a mighty force that blocked breathing, holding there, then somehow shattered whatever had held it confined and flowed free. Stark drew a ragged breath as the fire vanished, leaving nothing in its wake but a resolution cold and clear that filled him with calm certainty. He glanced at the HUD, where symbols flickered in time to the deaths of fellow soldiers, his mind suddenly seeing solutions with the cool precision of crystalline plates sliding into place. He called up a special file, the one he had asked Gomez to acquire for him, linked it with Captain Noble's symbol, then triggered the backdoor channel so the other Sergeants could hear what happened. "Captain, this is Sergeant Stark."

"Yeah." Noble sounded annoyed and aggravated. "What do you want?"

Stark kept his own voice formal and correct. "Captain, I am leading my Squad in to rescue the surviving members of Bravo

Company, First Battalion, First Brigade, Third Division."

"What?" Stark's words had apparently jerked Noble out of his self-absorption. "I didn't hear those orders. Who gave you those orders?"

"No one, Captain. I am acting independently."

"You can't act independently! What's going on?"

"I am going to rescue those soldiers," Stark stated implacably. "I will not sit back here and let them die uselessly while some idiots far behind the lines continue ordering senseless assaults."

"Stark, you're relieved of duties and under arrest!"

"I thought you might say that, Captain." Stark triggered the file he had called up earlier, a file with an innocuous name to help fool the watchdogs but that was commonly known as "frag." In the old days, the only way for soldiers to take out a stupid or hated officer had been to use one of their own grenades, a tactic known as fragging, after the fragmentation produced by the weapon. Now, with everyone dependent on electronics, soldiers had a simpler, surer, and at least initially nonlethal method of accomplishing the same thing. Stark had never imagined himself needing a frag file, strictly illegal programs hacked together by an unknown soldier decades ago and periodically updated by other unknowns, but thanks to Gomez he had one hidden and handy nonetheless. Now, targeted at Captain Noble, the frag virus froze his communications, his weapons, even the systems in his battle armor that assisted movement.

"Ethan?" Vic called, her voice horrified. "I've lost comms to the Captain. Did you frag Noble?"

"Yeah."

"Are you insane? When you killed his systems he dropped off the command and control circuit, too."

"That's the idea."

"Ethan, that means headquarters lost vid from him. We can't hide that, or explain it, because we're not directly involved in combat!"

"I know that. I don't care. I won't leave those guys to die out there."

"Ethan . . ." Vic's reply trailed out, as if bitten off with frustrated violence. "Don't be an idiot, Ethan," she finally pleaded.

"Too late." Stark bared his teeth in something that wasn't a grin. "I'm going in, Vic. Taking my Squad with me. Are you coming?"

"I don't—" Vic's exasperation melted into quicksilver uncertainty.

Stark could see her, in the smooth planes where his mind operated now, see Vic's face fixed immobile as her thoughts raced, balancing duty against loyalty and wondering where each lay. "I haven't got all night, lady."

"Shut up, you ape," Vic snarled back. "Yeah, I'm coming. I've had enough, too."

"Sanch?" Stark called. "How about you?"

"Are you certain of this, Stark?" The tone held the same impenetrable calm it always did, as if this were a normal conference on a normal comm circuit.

"Yeah, I'm certain. You going in? You with Vic and me on this?"

"I'm in." Sanchez might have been remarking on a poker hand.

"All right, Sergeant," Vic demanded, "you're in charge. What do we do?"

What do we do? No Tac with its hated but comforting orders, no officer calling out the drill. Just a noncom with a lot of experience in doing what he was told. Stark felt a shiver of fear and uncertainty try to break through the icy shield in his mind but fought it off. *Okay, I'll just do this backward. If I thought I was getting orders to do this, what would they say? Tac would show this, right? And this, and that. Yeah.* It felt good. It felt right. "Here, I'm sending you my Tac. What do you think?"

It took a few seconds for the transmission, and a few more for the other Sergeants to study the plan. Sanchez spoke first. "It's not enough. You cannot do this with a Platoon."

"It's a decent plan," Vic objected.

"It is," Sanchez agreed. "But we cannot do this with squads. We need Platoons. This plan requires company strength."

Company strength. Stark stared grimly ahead. He hadn't really planned on involving anyone else, getting anybody besides himself lined up for a court-martial, but now he had to try to convince six more Sergeants to join in. He braced himself, keying the Sergeants' comm circuit. "First Platoon, Third Platoon, this is Stark."

"Uh-huh." Podesta in First Platoon came back immediately. "Where do you want us, Ethan?"

"I . . . what?"

"Where do you want us?" Sergeant Podesta repeated. "We've been listening. We know what's going down. Our Lieutenant's been fragged and we're waiting for orders. How do we get those poor bastards out of there?"

"Third Platoon?" Stark asked.

"Here. We're with you, too."

Stark checked his HUD, suddenly wondering how far this might be spreading. All the Sergeants could talk and listen in to their own circuit. Perhaps, he thought, this was how a pebble felt when it started an avalanche, then shook his head. *Get this job done. I can worry about the rest later.* "Here's my Tac. Can you guys execute?"

"No problem." First and Third Platoons would move up on the flanks, providing pinpoint suppression on any enemy fire. Meanwhile, First and Third Squads of Second Platoon would advance far enough to overrun the trapped grunts of Bravo Company so that Third Squad could pass them back through Second Squad to safety.

"Ain't gonna be enough," Sergeant Tostig in Third Platoon observed. "Too much enemy fire coming down there. We can't hold it down with a company's worth of fire-power."

"I know," Stark agreed, voice flat. "Don't worry. There'll be more fire coming in. Get your people moving while I get support laid on." He felt it then, loyalty and obedience balancing again, hesitating before the final commitment.

Then the other Sergeants rogered up and the world shifted into a new pattern.

Stark made another call. Divisional artillery. An alien world, where men and women far behind the front lines, bunkered securely under the defensive umbrella, tended huge metal beasts that spat fire. Nothing like an infantry grunt's world, but maybe loyalty held across that gap in experience. "Grace?"

"Yeah. Master Sergeant Grace here."

"This is Stark."

"Ethan Stark? Long time no see, ground ape. What's with the back-channel call?" Despite the casual words, Grace's voice had a clipped quality, as if something were being held inside.

"I need everything you've got, laid on these positions," Stark added as he keyed in coordinates, "and I need it in ten minutes."

"Everything?" Grace's negative head-shake was somehow apparent over the circuit. "I need the Colonel to approve that, Stark. I can't commit Division Artillery on some grunt's say-so, even an old drinking buddy's."

"Sure you can."

"Bull. Have your Captain call in."

"No can do. He's out of action."

"Huh?" Now Stark could minds-eye Grace scratching his head. "You guys haven't been under fire."

"No, we haven't."

"Well, then have one of your other officers ask for it."

Stark took a deep breath. "All our officers are off-line."

"All of them?" Stark could imagine Grace at work now, calling up his own picture of the front to check individual stats. "How . . .? You fragged all your officers?"

"They're not hurt. Listen, we're going after the Third Division apes trapped out in front and we need artillery support to get them out of there. You got that, Grace? Do I need to spell it out?"

Silence lingered, while Stark studied the ground he'd have to cover with his Squad once they started moving, wondered how long it might take headquarters officers obsessed with their own activity to notice something strange happening, notice officers of units not in combat dropping off the vid feed, notice those same units acting without apparent orders, and mentally cursed rear-echelon noncoms as he waited. "Stark?" Grace finally questioned. "You guys did it? You're calling the shots?"

"Yeah. You turning us in? Gonna drop your rounds on us instead of the enemy?"

Low laughter sounded, bitter with anger. "The hell. It's about time. I had a brother in Third Division. Had. Give me a couple of minutes and our Colonel will be off-line, too. You've got your fire support, Stark. Get those grunts out of there."

Last but far from least, Stark called his Squad. "Third Squad, I have disabled Captain Noble and am advancing on my own initiative to pull out the Third Division soldiers trapped out front. None of you is obligated to follow my orders." Stark waited, watching as the timeline he'd created ticked toward "go."

"So, what are our orders?" Gomez finally demanded.

"You don't have to follow these orders," Stark repeated.

"They're from you, ain't they, Sarge?" Murphy asked.

"Yeah, they're from me."

"That's all we need to know. Let's go."

Stark smiled tightly, a warmth coming back into the coldness filling him. "Here's a feed for your Tacs. We start moving in a couple of minutes. Any questions?" He shifted to a private circuit. "Mendoza."

"Yes, Sergeant."

"What do you think of the plan? It look good to you?"

"Yes, Sergeant." Mendoza didn't try to hide his surprise at being asked.

"Good. Listen, if you get any command-level ideas, you pass them on to me on the double. No sitting back quiet and keeping your thoughts to yourself. Understand?"

"Yes, Sergeant." Firm this time, with more than a hint of pride.

Stark shifted back to the company-level picture, watching as his HUD counted down the seconds. It went green and he shouted "Go!" in the same instant. Bravo Company, First Division, surged forward, evading among the dead landscape with the skill of long practice. It took a few minutes for the enemy to spot the careful advance; then the fire pummeling the survivors of Bravo Company, Third Division, began lifting, seeking targets among the First Division soldiers.

Stark huddled behind a rock twice his size as a dumb, heavy artillery round slammed to the surface on the other side, the crash of its explosion transmitting as vibration through the rock in a dim echo of the shell's fury. *Come on, Grace.* Even as the urgent thought came, a massive barrage opened up from behind, American artillery plunging in to saturate the enemy defenses and blanket the enemy positions with a storm of fire. For a moment, Stark had a confused vision of Armageddon, the world ending in a final firestorm of combat; then his mind focused down on the job at hand, ignoring the distraction of death's messengers passing overhead.

The enemy fire faltered, dropping to almost nothing as the opposing troops went to ground. They could wait. Sooner or later the American artillery would have to let up; then the enemy would raise their heads again enough to target the attackers, waiting for this latest charge to carry another company of American soldiers within range. One more company repeating the pattern of attack they'd seen multiple times already. One more company to decimate while it futilely surged against defenses too strong and too strongly held.

But this time would be different. First and Third Platoons evaded forward on either side, then dropped and opened a murderous aimed fire on any enemy position still shooting. Second Platoon kept going, dropping Sanchez's Second Squad as it went, the other two Squads washing over the survivors of the Third Division Bravo Company, engulfing them, picking them up, and then receding like a wave hitting a sand castle and pulling its remnants out to sea.

Stark grabbed at a prone figure as Vic's Squad fired steadily around him. "Let's go, soldier." The figure lolled limply, and Stark realized one arm was completely gone. "Hell. Pass this one back," he ordered Chen, shoving the body his way.

Chen took the body automatically. "We recovering the dead, too, Sarge?"

"Yes. Damn it, Bravo Company isn't leaving any dead from Third Division's Bravo Company out here. We bring them all in, hear me? Alive and dead."

A cheer sounded, startling Stark, who half scowled/half smiled before seizing another battle-armored body. "You okay?"

"Who the hell are you?" The Third Division soldier quivered uncontrollably, nerves shattered by the torrent of violence rearranging the lunar landscape on all sides.

"Angels of mercy. Get the hell back. My people will help you." Stark shoved the man toward another member of his Squad, then moved to the next, swift and sure, finding far too many dead and far too few living. "You alive?" he demanded, hauling up another prone soldier. The soldier swung silently in his hands, trying to line up her rifle toward the enemy again, fingers tightening in endless reflex on the trigger of the empty weapon. Stark yanked the rifle free, sending it spinning off in a graceful arc, then slapped an armored hand against the shell-shocked woman's helmet. "Your fight's over for now. Get back." Another shove to the rear and she went obediently, almost falling into the arms of Billings.

"Ethan! It's starting to get pretty hot here again."

"Yeah, Vic." Absorbed in the evacuation, Stark had failed to note the rising intensity of the enemy fire, artillery and heavy weapons beginning to strike among them again as the enemy started to grasp what might be happening. Stark paused to check the picture on his HUD, scanning to determine how much was left to do. "We're getting the last ones now."

"I'll peel off half my Squad to help. Ethan, it is time to leave!"

"Okay, okay. Third Squad, let's go. Stop passing the Third Division apes to Second Squad. Just grab everyone left and head back to our positions." Stark reached out both hands, each locking onto a battered set of battle armor, both of which surely held no life within them, then gathered the two bodies to him, blessing lunar gravity, and headed for the American lines in a barely controlled rush.

They made it, to the bunker line where the defensive perimeter could offer some shelter, passing the shattered soldiers from Third Division back to waiting medical units. A few survivors, still too stunned to realize what had happened, to realize how many of the faces they'd seen this morning would never come back, never be seen again, not until Judgment Day dawned on the World below. Assuming, Stark thought bitterly, that that day hadn't already come and gone, with this portion of humanity damned to a special hell up here.

"Looks like the virus has spread," Reynolds remarked with feigned idle curiosity.

"What do you mean?" Stark checked his command scan, startled to see First Division units lunging forward around the perimeter to collect isolated pockets of trapped Third Division troops. "Headquarters finally came to their senses?"

Before Vic could reply, a strange voice called in. "Hey, Stark, what's next?"

Stark checked the ID tag on the transmission, seeing it came from a Sergeant he barely knew in another battalion on the other side of the perimeter. "Wha—?"

"Yeah, we need some follow-on orders here, Stark."

"Stark, what do we do with our fragged officers?"

"What if they counterattack, Stark? We gonna hit back?"

"Stark, we need more medical support over here. There's a lot of wounded from Third Division."

"Hold it!" Stark roared. "What the hell's going on?"

"They're asking for orders, Ethan," Vic advised. "Why the hell are they asking me?"

"Because you took charge. Better answer them."

"I didn't . . ." *Yes, you did.* Stark glared at the command scan for a moment. "Okay. How many units have fragged their officers?" A babble of responses clamored back. "Hold it! Let's try that different. Which units are still under control of their officers?"

A long silence stretched. "Stark?" someone finally called. He recognized this voice, the female Sergeant from headquarters who'd spoken with him after the Fernandez interview. "Every officer here is off-line and disarmed. We had to act when they realized what was happening, tried to order our units to attack each other, and started to call in the Navy to bombard our own positions."

"That's insane. Even if they'd succeeded, all they'd have

accomplished is stripping the colony of its defenses."

"Maybe. I'm not claiming they were thinking straight, but they tried. Right now they're mad as hell, but we've got them locked down. I'm not seeing any officer call-ins, either. I think you've got it all." *I've got it all.*

"Ethan," Vic urged, "tell people what to do."

"Okay." *What do I tell them? I don't want everyone calling me asking for orders. But if I don't give some orders, who will? No officers left, thanks to something I started. Yeah, I started it. So it's my responsibility, at least for now.* "Units still recovering Third Division personnel send support requests to neighboring units and Sergeant Grace at Divisional Artillery. Everybody else fall back into our defensive positions. Units without bunker assignments return to barracks and hold in reserve."

"What about the officers?"

"Make sure they're disarmed and put them under arrest. We'll load as many as possible in the stockade and improvise for the rest." A sudden alarming thought arose. "Is there anybody at the spaceport?"

"Yeah, Stark. Right here."

"The ground-based anti-orbital defenses. Who's got those?"

"We do. I sent my people in to make sure we owned them. The AO troops weren't too sure whose side they wanted to be on, so we removed the option for them."

"Thanks. Good job."

"Headquarters here," the female Sergeant chimed in again. "What do you want us to do with the vid feed?"

"It's still going out?"

"Yeah, on the link back to Earth. I don't know if anybody back there has figured out what's going on yet."

I'm not even sure what's going on. "Can you keep the vid going without letting anyone know the officers are offline?"

"I think so. We'll just send them a stream of vid from units recovering Third Division casualties."

"Good. That'll buy us some time. Do it."

"Stark," another Sergeant demanded, "what if the enemy counterattacks? What do we do?"

"We let them," Stark declared. "We let them try all they want, and we blow them to hell when they get within range."

"Sounds like a plan. We'll hold in reserve then, like you said, until we get new orders from you."

New orders from me? "Vic, what's happened here?"

"Congratulations, Ethan," Vic stated dryly. "You've got an army."

"I don't want a damn army."

"Well, you've got one. Better figure out what you're going to do with it."

Headquarters, again. The same overwide corridors, the same careful attention to every detail of construction, but feeling abandoned without those corridors filled with senior officers looking and acting important. A few enlisted soldiers stood around, some apparently on sentry duty and some obviously unemployed. One group of the unemployed grinned in a goofy fashion at Stark and received a hard enough glare in return to stiffen every one of them back into military posture.

The headquarters Sergeant greeted Stark outside a plain but

reinforced door. "Welcome back."

"Thanks. What the hell is your name, anyway?"

"Tanaka," she said with a grin. "Jill Tanaka. The General's inside," she added with a gesture toward the door. "This is the holding cell for people Fernandez fingered. I figured it'd be an apt place to lock up Meecham."

"Guess so." Stark grunted. "Jill, I don't want to tell you your job, but things feel pretty loose around here."

Tanaka's grin faded. "I know. The junior enlisted are a little giddy. Especially here. There were so many senior officers playing master of the universe around headquarters that the enlisted really built up a head of frustration. Now they figure they're in charge."

"They're not. We are."

"Hmmm." Tanaka thought a moment, then nodded. "Right. They were supposed to do what I said before, and they'll damn well do the same now, right?"

"Right. Now I guess I ought to see General Meathead."

Tanaka waved a security pass to open the lock, and Stark pushed through. In notable contrast to the rest of the headquarters complex, the holding cell hadn't been designed with comfort in mind. General Meecham, his heavily beribboned uniform noticeably wrinkled, stared grimly toward Stark from the bare metal chair that served as the sole furnishing of the tiny room. *Guess Tanaka had some frustrations built up, too, since she stuck Meecham in here instead of in the stockade. At least they've got bunks in the cells there.* "You wanted to see me, General?" Stark stated flatly.

"I wanted to see the traitor who has irrevocably stained the honor of the U.S. military, yes," Meecham declared.

"Fine. You've seen me. Anything else, General?"

"I should have had you shot a long time ago."

"General, you are one stupid son of a bitch, you know that?" Stark found himself smiling. "I guess I've wanted to say something like that for a long time. Anyway, you're stupid. Real stupid. You wasted the lives of thousands of good soldiers, and now you're dumb enough to threaten somebody who could have *you* shot. You got any other smart things to say?"

"Wait." Meecham made an all-too-obvious struggle to compose himself, then smiled in firm and apparently friendly fashion. "Sergeant, everyone makes mistakes. In the heat of action, with a temporary setback distorting judgment, even the best soldier can act perhaps too hastily, in a way they'd regret." Stark stared back, silent. "We can still put a lid on all this. Nobody wants a mutiny to go forward, right? Officially, nothing has happened, yet. Officially, nothing has to happen."

"Meaning what?"

Meecham leaned forward, eyes intense. "Meaning we can still pull back from this. Release me and the other officers, Stark. Let us reestablish discipline. There won't be any adverse consequences if this all gets called off, now."

"Why should I believe that?"

"Because it's in your best interest, Sergeant, just as it is in mine. What are you going to do now? You need supplies. You need ammunition. You need a way to pay your troops."

Stark kept his face impassive. "We can get all that."

"Can you? What about the enemy? Will they sit back and let you reorganize, or will they hit you as hard as they can when they realize you're isolated now? What about the civilians in the colony? How will you control them? And don't forgot the corporations, Sergeant. They run things. That's how the country works these days. You've just seized all their assets on the Moon, and blocked their chances of getting their hands on more. They'll make sure they get it back, no matter what it takes. What happens when the corporations make sure America retaliates, sending a punitive force to regain control?"

"I don't have answers to all that, yet," Stark admitted. "They're tough questions, but they're something we can handle."

"'We'?" Meecham questioned. "Is there a 'we'? Or is it you giving the orders now?"

"So far, it's me."

Meecham smiled, a fierce baring of teeth. "Fernandez gave you a clean evaluation. I should have him shot, not you. No, Sergeant Stark, you're too good a soldier, too important an asset to waste."

"What's that supposed to mean?"

"We can make a deal, Stark. I need people on my staff who can make things happen. People who are good leaders. That's you. You can be an officer. A senior officer. I can always use another Major, or better yet, another Colonel. Sound attractive?"

Stark laughed. "So I hand the troops back over to you, become an officer, and everything's fine, huh? You think nobody would ever find out what happened up here?"

Meecham nodded. "As I said, you're a smart soldier. Okay, maybe we'll need a scapegoat. Maybe two or three. It doesn't have to be you. You can come out of this smelling like a rose."

"What about those scapegoats? What'd happen to them?"

Meecham smiled once more, this time in a comradely fashion. "I'm sure you have enemies, Stark, people who you'd rather not have around anymore, people who've hurt you in the past. They can take the fall. Every way you look at it, you win."

"And why should you do all this for me?" Stark inquired in a soft voice.

"Because I'll win, too. That's how deals get made, Stark. Once you're a Colonel I'll take you under my wing, teach you what you need to know to make General yourself someday."

"Sure."

"Is that an agreement?" Meecham demanded, perhaps a little too eagerly.

"An agreement?" Stark shook his head, no longer hiding his disgust. "I guess you figured everybody has to be like you, huh? Out for themselves. Sorry. No deal. I didn't do this for myself."

Meecham reddened with anger, dropping all pretense of friendship. "You'll regret those words."

"I doubt it. There's a helluva lot I may end up regretting about today, but not those words."

General Meecham finally stood, nose elevated as if he were trying to look down on Stark. "You'll die a traitor's death. Loyal soldiers will come here and suppress this rebellion, wipe out this blot on the record of the military."

Stark laughed again, this time harsh and mocking. "General, you killed off all those loyal troops. Or didn't you notice back in your nice, safe headquarters?"

Meecham shook his head. "That's the price of victory, the burden of command, something people like you will never understand."

Stark clenched a fist, then lowered it slowly with an expression of contempt. "That's enough. Save your speeches for the civs on Earth."

"Speeches?" Meecham favored Stark with a special look, as if ostentatiously memorizing his face. "What is it you want me to tell the citizens of the United States, Sergeant?"

"I don't know. I'm no politician."

"Neither am I! I'm a soldier, one who still believes in honor, in loyalty, in—"

"Shut up!" Stark took a step closer, so his face was only inches from the General's. He felt his body shaking with repressed rage and fought it down. "You're no soldier. You're a politician, one who just happens to wear stars instead of a civ suit. You're loyal to nothing except your own career. What do you think the military's about? Lording it over us like you think you're some damn god whose decisions can't ever be wrong, let alone questioned? Playing games with other officers to see who can get the commands with the most prestige and impress the civ politicians? Talking about your big responsibilities but always blaming someone else whenever something goes wrong? Collecting medals for all the places you've been and not for anything special, let alone courageous, you've ever done? Treating the soldiers under your command like we're nothing but symbols on your worthless command-and-control systems?" Stark spun on his heel to walk out. "I'd kill you myself, right now, but you're not worth the trouble."

"You'd better be prepared for trouble," Meecham declared, flushing purple with rage. "You'd better be prepared to fight for yourselves, even if you're willing to disregard your oaths to fight for others!"

Stark stopped, then turned to face General Meecham again, shaking his head. "Our oaths? General, we'd fight for our oaths, to defend the Constitution of the United States. We'd even fight to defend the people of the United States, the civs who let us be sent to fight but won't pay the necessary costs, and so get to watch us die in places they'd never go. We'd even fight to protect the spineless politicians who give speeches about our noble sacrifices but never show any real desire to share those sacrifices. Maybe, maybe we'd even fight for the corporations who think having us fight and die is just one more way to increase profits. Yeah, we'd fight for all that, and die for it all, if we had to, because that's who we are. But you know what, General? We're sick and tired of fighting and dying for the likes of you." Stark exited, slamming the door behind him.

"Didn't go well, huh?" Vic Reynolds sketched a smile.

Stark glared, trying to get his emotions back under control. "What the hell are you doing here?"

"Trying to help you." She nodded toward the door of the holding cell. "Good job in there. I didn't know you could speak that well."

"What are you talking about? How do you know what I said in there?"

Vic sighed in resignation. "Ethan, a certain amount of naiveté is touching, but get a grip. That's a security cell. It's bugged."

"Oh." Stark slapped his forehead. "I should've realized that. So why'd you listen in?"

"Me and every other Sergeant, you mean?"

This time Stark's jaw dropped. "Every . . . ?"

Jill Tanaka came up beside Stark and patted his shoulder. "People wanted to see how you handled Meecham."

"The hell. They didn't trust me, did they? They thought I'd cut a deal."

Vic took Stark's other arm, shaking her head. "Very few thought that, but everyone figured Meecham would make a try and we wanted to see what you did, to prove a point to everyone."

"Right." Stark started walking away. "I'm tired."

"Can't rest yet," Vic advised, holding on. "We got a meeting."

"Who's got a meeting?"

"All the Sergeants. There's something important to decide." She pulled Stark along as Tanaka led the way into corridors even more elaborate than the standard at headquarters, walls lined with art and display cases.

"Hey, Vic," Stark asked as they walked, "Meecham must have known that cell was bugged. Why'd he make his offer knowing everyone could listen?"

She shrugged. "Maybe he figured you wouldn't turn it down right off and it'd sow mistrust. Or maybe he thought you'd deactivate the bug before seeing him."

"Oh." Stark scratched behind one ear. "I wouldn't have thought of that."

"No, you wouldn't have, Ethan." Tanaka reached an ornate door that automatically slid open at their approach, revealing a large, plush room beyond, a room dominated by a large table made not of cheap lunar metal or polished stone but of hideously expensive wood brought up from Earth. More wood paneled the walls, gleaming soft gold under polish. Most of the seats around the table were already occupied by other Sergeants, many of whom Stark knew by name or by sight. Vic led Stark to one of the last empty chairs, near the head of the table, then sat beside him.

"We've got two issues that won't wait," Reynolds announced. "Every Sergeant who isn't physically here is linked in so we can make decisions, and we've got to make them."

"So what are these issues?" someone demanded over the link.

"Number one," Vic stated calmly, "what do we do with the officers?"

"Shoot 'em," a voice in the room called. "Stand them up against a wall and shoot every one of the bastards." A rumble of agreement immediately erupted.

"No!" Stark's voice boomed through the room, cutting off the buzz of conversation. "Think about that. You're soldiers, right? Think about that," he repeated, pitching his voice lower so that the other Sergeants had to concentrate to hear him. "You wanna shoot defenseless people? We could do that. Then what?"

"What's your point, Stark?" Stacey Yurivan demanded from her seat.

"First of all, some of them don't deserve it." Stark hunched forward slightly to stare at the others, swiveling his gaze around the table like a turret-mounted main gun. "A lot of officers went forward with Third Division. Some officers have gone into battle alongside us. Sure, that's the junior officers, but where are you going to draw the line if you start killing them in cold blood? You shoot all of them and you're no better than the worst of them are."

Stark took a deep breath, feeling the hostility in the room and somehow that of the linked-in Sergeants as well. "More importantly, much more importantly, if you decide to purge our officers, you're heading straight to hell. I promise. A military needs officers, needs people in charge. Just because the ones we've got locked up are worthless doesn't mean we don't need better ones. Shoot these, and anybody else who's in charge will always know they could get the same treatment, even if it's you and me. They'll be scared, and wondering constantly when they'll be purged for whatever reason. You want untrustworthy officers? You want units running around without anyone in authority to keep things under control? You want to establish a precedent that enlisted can kill their superiors just because they don't like them? Think about it. Don't create something worse than we had. Don't start a cycle of terror. It'll eat us all before it runs its course."

His words hit home. Anger dissolved into uncertainty as Sergeants exchanged glances. "Very good points, but there's another factor," Vic noted in the silence.

"What's that?"

"A lot of the soldiers up here have people back home. Family. Right now, they're hostages for the authorities on Earth. But if we have a lot of hostages of our own to trade for them, we might get all those families up here safe."

A thin Sergeant nodded rapidly. "Right. Damn right. Good thinking."

Grace, far down the table, raised a fist. "Okay, we can do that with the rest. But I want to personally kill Meecham for wasting the lives of my brother and thousands of others."

Stark stood slowly. "I've lost plenty of friends, Grace, but I've been lucky enough not to lose a brother, so I can't preach to you as an equal on that. But killing Meecham would be doing him a favor." A murmur of comment arose. "I mean it. Right now, he's lost his battle, lost the troops the United States has depended on for decades to defend its own territory, lost control of the rest of us up here, and lost the lunar colony, if we hold it. He's toast. We send him back and they'll eat him alive, the brass in the Pentagon and the civs and the politicians and all the corporations whose assets are now ours if we need them."

Yurivan grinned with delight. "Generals always get high-ranking jobs at corporations when they retire. I don't think Meecham's gonna get one."

Stark nodded. "Hell, there's even a chance the authorities back on Earth will shoot him instead of locking him in a small, cold cell in Leavenworth for life. Either way he's gotten a payback, and our hands are clean."

"Let's do it," Tanaka declared. "Vote. Anybody object?"

Grace scowled but remained silent. No one else spoke. "Then that's what we'll do. Hold the whole bunch for bargaining chips. So, what's your second big issue, Reynolds?"

"Who's in charge?" Vic asked.

"We are."

"What?" Reynolds questioned. "We are? So this army's going to be a democracy now? We vote on everything? Which units go on the line? What punishment a junior enlisted gets for a court-martial offense? What soldier goes out on patrol? Whether we provide fire support to a sector, and how much? Anybody think that'll work?"

Silence greeted her words, along with a lot more scowls. "So what do we do?" a linked Sergeant demanded.

"We choose a boss."

Stark stood again, drawing the attention of everyone in the room. "That's not enough, Vic. We don't need a boss. We need a commander. We need someone who's in charge. Without question. Without that, we're not mil."

"I've had enough commanders," someone groused.

"No," Yurivan agreed with visible reluctance. "Stark's right. We lose discipline, and we're damn close to that in the ranks, and there'll be hell to pay."

"I'll concede that, too," the thin Sergeant added, "but if that commander is going to function, he or she will have to have real authority, as Stark said. Who do we appoint to that job?"

"Somebody with good tactical smarts," Stark suggested. "Like Vic, here."

The thin Sergeant shook his head. "Even if Reynolds wasn't your friend, I'd still disagree. Commanders can get tactical smarts from their subordinates, if they listen. No, what we need in a commander is somebody who realizes those stars on their shoulders are a reminder of their responsibilities, and not just a symbol of all their privileges. Somebody who isn't going to stab us in the back as soon as they get the power. Somebody who's a good leader, and who won't forget us and the rest of the troops."

"Somebody we can trust, you mean?" Yurivan questioned. "Somebody we know isn't out for themselves?" She swung an arm to point toward Stark, grinning wickedly. "There's your commander, then."

"The hell!" Stark denied furiously. "That's not why I talked about this! I don't want the job!"

"That makes you qualified," somebody noted.

"I'm not qualified. I'm just a squad leader. I can't command a division or more worth of soldiers."

"I think you could," Sergeant Manley noted. "With the help of specialists like me. That's why commanders have staffs."

"Thanks a lot." Stark glared around the table. "I'm not asking for the job, I don't want the job, and I can't do the job."

"Vote," Tanaka announced implacably. "We can work out the details later. I want a commander to hold things together starting now, before our Corporals and Privates decide they can run amok without anybody officially in charge."

"Absolutely," Manley stated. "We've got Stark nominated."

"I do not agree to that!" Stark insisted.

"Are you saying you won't take the job if we appoint you to it? You'll reject the responsibility?"

"I.. ." Stark bit his lip. "I can't say that. You know that. I don't reject responsibility."

"Fine. Any other nominees? Come on, people."

"What about Maria Vasquez in Third Battalion, Second Brigade?"

"I don't want it, either," Vasquez hurried to announce.

"There's Smith in Second Battalion, First Brigade."

"Which Smith?"

"Richard. Richard T. Smith."

"No way," Smith chimed in. "Leave me out of this. Most people don't know who I am."

"Same here," Vasquez added. "The new commander has to have a Name with a capital N so people will believe in him or her, right?"

"Right," Manley agreed. "That brings us back to Stark."

"Do you people think I'm the Second Coming of Christ or something?" Stark demanded.

"Hell, no," Yurivan observed. "But you'll do until He shows up."

"Let's vote," Manley stated. "Motion is to appoint Ethan Stark commander of the entire force up here, with all the authority normally vested in a commanding officer."

"With the understanding," the thin Sergeant added, "that he will continue to consult with us whenever appropriate. You agree to that, Stark?"

"If I'm gonna be in charge, I'm damn well gonna be in charge," Stark declared. "But talking to you guys and listening to what you have to say? I'd want you to take me down if I stopped doing that."

"Fine. Anybody object to the motion?" A long period of silence stretched. "Guess you're our new commander, Stark. What do you want to be called?"

"Sergeant."

A chuckle ran around the room. "That can stay your honorary title," Manley noted. "For now, let's call him Commander. Better get used to the idea of General, though, Ethan."

"That's going to take one hell of a lot of getting used to," Stark grumped.

"Congratulations, Ethan." Vic offered her hand with a broad smile.

"Thanks so very much," Stark smiled back. "Hey, you know what I'm gonna need now? I'm gonna need a chief of staff."

Vic's smile shaded to alarm. "Now, Ethan, there's a lot of other—"

"One with good sources and tactical smarts," Stark continued. "Congratulations to you. And you, Manley. You said I needed somebody like you for the administrative junk."

Yurivan stood dramatically. "I'm getting out of here before Stark taps me for a job, too."

"Like there's a chance of that, Stace," someone joked.

"Hey, how about Security Officer?"

The laughter came louder this time, with a sharp edge. Stark took a good look around the table, trying to assess the mood. *Tired. Scared, more than a little, but then we all should be.* "People, I recommend you get back to your units and reestablish routine. They need it, and you need it. We've thrown out a lot of what we've always taken for granted, and we've got to take some comfort in how much of what we've got is still there, just like always."

"Good idea." An awkward moment followed; then Yurivan walked up to Stark with another mischievous grin before bringing her arm up in a precise salute.

Stark returned the courtesy, shaking his head in exasperation. "Get the hell out of here, Stace."

"Yes, sir, Commander." The others followed, many repeating Yurivan's salute, so that Stark had to hold his own salute in acknowledgment.

As the door whisked shut behind the last of the other Sergeants, Stark noticed an outside monitor on the opposite wall of the conference room. He strode over to it, then stopped, gazing at the rocks and the dust, the night black as only emptiness can be, the light and shadows unnaturally sharp. The vicious bedlam of battle had died down, leaving the false impression of peace where exhausted combatants rested before renewing their struggles. Nothing moved in the barren landscape now, nothing except the slow wheel of stars overhead and the even slower progress of the shadows across the lifeless surface. Somehow it seemed different now. "I could live with it, I guess," he noted to himself.

"What's that, Ethan?" Vic asked.

Stark turned to see her still standing nearby, a questioning look bent his way. "Ah, nothing. Battle fatigue, maybe." He returned to his chair, sitting carefully. Somehow, the weak gravity of the Moon seemed to have suddenly multiplied, so that it bore down on him with a weight greater than that of Earth-normal. "I never expected this. Never thought any of it would happen."

She came to sit beside him. "I warned you about that demon, Ethan. Warned you to be ready to live with whatever it made you do."

"I can live with it. I guess. I couldn't let lives be wasted anymore, not when I could save them. But I really didn't want this, Vic."

"What *do* you want, Ethan Stark?"

"What do I want?" Stark looked down at his hands, thinking, then back up at Vic. "I want to wake up in the morning knowing what to do, who to take care of, and who to report to. I want officers who care about me and my troops more than they do about their own promotions. I want everything to happen by regulations, unless the regulations are screwed up, and then I want the senior enlisted to handle it right. I want to know what little box everything belongs in and what big box the little boxes all go into."

Stark paused, noting Vic's unwavering attention. "I want to know I did the right thing, when everything I was ever told about honor and loyalty says maybe I betrayed the stuff I'm supposed to believe in. But none of that can happen. Not anymore. Now I've got to make decisions for others, and make sure I look out for them, and sometimes that's going to mean sending them into situations where they might be killed. I want someone else to be responsible for all this, but I also want to justify the trust my fellow soldiers placed in me, so I'm going to do my damnedest to get it right."

Vic smiled sadly. "Ethan, I can't help you with everything, but I'll try. As for honor and loyalty, nobody anywhere can tell you a thing about those qualities."

"Hell, Vic, we've got to worry about the enemy, about the civs in the colony, about how to get basic supplies, and about our own government and our own military."

"That's right. The corporations are going to be foaming at the mouth at the thought of losing everything up here. They'll tell the government to get it all back, and the government's going to do just what they say, just like always."

"So," Stark concluded, "I won this battle. Saved some people. Now I've got to win a lot more battles."

She nodded back. "Tough jobs only get tougher, Ethan. Think of it as an opportunity to excel."

He laughed at the old joke, then rose from the chair. "A million things to worry about. So what do I do first, Vic?"

"Set priorities."

"Fine. What's first?"

"It's been a long day. How about a beer?"

"Make it two."

"Deal."

STARK'S COMMAND
JACK CAMPBELL (WRITING AS JOHN G. HEMRY)

THE SECOND VOLUME IN THE GRIPPING
STARK'S WAR TRILOGY

Sergeant Ethan Stark is placed in command of the US military forces that have overthrown their high-ranking officers. Instead of issuing orders, Stark confides his hope of forging an army based on mutual respect. Now, in addition to fighting a merciless enemy on the moon's surface, Stark must contend with the US government's reaction to his mutiny.

"A fascinating, complex look at the military mindset … and a damn fine story. For those who like military SF, this book more than serves the purpose, clearly claiming Hemry's place at the Round Table of military SF writers."
— *Absolute Magnitude*

STARK'S CRUSADE
JACK CAMPBELL (WRITING AS JOHN G. HEMRY)

THE THRILLING CONCLUSION TO
THE STARK'S WAR TRILOGY

He was sent into space to protect the US Lunar Colony. Instead, when faced with orders that would do nothing but get his soldiers killed, Sergeant Ethan Stark lead a rebellion. Now he and his soldiers must fend off deadly aggression from their own country without igniting a full-scale civil war.

"In a gripping space opera, Hemry delivers an intensely satisfying read. Strong characterization and well-executed action keep the pages turning." – RT Book Reviews

"Hemry has combined a keen sense of action with a fine look at the morality of following orders, and produced a groundbreaking story in the same vein as *The Forever War* or *Starship Troopers*."
– *Absolute Magnitude*

WWW.TITANBOOKS.COM

THE LOST FLEET SERIES
JACK CAMPBELL

DAUNTLESS

FEARLESS

COURAGEOUS

VALIANT

RELENTLESS

VICTORIOUS

After a hundred years of brutal war against the Syndics, the Alliance fleet is marooned deep in enemy territory, weakened and demoralised and desperate to make it home.

Their fate rests in the hands of Captain "Black Jack" Geary, a man who had been presumed dead but then emerged from a century of survival hibernation to find his name had become legend. Forced by a cruel twist of fate into taking command of the fleet, Geary must find a way to inspire the battle-hardened and exhausted men and women of the fleet or face certain annihilation by their enemies.

Brand-new editions of the bestselling novels containing unique bonus material from the author.

"Black Jack is an excellent character, and this series is the best military SF I've read in some time." – *Wired*

"Fascinating stuff... this is military SF where the military and SF parts are both done right." – *SFX Magazine*

"*The Lost Fleet* is some of the best military science fiction on the shelves today." – SF Site

THE LOST FLEET:
BEYOND THE FRONTIER: DREADNAUGHT
JACK CAMPBELL

THE FIRST VOLUME IN THE BRAND-NEW FOLLOW-ON SERIES

Captain John "Black Jack" Geary woke from a century of survival hibernation to take command of the Alliance fleet in the final throes of its long and bitter conflict against the Syndicate Worlds. Now Fleet Admiral Geary's victory has earned him the adoration of the people and enmity of politicians convinced that a living hero can be a very dangerous thing.

Geary is charged with command of the newly christened First Fleet. Its first mission: to probe deep into the territory of the mysterious alien race. Geary knows that members of the military high command and the government fear his staging a coup, so he can't help but wonder if the fleet is being deliberately sent to the far side of space on a suicide mission.

"Campbell combines the best parts of military SF and grand space opera ... plenty of exciting discoveries and escapades."
– *Publishers Weekly*

"Another excellent Addition to one of the Best military science fiction series on the market."
– Monsters & Critics

WWW.TITANBOOKS.COM